BOOHOUSE **BHB** BOOKS

boohousebooks.com

MARK STEVEN NORDLUND

WHERE TOY BOATS SINK

A COLLECTION OF DARK STORIES

This is a work of fiction. All of the characters, organizations and events portrayed in this collection are either products of the author's imagination or are used fictitiously.

WHERE TOY BOATS SINK

A COLLECTION OF DARK STORIES

BY MARK STEVEN NORDLUND

Copyright © 2025 by Mark Steven Nordlund

All rights Reserved.

A Boohouse Books Book

www.boohousebooks.com

ISBN 979-8-9895864-4-8 (Paperback)

For my wife, Jen.

Years behind every horror fan
is a child who saw something on TV
that shook their innocence, cracked their
bedroom doors and turned them into
the monsters we became as adults.

PREFACE

This book represents the end of a very dark time in my life, the beginning of a climb and the brightest days I never thought I'd see. I don't mind admitting, my recent past was a series of terrible decisions and self-destructive behaviors that hurt myself, as well as the ones I love the most. It took more hands than my own to pull me out of the spiral I was plummeting into, and to them I say, *Thank you, from the very bottom of my heart.* In the past year, I've let go of what was inevitably killing me, built a new future and reunited with loved ones I never thought I'd talk to again. Beginning in 2025 I've turned myself completely around, in *more* than just one context. For the longest time I lived facing backwards, focusing on the past and what I could have done differently. Doing so played a big part in my recent fall. Moving into the future, I've decided to look ahead and never glance back. With the upcoming years that remain in my life I plan to work toward my ambitions, create art and embrace the people who still stand beside me. *You only live once,* the cliché goes. And it's very, very true. Follow your dreams, do what you love and hold on tight to the ones you care about. *That,* in my experience, is the only way to live.

Where Toy Boats Sink is my analogy for leaving childhood and entering adulthood. Many of the stories you are about to read deal with the fall of adolescence and the beginning of responsibility. However, they also illustrate the importance of never *fully* growing up. In the rat race of grown-up life, we can often lose ourselves in the burdens of work, money and reliability. The key is finding a happy medium, at least, in my opinion.

This collection of six stories holds some of my worst nightmares, darkest visions and assorted, irrational fears. Also, obliquely, some of my fondest memories and hysterical recollections. There is a piece of me or of someone I know in every character, every conversation and every situation. It artistically displays who I am, what I believe and the twisted, whimsical darkness I have come to love as a horror fan. Please enjoy this collection and what it has to say. I've *lived* many of the horrors it has in store for you.

FORGOTTEN TOYS
A Short Horror Story

Theo kicked a plastic horse and a die-cast monster truck away from his path across the carpet. He slapped his open palm on the top of a fresh beer bottle and pried the cap off with his chewed-up, silver wedding band. Falling into the trashy, stained heap he called his easy chair, Theo turned his head towards the stairs and growled, "Desi! Pick up your shitty toys before I pick them up for you!" He burped loudly after taking a heavy swig. "...and take them out with the garbage!" He added cruelly. He selected the television remote from a uniformly-aligned row of device controllers and turned on the TV.

Theo strictly believed there was a place for everything and hated when anything was *out of place*. There was a place for playthings, a place for the discarded and a place for his ass. And *that place* was in his easy chair. That's how they did it in the service and that's what he was used to. As far as *he* was concerned, it was the one and only way for everyone.

Hurried footsteps descended the stairs and the sound of small hands gathering toys could be heard from the hoppy belch cloud and airborne dust from the inhabited chair. Desi quickly stowed his trinkets in a wooden chest placed in the corner of the small living room and cautiously approached his father. He stood quietly beside him like a ghost, waiting to be noticed. Theo knew his son was there but ignored him, hoping he would pick up on the non-verbal hint and leave him alone, as any perceptive adult would. But Desi was only three and had not yet attained such a skill. He just stood, his blonde head inches from the electrical-union patch on his father's shoulder as the seconds became a minute. Stinging tension filled the room.

"What the hell?! What? What do you want?!" Theo shouted. His son winced when his father reacted but stood his ground out of pure desperation.

"Are we going to the park today?" Desi asked. His big, blue eyes stared up at his dad, begging for a yes in response.

Theo sighed dramatically and rolled his eyes behind his eyelids, feeling the hard pressure of aggravation combined with annoyance. He wished his son knew what it was like to be an adult and understood that after a ten-hour shift after nine straight days of work, you just want to come home and *not do shit.* His expression hardened after another gulp of beer. "The park isn't going anywhere, bud. It'll be there tomorrow and the day after and the day after that. Dad just wants to relax. We'll go to the park another day, Ok?" He answered coldly.

Desi's disappointed eyes fell to the floor. He rubbed his nose and gathered enough understanding to outweigh his disappointment with forgiveness. He may have been only three, but empathy was a perception he had attained very young. Desi placed his arms around his father's sleeve and hugged his arm. "I love you, Daddy," he said sincerely.

Switching the beer bottle from one hand to the other, Theo ruffled his son's hair and patted him on the back. "You too, bud," he said. "Why don't you grab Daddy another beer. The tall ones, like this." He displayed his bottle, making the silver label visible.

"Ok," Desi said happily. His little footsteps slapped against carpet and then tile as he approached the refrigerator. Theo heard the fridge door open and the momentary quiet of his son searching diligently.

"The ones on the door?" Desi yelled.

"Yeah! In the door!" Theo answered. The sound of glass tapping against hollow plastic sounded before the door closed. The slapping steps approached.

"This one?" Desi asked.

His father euphorically took the bottle with a smile. "Yeah, that one. Great job, buddy." He said. "You're really good at following directions," he praised.

Desi's face lit up with pride. He jumped up and down on the tips of his toes. "I really am!" He happily agreed. In Desi's other hand, he held a bottle of red Sports-Ade. Theo hadn't seen it. He finished his first beer and popped the top off the new one, taking a sip. "Dad?" Desi asked reluctantly.

Theo swallowed. "Hm?" he inquired.

"Can I have this?" His son asked, showing off the drink. His eyes begged again.

His father shook his head. "No, no. Those are for Dad for work. Where's your water cup? Drink that. The one your mom always gives you." Theo noticed the sadness in his son's silence again and felt a modicum of sympathy. He decided to compromise. "You can have one of the blue ones. Dad doesn't like the blue ones, you can have one of those."

The little boy jumped with delight and raced into the kitchen. The fridge door swung open again.

Theo was glad when he could serve up pure happiness with just words. Desi was at that age where words alone could induce profound elation without Theo having to actually do anything or perform any kind of action. Telling his son he could have a Sports-Ade sure beat taking him to the park, setting up a train set or having to get out of his chair. He dreaded the day that kind of service would no longer yield jubilation due to Desi's increasing age and inability to impress so easily.

Desi shouted from the fridge, "There's blue ones, purple ones, red ones and orange ones!"

"Take a blue one!" Theo shouted back. "The others Daddy brings to work!"

"Blue?" Desi asked, just to be double sure.

"Yes!" He answered. "If it's blue you can drink it, It's ok if Mom didn't tell you you could have it."

"Ok!" Desi shrieked happily.

Theo's eyes fell back on the TV as an ad for potato chips danced across the 60-inch screen. His stomach growled. "Grab me a bag of chips while you're in there, will ya'!" he requested loudly.

"Ok!" his son repeated. The pantry door creaked open. More silence. Theo's eyes wandered the room as his son searched. He eyed the painting of The Mother Mary on the wall above a mantle decorated with photos of himself from his days in the army. They sat beside a National Defense Service Medal, his service patches and a small, worn teddy bear holding a red heart, he received from his mother after basic training. She had died a week after giving it to him of a sudden brain hemorrhage. The bear was the only item he decided to keep in remembrance of her. He planned on giving it to his son when he learned how to take special care of things. According to Theo, that day was a long way off. A very long way off.

As an unwelcome addition, a crucifix was added to the mantle by his wife. Theo scoffed at the meaningless trinket every time he laid eyes on it. This moment was no exception. The gold, catholic cross had no place among his coveted, earned trophies that *actually meant something real* and he hated the idea of the symbol included in his shrine to hard work, sacrifice and achievement. The scam of faith, praying to a bearded man in the sky and the man-made ideas of true reverence and true evil repulsed him. When his wife would go to church, she'd be gone *all day* praying, bible-studying, eating stale crackers and handing out *his* hard-earned money to the world's oldest pyramid scheme. He drove the thoughts from his mind before they sent him into an unnecessary animosity spiral and focused on his beer. He took another swig.

Desi returned holding the blue Sports-Ade but no bag of potato chips. "I can't reach!" Desi squeaked with frustration.

Theo burped again then grunted. "All right," he groaned. He reached over and unscrewed his son's bottle cap for him, breaking the seal. Desi took a long, happy drink and then a big breath. A little, blue mustache was left above his upper lip. Theo leaned forward and hauled his aching body off the dirty chair and got to his feet as his son ran back into the kitchen. He sighed at the thought of taking the long walk to the pantry and back, just for a snack.

Desi pointed at the pantry, taking another drink of blue sugar. "It's on the top, I can't reach!" He said.

"All right!" Theo snapped. "I'm coming." After two steps across the rug in his thin socks, he stepped on a razor-sharp, plastic building block with the corner positioned directly at his heel. The toy pierced his fleshy padding and made him scream in pain. *"Goddammit, Des!"* Theo roared. "I thought I told you to pick up these damn toys!" Desi stumbled back, shaken by his father's outburst and dropped his drink on the floor. Azure liquid splashed across the tile. The empty bottle rolled, pouring Sports-Ade in a curve from the pantry to the oven. Tears welled up in Desi's eyes, his mouth frowned sadly and his breaths became heavy. *"I told you to clean this shit up!"* His father screamed, kicking the block at him. Theo's rage drove him into madness, fueled by lack of sleep and long work hours. "I was wrong! *You're terrible at following directions!"* He exclaimed. His words spewed like acid. Desi covered his face with his tiny hands and sobbed with disgrace.

The front door flew open. Allison's voice called out from the sharp sunlight pouring down the hall. "More bags in the car, I need help!" She announced. Upon hearing his mother's voice, Desi sent himself into loud, unhinged crying. The type of crying he only exhibited for Mom. Allison quickly paced down the hall holding grocery bags. Her purse hanging from her shoulder and keys jingling from her fingers. She eyed the spill, her crying son and her husband standing in the living room. Desi ran to his mother and wrapped his arms around her leg, wailing madly. "What happened?" She asked. Theo wasn't about to tell her about the sports drink he allowed Desi to take after repeated, strict instructions regarding what his son was allowed to consume. He wasn't in the mood for her bullshit or another lecture regarding his carelessness, temperament or ignorance. His son's cries eased, reduced to breathy sniffles.

Theo lied, "I told him to get his water cup from the kitchen and he snuck one of my Sports-Aides. I caught him when he was half-way through the bottle and he spilled it on the floor." Desi turned his eyes up to his dad with tearful humiliation and betrayal. He continued to sob. This time, for the questions and confusions that raced in his innocent, adolescent mind. Why would his daddy say those things when he had made him so happy just minutes earlier and after their enormous hug in the chair? Desi was sad, bewildered and heartbroken. "And he's constantly leaving his shit everywhere. How many times do I have to tell him to pick up his toys?" Theo added.

Allison rested the bags on the counter and picked up her son, holding him close. She whispered sharply to her husband, "Children make messes. That's what they do. It's up to us to teach them and clean up after them most of the time. That's what *parents* do." Her voice returned to normal as she addressed her son, "Sweetie, you know you're not supposed to touch Daddy's drinks. They have too much sugar. Where's your water?" She searched the kitchen briefly before grabbing a yellow sip-cup from a cabinet and filled it with the filtered dispenser in the refrigerator door. Desi took the cup and drank from it eagerly, his eyes reddened and tired from stress. Allison pointed towards the hall. "There's more bags in the car. Can you bring them in?" She asked. "I'll get the mess."

"Yeah," Theo said, not too eagerly. "Oh, What did the doctor say?" He asked.

Allison sighed. "He said I need to quit smoking ...for the thousandth time. It aggravates the CVD. He said stay on the ACE inhibitors and beta blockers, maybe take up running. Fat chance," she said with an eye-roll. "I disagree. Smoking always calms me. *Stress* is what is going to kill me."

"I'm sure you'll be fine." Theo waved his hand dismissively. He dragged his sore carcass toward the front door to unload the car as his wife took a mop from the closet. She slapped the mophead into the blue spill and took a second, examining the sports bottle on the floor. She sighed and shook her head with irritation.

Dark filled the living room. The only light blessing the space was the dim glow of the TV displaying a muted infomercial. Theo sat in his easy chair, wide awake with an eighth beer in his hand and the remote control in the other. He stared at the floor as he thought about what he had done to his son. For some reason the look on Desi's face when he had lied about the stolen drink bothered him. His pondering was interrupted by the familiar sound of Allison's approaching steps on the stairs. The living room light illuminated above. He listened for words but heard nothing for a few, drawn-out seconds. "Here we go," he mumbled to himself with pressing discontent. "What is it *this time?*"

"I want you to go to church with me on Sunday," Allison said sternly. "It'll be good for you."

"And why the hell would I do that?" He asked. Enmity grew in the back of his throat. His body tensed.

"Or go to therapy, counseling or get some kind of help for your abuse to yourself and to your son. And to me," she stated.

"What the hell are you talking about? What did I do now? What in the *God damn* did I do now? There's always something, what is it this time?!" Theo growled.

He heard her swallow hard. "You know I hate it when you talk like that. I know you do it because it bothers me. You never used words like that until we started fighting," Allison asserted. "I'm not going to complain about the hours you work. I know you can't help that and I appreciate that you work so hard. But when you're *here,* you're always drinking, you're always in a terrible mood and you're always snapping when I ask you to do something you should be doing anyway, as a father and as a husband. You need some kind of moral compass. A standard, an example to live by. You don't even have friends you hang out with once a week, or at all. The husbands at my church go out together, they play golf, they go hunting, they talk about their families with one another and share insights with each other about running a household."

Theo laughed at her. "Oh yeah. I'm sure that's what they're doing together, sharing insights," he mocked sarcastically. "I've seen what catholic, bayside men do together and their families are *no* part of it. They're taking off their wedding rings and sharing their dollars with strippers and bar floozies. And the only racks they're bringing back to their hunting cabins are attached to long legs and shaking asses. *There's* your moral compass. I *come home* after work. *I'm here, I'm present,*" he argued. "And I can't afford the quality of prostitutes your Dans, Skylers and Bryces share at their ocean-view penthouse downtown," he joked.

"I'm not asking you to join *them specifically.* I'm asking you to interact with someone other than us and your foreman at work. Father Francine said that a head of a household needs to surround himself with positive examples to properly—"

Theo explosively cut her off mid-sentence. "Father Francine! There it is. That's what this is all about!" He complained. "Tell me, what wise, Godly words did Father Francine bestow on you when you went to him *complaining about me?* Tell me! I'd love to know!" He spat.

Allison took a deep breath, gathering her courage after his ridicule. "He said that you need to interact with other fathers and husbands with a right-facing moral compass to calibrate your awareness of duties as the head of our home," she stated. Theo rolled his eyes so hard his wife could see the expression through the back of his head. "You come home from work and you disappear into your beer and your TV. I'm afraid to go out, go to appointments, run errands and *leave you alone with our son.* You don't feed him, you don't give him anything to drink and some nights I find him asleep on the floor and you asleep in your chair with the fridge left open and beer spilled on the carpet. You still haven't installed that child lock on the garage door and you leave your tools and car parts where Desi can get to them. What happens if you fall asleep and he gets into the garage and puts his hands on that chop saw you keep on the floor? Or the half cans of oil you leave everywhere?" She asked. Her breath trembled with trepidation. "I'm tired of the carelessness, the temper and the ignorance. And most of all, *the lies you tell* to avoid confrontation that eventually lead to further arguing. Worse arguing than if you told the truth."

Theo clenched his fist to keep from screaming. He spoke harshly through his teeth, "Our son isn't stupid, he *knows* to stay out of the garage. I've told him again and again not to touch anything in there! I am *not* careless, the only *temper* I have is towards *you* and the only *ignoring* I do is because of your constant and narcissistic preaching about church, heaven and *God bullshit!* Head of the household my ass! Everyone knows that the head of every household is the wife. How do I know that? Because the only way husbands can have any fun, is when they have to leave their *own households* to do it!" Theo leaned forward, turned his head and faced her. "And I have *never fucking lied to you,"* he snarled.

Allison shook her head with blatant disgust. She threw her palm into the air and slapped her thigh. "That's exactly what I'm talking about," she said flatly.

"What?!" He barked.

"How on earth could Desi drink half of one of your Sports-Ades if you didn't unscrew the cap and break the seal for him? You know he can't open one of those by himself." She finished. She wiped a tear away from under her eye and turned her back. "I've said my peace," she said softly.

Allison ascended the stairs and disappeared around a corner. Theo was left speechless staring at the wall she had been standing in front of. The words *Faith, Love* and *God* were painted decoratively on the white drywall beside a floating shelf covered in artificial flowers. The message mocked him as he glared. Rage boiled in his gut and his hatred for her, this house and his needy son sent his blood racing through his veins.

Three days later, Theo trudged past the trash cans on the curb and up the path to his front door. He struggled to find his house key in the dark. It was five o'clock in the morning and he had just finished eleven hours of pulling wire for a new apartment complex on the south side of town. All he wanted was a shower, a beer and to fall asleep in front of the TV. He figured he was lucky this morning, Allison and Desi didn't get up until seven and he had a good two hours to himself. Not that it mattered. Allison hadn't spoken to him since their argument and she was keeping Desi out of his way for the time being. He found the key, unlocked the door and walked into blackness. Theo shut the door behind him and made his way down the dark hall, headed for the lightswitch.

Suddenly, he slipped on what felt like ice under his boot and hit the ground hard. His head collided with the wall. Sharp pain surged from his head and shoulder as he sat up. His ankle was twisted and throbbing. He got to his foot, hobbled to the living room and turned on the lights. A coloring book laid open beside him on the tile. The exposed page was stamped with a perfect boot-print. The book had been the ice he had slipped on. His complexion reddened with fury and what he beheld in the rest of the house sent his brain into irate spasms. Trucks, blocks, plastic food items and crayons were scattered like confetti across the rug and furniture. A miniature kitchen set was tossed into his easy chair and a row of rubber dinosaurs were placed uniformly on the entertainment center, blocking the TV. He wiped them onto the rug revealing irremovable, farm animal stickers covering the bottom of the plasma screen. He took the mini-kitchen out of his chair and tossed it across the room. It smashed into plastic fragments against the wall and heaped into a pile on the floor.

Theo's heart palpitated at the state of the room but the last fiber suspending his sanity above madness snapped when he saw the remote controls. They had been placed one-by-one, into a small row of play-putty cups, bathing in green slime. He pulled the TV remote out of its cup as strings of goo dripped from the hard plastic. He pointed the controller at the TV and pressed one of the gooey buttons. The TV's screen did not illuminate. The remote no longer worked. Theo lost his mind.

He threw the door leading into the garage, wide open and dragged a brown trash can into the living room. He began kicking all of the stray toys into a pile around the can, stomping on some of them and breaking them into shards. Theo booted the dinosaurs, play-food, horses, blocks, trucks and crayons into the center of the room until an assortment worthy of a yard sale was stacked around the dirty, oil-stained can.

Trying not to wake Allison, he crept up the stairs, passed the corner and opened Desi's bedroom door. The room was in the same state as the calamity downstairs, but Theo ignored it for now. He took the three-year-old by the arm and pulled him out of bed. Desi woke up on his feet and began hyperventilating from his sudden arousal. "Let's go!" Theo demanded in a whisper. The boy began walking while being pulled towards the landing. His confusion and discombobulation sent him into whimpers. "Shut up," his father spat through his teeth.

Theo lifted him and descended the stairs, bringing his son into the bright light and before the pile around the can.

Desi tearfully eyed the sight of his playthings surrounding the trash bin and began to cry. His father stopped him before he made a sound, "Stop it, right now!" The boy choked back his tears. "You will put *every single goddamned toy from this living room floor* into this barrel in five minutes or your bedroom will be next! Do you hear me?!" Theo belted. Desi's breaths heaved again. His father pointed to the clock on the wall. "You have four minutes and fifty-five seconds left. Move!" He ordered. Salty water poured from the boy's eyes as he reluctantly placed each one of his toys one by one, into the bin.

Theo charged down the hall, opened the front door and jogged down the driveway, looking down the street. The sun was on its way up and the large headlights of an oversized, green truck could be seen far off. He turned on his heel and returned to the house, entering the living room. Desi was hurriedly filling the can. "Four minutes left, move it!" The clock ran down to time-up as the child tossed the final, broken truck into the trash can.

Theo grabbed the bin by its handle and dragged it out the front door. He placed it on the curb just as the garbage truck pulled up. The brakes hissed as a man got out wearing brown gloves and dumped the plastic trove into the back, on top of black and white bags, wet cardboard and rotten food. Theo walked up the driveway, shut the front door behind him and saw his son at the window. Desi was crying softly with his tiny hands pressed against the glass. He had just witnessed half of his things tossed away like trash into a big, scary truck and would now have to watch it drive away. He sobbed into his little fists.

The arson-like madness within Theo fizzed out after a few remaining sparks. A weight grew in his chest as he came back down into sanity and reason. The fury, the outlash and the mania vanished like a satisfied spirit and Theo was left with the horror of what he had just done. He stared at his weeping son. The sympathy he felt about the lie from days ago was nothing compared to the twisting regret and burning repentance he felt now. He wanted to apologize, he wanted to stop the truck and get his son's toys back, he wanted to make that little face light up with euphoria again. But it couldn't be done with words alone this time. Theo's eyes glazed, he felt a lump in his throat and, for the first time in years, he *almost* cried. He searched around the room for any toys that may have survived to salvage any kind of bond he had left between him and his child.

The only toy left in the entirety of the room was his treasured teddy bear on the mantle. Theo's eyes rose to the bear's sacred spot beneath the painting. His heart sank into his stomach and dread filled him. All at once, the rage returned. His mother's bear was missing. The photos, the medal, the stupid crucifix and the army patches were all present and accounted for but the bear was absolutely nowhere to be seen.

"Des! Where is my bear?!" He asked his son. Desi turned his head away from the window and looked upon his dad with a bright, red face and tired, sopping eyes. He sniffled and wiped his nose with his sleeve. "Where is Daddy's bear?! The teddy bear on the mantle, did Mommy move it?!" He asked in more detail, frantically.

"M-m-mommy. She let me..." Desi began. He wiped his face again.

"Mommy let you what?!" Theo snapped. "Mommy let you play with it?" His son just stared at him. Theo panicked. His voice cracked. "Where is my bear!" He thundered loudly.

Desi lifted his hand slowly and pointed to the garbage truck outside by the curb. The truck's engine howled like a demon as the brakes released and the monstrous tires turned. "It's in there," Desi squeaked.

Theo darted down the hall, yanked the entry door open and sprinted across the lawn, chasing the truck. His boots were heavy and the pain in his head, shoulder and ankle burned like white fire. The truck passed the next house where Theo assumed it would stop next, but kept on driving. All of the cans he was running by had been emptied, the terrible thought occurred to him. *His house* had been the last on the pick-up route, and the massive vehicle wasn't stopping anytime soon.

He quickened his pace but so did the truck. He peered into the back of the trash-hold, searching for any sign of the bear amongst the banana peels, foam cups and torn bags. A hint of red could be seen in the deep corner just below the hydraulic, compactor press. It was the heart the teddy bear held at its chest. He located his beloved toy and grabbed onto the cold steel of the rim. Pushing himself up, Theo got his chest over the edge, his boots dangling above the moving street. Without warning, the brakes hissed and the truck stopped, throwing Theo onto the pile of rubbish. One of the bear's legs was pinched in a corner between two metal plates. He pulled the bear free, tearing off the leg. He tossed the toy out of the truck and onto the street. Now, all he had to do was climb out of the truck and make it to the pavement. Dark engulfed him as the sound of motors pumping hydraulic fluid screeched from the truck's crushing jaws.

The piercing sound, the smell of rot and the black was the last thing Theo remembered.

Remembered was the key word. Remembering meant you could recall an experience later. If he had died in the truck, he wouldn't be remembering anything. He'd be dead. But he did remember. According to Theo, that had to mean he was *alive.*

Theo's eyes opened. Or he woke up, or both. He wasn't sure. He was sitting in his easy chair. It faced the center of the living room instead of the TV. Someone had moved his chair. The living room was clean. Very clean. Everything was in its place as it should be, with the exception of his chair. Only, the room was different, very different. The mantle still held his Army trinkets, the remotes were lined uniformly as he had always kept them and all of Desi's toys were cleaned up and put away. *Toys,* he thought. He looked to the end of the mantle. The bear was still missing. He felt his gut boil, but was distracted by other peculiar changes in the room. Big changes.

White folding chairs were placed carefully around the room and flowers were set out against a wall, surrounding an enlarged photo of himself wearing his Army, service uniform. He remembered the picture. He was only 22 when the photo was taken, but why the hell was it surrounded by red white and blue carnations and lilies?

He attempted to pry his body out of his chair. His arms wouldn't move. Terror struck him. He tried turning his head. Nothing. He felt his lungs breathing, his heart beating, his head and shoulder pain, but did not feel his sore ankle. It must have healed. Theo couldn't move his fingers, wiggle his toes or even blink. Was he paralyzed? *That's what happened,* he thought. He was crushed by the truck and paralyzed from the neck down. That had to be the reason for his inability to move. But, wouldn't he still be able to blink his eyes and speak if he had control of his face? He couldn't feel his tongue or his jaw. Just his eyeballs, heart and lungs could be felt and accounted for. Was this somehow a full-body paralyzation that took away all voluntary control? He would sooner choose death, any day. Theo just sat in his chair, facing the room, examining its details. It's all he had the ability to do. *Why does this look like my funeral?* He questioned internally. The idea made him ache. His breaths quickened and his pulse raced. If he could tremble, he would have.

Allison walked silently into the room. She was wearing a long, black, pleated dress and charcoal heels. A lit cigarette was held between her fingers. Her eyes were exhausted and almost looked bruised from grief. He knew that look. That's exactly how she looked when her father died four years ago. She had spent an entire week in bed and he felt helpless the entire time she mourned the loss alone, refusing to allow him by her side. Allison sat in the folding chair closest to the Army photo and covered her face with her hand. She wept and smoked, just as she had for her father.

Theo wondered why she wasn't looking at him. He couldn't be dead, he was alive. He couldn't move but he felt alive. He could see, think, move his eyes and experience emotion, extreme emotion. For the next seventeen, painful minutes he felt nothing but somber, terrible bereavement as his wife cried into her hand. She never once laid eyes on him as he sat desperately and furiously in his chair, unable to move a muscle.

Allison stood. Her eyes glanced in his direction. *Finally,* he thought. *I'm here, I'm right here!* He screamed in his brain. Her tortured expression did not change as she approached the chair. She lifted Theo out of his seat and took him into her arms. Baffled beyond any words, he went mad with confusion. *How had she picked me up?* He pondered wildly. He was distracted by the warmth of her arms and the smell of tobacco smoke combined with a soothing pinch of perfume. She had only worn that perfume for special occasions. He had not smelled it in years. Two *new* realizations hit him. He could feel and he could smell. Tiny steps but at least they were in the right direction. But why couldn't he move, how could she be holding him and why was he so high above the ground?

The carpet looked as though it was twenty feet away and she was moving freely while clutching him like a baby.

A thought occurred to Theo that hadn't before. The thought struck like a club to the head and made him feel incredibly stupid. He took a breath of relief. *This was a dream,* he concluded. One of those dreams you hear about but don't understand until you have one yourself. Sleep paralysis and night terrors. He always heard them mentioned and felt sorry for the poor saps that had them. Now he was having *his* and it was awful. However, understanding the condition gave him comfort. Enough comfort to help him deal with the nightmare until he woke up. It's not like he had a choice. *Sleep paralysis,* he thought. *That's what it had to be. There was no other explanation.* He was dreaming about his own funeral and it felt real as hell.

Desi entered the living room. He wore a black jacket and a small necktie with gray pants. His expression was flat and lifeless. He hugged his mother the same way he had when she came home that day with groceries. Theo could see him below from his wife's tight embrace. Desi sniffled and wiped his eyes. A sound Theo knew all too well and still fresh in his mind from the trash bin incident yesterday. Or days ago, or a week ago for all he knew. He wasn't sure how far in the future he had traveled in this dream. He shrugged off the thought. Allison sank to one knee. Theo was now eye to eye with his son, examining his sad face. He sorely wanted to hold his son and tell him how much he loved him. If he could move, he'd take him to the nearest store with a toy section and buy him everything he wanted. He'd even take out a loan for it. A small loan, of course.

Allison spoke, "Your dad wanted you to have this when you were older. It was very special to him and he wanted you to have it. I think you're ready now. I know you'll take good care of him," she whispered. Theo felt more confusion as his son took him into the crook of his arm and held him close. Allison stood and ran her hands through her son's blonde locks. "Why don't you go brush your hair, sweetie. Look good for Daddy, Ok?" She asked kindly.

"Ok," Desi said. Theo's son proceeded to carry him across the room, up the stairs, around the corner and into the master bathroom, located in his and Allison's bedroom. Theo was placed on the long, vanity sink. The light was flipped on and his son took a comb from a drawer. He began meticulously combing each follicle, individually.

Theo's heart drummed. It almost burst from his chest due to what he saw before him.

He was sitting on the cold marble of the counter. He could feel it icy against his ass and one of his legs. He was facing the mirror. His reflection looked *nothing like him.* He didn't even look human. Everything he had experienced since waking up made grisly sense and all of the pieces came together before his round, black eyes. In the crystal-clear reflection, his mother's teddy bear stared lifelessly back at him. He clutched the red heart against his fuzzy chest and his leg had been torn off, just as it had in the garbage truck. He ran through every painful detail in his throbbing head and everything fit perfectly and seamlessly like a jigsaw puzzle. *He* was the teddy bear. That is why he couldn't move, that is why he was given to his son and the missing leg was the reason he couldn't feel the pain in his ankle. The bear was missing from the mantle in the living room and he was thoughtfully placed in his easy chair because the bear was the one thing in the house that represented himself other than his real body. No doubt he was put there by Allison.

This nightmare made too much sense. Dreams are supposed to be a mismatched stew of random thoughts that make absolutely no sense at all. That's what made them dreams. Theo refused the idea of any of this being real and he refused to even consider that his human body could be in a coffin somewhere. Ignorantly, logically, he clung to the sleep paralysis hypothesis like a grounded water pipe during a typhoon. His miniature heart still raced.

Desi finished crafting his hairdo, replaced the comb and took his dad from the sink. Theo was carried to the bed and gently laid on his own pillow, facing the ceiling. His son pulled the covers over his tiny body. Allison entered. "Uncle Lewis and Aunt Carol just got here. Grandma is on her way. Let's get downstairs and greet everyone as they arrive, ok?" she requested softly.

Desi placed his hand on his father's chest, upon the silk heart below the comforter. "I'm going to put him here. In Dad's spot," he said lovingly.

Allison nodded and smiled. "I'm sure he would have loved that," she replied. The child caught up to his mother as they both stepped out of the room and closed the door. Theo was left to his thoughts.

Reason, fear and paranoia battled for countability in his mind. The ceiling fan turned slowly as his ideas churned, processing everything he had witnessed in the last hour, or however long it had been. He knew he was in the living room for about twenty-eight minutes because he could see the wall clock from his chair. Any time passing after that was a guess. He was exhausted from worry, stress, confusion and aggravation. His eyes felt heavy but he couldn't close them. He was blessed with fatigue. He smiled internally at the thought of falling asleep and was elated to realize he was slowly fading into slumber. The white ceiling dimmed and the fan blades blurred. Theo would wake up soon and this nightmare would end.

He woke up again. The ceiling was dark and the fan still turned. The sound of distant chatter flowed into the room from under the closed door. He heard the toilet flush from the bathroom in the hall. A door opened, closed and footsteps jogged down the padded stairs on the other side of his bedroom wall. Tapping plates, a laugh here and there and young squeals from stray children peppered the cocktail of barely audible pressures his ears picked up and translated for his brain. *No,* he thought. *This can't still be happening!* Insane screaming from inside his little, felt head exploded into the air around him in complete and total silence. He shouted, roared, cried and groaned with unbridled agony with not so much as a whisper to the room around him. His eyes were frozen open. The movement of the blades and the noise from the living room was his only concept of time. Hours or seconds or weeks seemed to pass. The ceiling stayed black, the fan spun and chatter continued as the nightmare unceasingly drew on.

The bedroom door opened. He couldn't see who entered. Two voices spoke in whispers from the foot of the bed. He recognized Allison's musical tone but had no idea who the older male's voice could be. He listened intently, examining every word.

"I'm proud of you, Allison," the man said. "You're holding your composure for the sake of your family and it's something to be admired. But it can be damaging as well. It's ok to cry, everyone will understand. Don't keep it all pent up, you need to ventilate or the backdraft will hit you with a vengeance when you're left to your own, tonight."

Theo heard the flick of a lighter. The waft of cigarette smoke filled the room.

"I know," Allison replied. "I'll deal with that my own way. I just want to get through today without making a mess of myself in front of my mother and my son. Is that wrong?" She asked.

"That's between you and God," the man said. "I'm just an extra hand, a vessel, if you will. I'm here to help in any way I can."

"Thank you for that beautiful service, Father," Allison whispered. "You're blessed with an incredible way with words. I just wish he could have been there to hear it."

Father fucking Francine! Theo roared. *That son of a bitch! What the hell was he doing speaking to Allison in private and why the hell was he in my bedroom?!* He thought violently. Hatred seethed through his miniature, bear body and he wanted to choke the priest out with his undersized, bear hands. Theo imagined all the things he would do to that righteous prick as soon as he woke up and had his body back. He knew the thought made no sense at all but he decided to ride out his anger and let it flourish, even if it *was* vastly unreasonable.

"Theodore was a good man," Father Francine said sincerely. "He just didn't realize it. If he would have given me the time of day, I could have talked to him as a man, not as a priest. God's voice can reach out to us in many forms, no matter where we are or what state of mind we're in. But, it's up to *us to go to him.* Nobody is dragged to his grace, kicking and screaming. Sometimes we need to close our eyes, let go of our pride and just trust."

Allison replied, "Talking to him wouldn't have changed what happened. Don't assume it would have, this wasn't your fault."

"I guess we all blame ourselves when a travesty happens, partially or wholly," the Father stated. "It's in our nature to regret. It can keep us focused on what we can do now to prevent, or it can keep us sightless, suck in the belief that there is nothing we can do to change things. Theo is a smart man. I just pray he kept his mind open, just a little, in this world and the world after.

Theo didn't dare admit to himself that he was touched by what the priest had said, or maybe he had already. Based on the current circumstances and in the light of his present suffering, he almost wished he had spoken to Francine. As a man, not a priest. Obviously, not as a priest.

No, Theo thought stubbornly. *Father Francine is a complacent ass.* He had already duped his wife and he had almost hooked Theo as well, just now. Religious figures always had their tricks, agendas, schemes and their ways with words, as Allison had *just stated* not a minute ago. Theo built a metaphorical wall around his mind and decided to dismiss anything the priest had to say. He wouldn't become a blind sheep, obeying every word set before them by a shepherd. If someone is preaching obedience, they're selling you something, every time.

"Thank you so much, Father. You have no idea how much I appreciate you being here. For me, for Theo and for Desi. It means more to me than you know," Allison's breath was barely audible.

"Of course, my child," he said. "Anything you need, always."

"Father?" She asked. Desperation lingered on her breath.

"Yes, Allison," he answered.

"Do you think..? Do you think you could be here, right now... for me. As a man, not as a priest? Could you *do that* for me?"

What in the holy hell did that mean?! Theo bellowed. His blood boiled over with outrage and blind indignation. He tried convincing himself that he had misunderstood his wife's words but there was *no wholesome way* to interpret Allison's breathy request. He tried moving his three, mini limbs through sheer will and intense, searing emotion but the stuffed bear laid motionless on the pillow, under the covers, writhing with hate.

"Of course," Father Francine said.

Theo swore he heard the sound of hands moving against fabric and the taps of light, passionate kissing. Their breathing became heavier and motions became louder. Suddenly, something heavy struck the bed and Theo was knocked off the pillow and onto the floor. Breaths became gasps and a pair of Allison's panties fell right before Theo's wide, outraged eyes.

All he could do was stare at the lacy pattern on his wife's black lingerie as the sounds of their lovemaking echoed against the walls and into his impeccable, perfect, furry, little ears.

Theo sat at a round table seated in a chair sized perfectly for his stature in Desi's messy bedroom. A wicker, picnic hat rested on his fuzzy, brown head and a cowboy kerchief was tied around his neck. His dinner guests included a green rabbit, a wind-up robot and a yellow triceratops sporting a pair of aviator sunglasses. A thick, foam slice of pizza was served before him on a paper plate with a side of plastic carrots as a supplement to counter the carbs in the Chicago-style entree. Desi was dressed as a fireman, pouring imaginary coffee for each member at the table. Decaf for the rabbit. He evidently had an allergy to wheat as the three-year-old host had announced just minutes ago over dessert, which was butter on ice cream with snow peas as a garnish. Desi hummed a song to himself he had heard on the TV as he added french fries to the coffee. He had heard the song about four weeks ago and was still humming it today. Theo longed for the next childish tune that would catch his son's fancy. To what, he did not care, no matter how repetitive or monotonous it would be. At least the next song would be different.

Theo had somewhat of an idea regarding the amount of time that had passed since he was blessed with an adorable, yet inoperable body. He had lost his precise count at around 22 days and Allison was beginning to talk about her mother's birthday, so he figured he was at about five weeks since the transformation. He had long abandoned the idea of sleep paralysis, unless he was in some kind of coma. He was convinced this was real. It was real everyday and every day was the same. He'd wake up at eight in the morning, cursing God's name for another day in purgatory. Breakfast was watching Desi play with his food. He'd take a walk around the block with the family at 10 and visit the park on Sundays, and Wednesdays, attendance mandatory. Lunch was at noon followed by pizza and carrots with his three friends, and dinner was at six. Desi would pick at his food again. At least one night a week, Father Francine would show up, visit for 10 minutes, then disappear upstairs with Allison for another session between the sheets. Bedtime began with a story read by his cheating wife and it was lights-out twenty minutes later. Theo would fall asleep beside his son, awaiting another inevitable repeat of the day he had just involuntarily participated in.

His mind was turning to mush. He knew he should be appreciating the newfound time he was spending with his son, but he did not. Not from the end of day one of the humdrum. He wondered if this could go on forever. After about 35 days of this bullshit, he was damn sure that it would. What would happen when Desi grew up? Would Theo end up with his grandkids or on a shelf in a dime store, gathering dust and waiting for the next child to begin the process all over again? Child after child, decade after decade?

Theo hated. He hated harder than he had ever hated before and wished nothing but death to every member of the human race, including his family. He longed for the destruction of Earth so he would finally be put to some kind of rest. He wanted *that* far more than he wanted his easy chair, his TV and a beer. His mind was a vengeful lump of excrement, begging for death and blind to any form of change or hope.

Desi approached the little table holding a plastic treasure chest filled with "fairy dust" and announced to the group that happy thoughts would activate it. What Desi would use the dust for after that, Theo had no idea and didn't give a damn.

"What is your happy thought, Robert?" Desi asked the green rabbit. He leaned in close, smiled and shouted, "Birthday parties? I love birthday parties!" The boy bounced on his knees and inched closer to the triceratops. "What is your happy thought, Cameron?" He leaned in again. "Football? I love football!" He cheered.

Desi got to his feet and came up behind Theo, whispering into his ear, "What is your happy thought, Teddy?" It wasn't until that very moment that Theo realized that *Teddy* was short for Theodore, the name appearing on his birth certificate and possibly, by this point, his death certificate. He had always gone by Theo. The irony of his transformation into a stuffed bear relating so directly to his given name should have intrigued him. But it did just the opposite. It infuriated him. Desi repeated himself, "What's your happy thought, Teddy?"

Fuck your happy thought, Theo snapped. *And fuck this picnic and fuck this day-after-day bullshit!* It didn't matter what he thought, happy or otherwise. Nobody could or would ever hear him.

"Do you have a happy thought?" His son asked a third time. Theo was so beside himself with white-hot anger he wished his son could hear him say *Go screw yourself* just once, out loud and he'd be satisfied, at least for a few days. Desi gave up and bounced on his knees, in the direction of the robot. All at once, chills ran through Theo as an observation hit him like a punch to the gut. Desi got an imaginary answer right away from the rabbit and the dinosaur, but asked Teddy three times with no made-up response. If Desi was simply playing pretend with his toys, he would have made up an answer for Teddy, just as he did with the others. The thought was daunting. There had to be a reason for it.

Just as Desi asked the robot what *his* happy thought was, Allison let out an odd, intense shriek from downstairs then a crack rang out like the sound of a chair falling over. Something was wrong. Desi jumped to his feet and disappeared into the hall. His feet hopped down the steps and the thuds grew distant. Silence followed. He didn't hear Desi, he didn't hear his wife. No banging, no knock at the door, no footsteps and no phone ringing. Just silence for minutes now, as though the house was completely abandoned.

The light cascading through the bedroom window faded and night fell. Theo sat awake in his little chair through the hours until blue then orange dawnlight emerged. Something was very, very wrong. Not a sound for at least 12 hours. He pondered fearfully, desperately considering every possible scenario that would lead to Allison's shout, Desi's absence and utter quiet throughout the night as he sat at his extended picnic. And why had Desi not received a happy thought from Theo when asked? Nothing made sense. But, considering everything since the garbage truck incident, being transformed into a bear made equal sense.

The day passed and night came again. Another day, another night. Two days now. Absolute hell. Where was Desi? What had happened to Allison? Around late afternoon, Theo heard footsteps. Little footsteps. *Thank God!* He thought. Desi walked through the door slowly, rubbing his eyes. His hair was disheveled. He looked like he had just woken up from an extended nap and he was still in his fireman uniform. Dry chocolate and crumbs were smeared across his mouth and cheek. What had he been doing for the last two days? Was Allison dead? Father Francine's last visit had been just a few dawns ago so he wouldn't be returning for another booty call for another four or five days. Someone had to call or visit. Anyone. Some competent adult had to realize that something was wrong.

Desi lazily took Theo by the foot and carried him slowly into the hall. His hat and kerchief fell to the floor. Desi descended the stairs and Theo finally got to see the living room again. It looked the same as it had the last morning he had come home from work. A mess. Toys and playthings scattered the floor with coloring pages and crayons littered like debris. But no Allison. Theo smelled a foul and pungent odor as he was carried to the kitchen. Then, there she was.

Allison laid on the tile beside the counter where the blue spill of Sports-Ade had been. A large, silver kitchen knife rested beside her limp palm. Her skin was a greenish-yellow tint and fluid had dripped from her nose and dried on her cheek. She was dead. For a split second he wondered how it had happened but he quickly remembered her heart condition. It must have been a stroke or heart attack. At least that's what her doctor was always warning her about.

Every hateful thought Theo had towards his wife burned to cinders and terrible sadness engulfed him. If he was able to cry, he would have. He sobbed with heaving breaths and his mind screamed with anguish as his teddy bear face remained still and motionless.

Desi approached the body and wiped his eyes. "I'm hungry," he moaned.

Theo roared with agony. His wife, who he loved was dead and his three-year-old son was now left to his own devices alone. Alone for two days now. Desi stood over his dead mother waiting for a response and kept repeating, "I'm hungry, mommy and I want water" over and over again. A chair had been pushed against the open pantry and the open refrigerator. Cookie, pretzel and granola bar wrappers covered the tiles like the toys in the living room. Desi had eaten like a king for most likely a day and was now out of food. He hadn't had anything to drink since Allison had died. There were no open bottles and he knew his son couldn't reach the sink or the fridge dispenser.

Desi approached the knife. *No, no, no,* Theo thought. *Don't touch that!* He took the knife from the floor and looked around the kitchen. He reached up and placed it carefully on the kitchen table and let it be. *Good boy,* Theo sighed. At least Desi was smart enough to know that knives were dangerous and had to be put away.

Theo was carried around the house as Desi searched the bedrooms, bathrooms, halls and dining room. He was mortified by the feeling of helplessness. There was absolutely nothing he could do to help his son. He wanted so badly to help. Their tour ended in the downstairs hallway beside the front door. Theo dangled from Desi's fingers as he attempted to turn the doorknob.

He grunted as his small hand helplessly pawed at the brass, but it wouldn't matter anyway. The dead bolt was locked and Desi wouldn't be able to reach or undo it. Desi gave up and stopped in front of the garage door. He just stood there, staring at it. *Oh, God no. Leave the garage alone,* Theo whispered. He was placed on the floor as his son ran into the kitchen. Wood scratched against ceramic as Desi pushed a chair from the kitchen table, down the hall and to the garage door. He climbed onto the seat and used both hands to turn the knob. The door opened. The chair was removed and the door was swung wide open. Theo sat in front of the open boundary as the little boy flipped on the lights and examined the deadly state in which his father had always left his garage. The chop saw sat on the floor, two gasoline canisters beside it. A rusty, tetanus-covered muffler, an open bag of lawn fertilizer, three open cans of motor oil and a pouch of rat poison were all exposed and available for Desi to do as he pleased, with extreme hunger and thirst raging within his throat and belly.

Theo's thoughts went into a frenzy. He clung to the one concept that could keep his son from certain death and that was his repeated, past instructions, "Don't touch anything in Daddy's garage." Desi wasn't stupid, he was a smart kid and he could remember absolutely everything. Especially the things he and Allison hadn't wanted him to remember. Theo watched Desi softly approach the open container of lawn fertilizer. The pellets were brown and looked like pretzel rods. Theo's heart raced. Desi stared at the pretzels and took a long, hard look. Then, he took a step back. He pointed at the bag and shouted sternly in his squeaky voice, "Daddy says don't touch!"

Theo sighed with exhausted relief. He *was* a smart kid. That deterrence would hopefully keep Desi safe from everything else in the garage, if he held to it. But if someone didn't show up soon, his son could starve to death or die of dehydration. Desi headed back to the open door. He placed his hand high up onto the light switch and took one last look around the garage. He glanced at the tools, car-parts, open bottles and yard tools and paused. Desi said one word that made Theo die inside. "Blue?" His son said curiously. Against the far wall, beside the lawn mower, sat an open, half-bottle of antifreeze. The liquid was blue. The words Theo had spoken to Desi weeks ago, came back like a vengeful phantom and repeated in his head, *"If it's blue you can drink it. It's ok if your mom didn't tell you if you could have it."*

Insane screaming resonated inside the helpless, little bear's head as Desi walked across the cold, concrete floor and easily lifted the antifreeze bottle from the floor. He drank, eagerly. Just like he had with the Sports-Ade. He pulled the bottle away from his mouth and took a breath. A little blue mustache appeared above his upper lip. Immediately, Desi's eyes went wide. His body shook as if experiencing a shiver from cold. He began to cry, but stopped. He just stood there, holding the bottle in both hands. He opened his mouth and blue liquid spewed onto the floor. Desi shook again. His body continued to vomit until nothing was left in his stomach. Heaving spasms overtook him. He dropped the bottle onto the floor and collapsed, his mouth still open and heaving. Theo watched his son tremble on the floor and ease into stillness. He laid on the cold floor beside the lawn mower and died in his fireman costume, under the silent hum of the garage light.

Theo had passed sadness, turmoil and madness, and plummeted straight into paralyzing delirium. It was as though a teddy bear lobotomy had been performed. The part of his brain that allowed him to rationalize, shriveled up and rotted between his fuzzy ears. He could only think in brief, short whispers and his mind grew further and further away from coherence. Anger, sadness and hostility took over completely, leaving patience, understanding and solicitude to decay.

For five days, Theo sat on the floor facing the open garage between the bodies of his wife and his son. Cursing, hateful banter and screams of grief and unrelenting misery erupted behind his round, shiny eyes.

One day, around mid-afternoon, a knock came at the door. Theo's head finally silenced after 120 hours of angry noise. The knock came again. He remained silent, just listening. The dead-bolt unlocked and so did the knob. The door swung open and Father Francine peeked his head inside. "Allison?!" He called out. Silence. He stepped into the hall and swiftly made his way to the kitchen. "Oh, gracious, no!" He shouted. Theo heard the priest begin to sob then inhale sharply. "Desi!" He cried. Then, called the name again. His shoes tapped across the floor, down the hall and up the stairs. "Desi, where are you?" He screamed desperately as he ran back down again.

He stopped suddenly beside Theo and before the open garage door. The priest yelped sadly and ran to Desi's side. Taking the boy's head in his hand and covering his mouth with the other, he cried over the deceased mother and son. Theo just stared, wide-eyed and lobotomized.

The authorities were called and the bodies were taken downtown. Father Francine made funeral arrangements for the both of them. He brought Allison's mother to the house to go through personal things and prepare for the burial. Their final resting place would be Saint Alexander's cemetery, located a few blocks from Allison's church. Theo's mother-in-law cried as she clutched an armful of documents and a few treasured items, including the crucifix that Theo had so hated. She thanked the Father for coming with her and left the home, unable to bear staying in the house for another minute. The priest took one last look around before closing the door to depart and noticed the bear on the floor. He stepped over, picked up Theo and took a long examining look at his eyes, heart and missing leg. He raised his eyebrows and took Theo with him, placing him in a pocket and locking the door.

Theo was placed on the mahogany podium as Father Francine gave an extended eulogy before two, open caskets to a filled church. The service went on as Theo looked upon all the faces present. Some of which he hadn't seen in years, along with many members of his own family. The priest closed with a reading from the book of John and closed with a prayer. The congregation rose softly and slowly filed past the decorated caskets, giving their final respects.

The church emptied and Father Francine remained at the podium. He took the bear into his soft hand and looked upon its eyes. "Theo," he said to the stuffed toy. "Are you ready to come home?" He asked in a gentle voice.

Deep in the recesses of Theo's barely-operating mind, he muscled out one, conscious answer. An answer that would be the one, final cognitive thought he would ever muster. Theo reached deep down into his soul and pieced together his last, final, inaudible words. *Fuck you, priest!* Theo roared. Father Francine sighed, looked upon the bear as though he had just lost a child and a tear fell from his eye.

He slowly walked to Desi's open casket, placed the teddy bear in the crook of his little arm and shut the lid. Theo would go to his son's final resting place, awake, sentient and tormented for the remainder of eternity by his own carelessness, temperament and ignorance. There was indeed a place for everything, as Theo had so strictly believed. A place for playthings, a place for the discarded and a place for his ass. And *this* place was where he would remain in the dark, forever.

One hour after the garbage truck accident, Theo's body was loaded into an ambulance beside Allison and Father Francine's parked vehicles. Theo's wife cried into the priest's chest as he comforted her, a lit cigarette pinched in her fingers. Desi stood beside his mother, holding her by the hand, his face flat and expressionless. "Don't worry," the Father said kindly. "Theo was a good man, he just didn't realize it. God can speak to us no matter where we are, in this life and the next. But it's up to *us* to go to *him*."

THE VISITOR
A Haunting Yarn Of Insomnia

Evan argued with his parents in their suburban home. The disputes had become ongoing for several months, without missing a single night. Each evening, the boy was terrified of retiring to his bedroom. He felt safe during the day, but when the sun had long passed and the hours deepened into darkness—something visited him. Something sinister. Something evil. The altercation was muffled from the blackness of his foreboding room. The childish optimism of toys, games and cheery decor was muted by a haunting and deathly presence. Dread hung thick in the air.

Abruptly, the argument ended and a door was slammed closed. Evan sobbed as he slowly made his way down the hall. Pausing in the shaded doorway, he checked his space thoroughly before sprinting to his bed and ducking under his comforter.

He laid in bed, wide awake. It would be hours before he fell asleep. Dismay reflected in his wide eyes as he stared into the darkness, fearful of any movement, any disturbance and any sound. For roughly ten, deafening seconds, silence ensued.

"Saludos, Evan." A gruff voice made him jump. He threw his blanket over his face and whimpered audibly.

Evan prayed for just *one night* of rest without a formidable disturbance. Tears soaked his eyes. "Don't worry, Evan. I'm not your ghost," it said. The sound of a lighter tinged and sparked. The faint light of a flame cast a shadow of a figure against a far wall. The sour odor of cigarette smoke bit the air. Evan peeked over his blanket as the flame doused. "Having trouble sleeping?" The voice asked. The intruder sounded friendly but indifferent at the same time. Its deep tone and funny accent reminded Evan of Puss in Boots.

"Yes," Evan replied with a whisper.

"Mom and Dad don't believe you?" The voice asked.

"No," he wheezed.

The visitor took a long puff on the tiny, glowing ash and exhaled, "Most parents don't." Evan sat up in his bed. His fear had subsided from the moments before. The calm voice and the comforting words it spoke was a vast improvement over what Evan typically experienced each night. It continued, "Most grown ups are scared. So they don't believe. It protects them. But it also makes them stubborn." Another lungful of smoke, then a long exhale. "Unfortunately, stubborn parents can often make their little boy feel *stupid* when he sees something real."

Confusion and intrigue danced in Evan's head. "Who are you?" He asked. A small, dinosaur lamp clicked on in the corner of the room, illuminating the visitor. The man looked to be in his mid-thirties, with days of scruff on his chin and wavy, black hair. He had a dark vigilante look about him, like an outlaw cowboy or Zorro without a mask. Evan did not recognize the folding lawn-chair the visitor sat in, nor the tall bottle of olive oil and plastic grocery bags at his feet. The sharp scent of basil and rosemary added to the pungent tobacco.

"I'm another little boy," the man said. Cigarette pinched between his knuckles, he unwrapped a sandwich covered in plastic and took a bite. "Like *you*," he added with a full mouth.

Evan eyed the man and then the sandwich. "Those are my dad's. For work." Zorro lifted the turkey on swiss with ciabatta and examined it. "My mom makes them for him," Evan said.

"She's good," the man praised. "Good mustard. French's dijon?" He asked.

"Store brand," Evan answered.

The stranger lifted the bread and observed the item's inner-ingredients. "*¡Desplumador! Hijo de puta,*" he remarked.

"What does *that* mean?" Evan squawked.

The man feigned incognizance. His eyes darted innocently. "What does *what* mean?"

"Those words you used," Evan clarified. "In another language."

He took another large bite before stowing the sandwich in the inside pocket of his long, brown jacket. Evan briefly noticed a necklace of small, dehydrated animal bones around the man's neck as he pocketed the plastic and bread. "It means ...I love sandwiches," the man fibbed. Evan rolled his eyes, the lie was visibly noticeable. "But I *did not* just come here for a snack." He doused his cigarette on the clean, white, finish of the lamp-table. The man sat back in his lawn chair and straightened his coat. "I've been looking for you for a long time, Evan," he said. He cocked his head to the side. "Well, not *you* in particular," he clarified. *"Your friend."* Evan's confusion grew. "You have a ghost," the man growled. Evan nodded. His fear returned as he thought on his blight. His fingers tapped the bedsheets as he frittered. "When does it come?" The visitor asked.

Evan frowned. "Every night. When it's dark and my mom and dad go to bed."

"Where does it come from?" The man asked.

Raising his little arm, Evan pointed hesitantly toward a large, hanging quilt on the wall opposite his bed. The unsightly, 19th century bedspread was decoratively displayed, taking up a good six by five feet of vertical space. "From my mom's blanket. It's haunted," Evan whimpered.

The visitor beheld the tapestry. *"It's ugly,"* he quickly off-handed. His seat creaked as he stood and neared the quilt. Evan grew nervous. "Does the ghost talk to you?" He questioned.

"Yes," Evan answered.

"Do you talk back to it?" He asked.

The child shivered with dismay. "No. I can't understand what it's saying."

"Good boy," the man said. "Your friend only speaks Spanish. It needs to know that you can see it before it acts. If you had spoken back—in any language—It would have taken you with it."

"Taken me where?" Evan inquired with a tinge of panic.

Ignoring the question, the man placed his open hand gently at the center of the decoration. "It comes from here?" Evan nodded again. The man took the edges of the quilt into his fingers.

"Don't touch it!" Evan whispered loudly, throwing out his hand.

An assuring finger was brought to the man's lips. "Don't worry, Evan. I'm a professional." He showboated with dramatic hand movements like a street magician to play to the boy's naivete. He slowly felt the fabric, rubbed its worn texture with his palm and sniffed it thoroughly as Evan watched with intrigue. He released the tapestry and dropped his hands to his sides. He turned to Evan. "This blanket is not haunted," he concluded. "I think you may be mistaken."

Evan became frustrated. "It *is haunted!* The ghost comes out of there *every night!* It's old! Really old! My mom's grandma gave it to her and her grandma gave it to—" As Evan spoke, the visitor whirled around and tore the quilt from the wall, exposing a splatter of black ectoplasm, infecting the drywall with a frightening and transcendental energy. Evan's eyes went wide with shock. The man examined the blemish as he carelessly gathered the quilt and tossed it aside.

An expression of awestruck familiarity and cynical joy shined in the man's stare as he looked upon the heinous portal. He lifted his hand and felt its current as the substance oozed and breathed. "Por fin te encontré hijo de puta," he whispered with a grin. *"This,* is where your friend is coming from, Evan." Taking a step back, he returned to his squeaky chair and made himself comfortable.

Evan's gaze snapped back and forth between the seated stranger and the black, searing mass. "What happens now?" He asked.

The visitor reached into one of his grocery bags and pulled out a tall, glass bottle of Mexican Coke. He twisted off the top and took a swig. He tilted the bottle, pointing it in Evan's direction. "This time, don't cover your face with your blanket when your ghost approaches you," he instructed.

Evan winced, *"It's still coming?"*

"You said it comes every night," the man spat. The boy's expression went dead-pan. "Now, lay on your pillow and make believe I'm not even here," he ordered. Evan just stared at him. He didn't know what he had expected the man to do about his supernatural problem, but he was hoping for more than *this.* "Beddy-bye time, Evan," the intruder encouraged. "Go to sleep. Ve a dormir. Arrorró mi niño."

Evan didn't appreciate the condescension but he had no other options. Telling his parents about the visitor would result in him facing the ghost by himself again. He slowly leaned back and laid his head flat against his pillow. He pulled the blanket up under his chin. "Are you going to kill it?" Evan asked.

"Nobody can kill a ghost," the man growled softly. "And if I did kill it, it would be of little use to me."

Evan heard the Coke bottle tip back, followed by a hard swallow. "When the ghost speaks to you tonight ...answer," he whispered.

"But won't it try to take me away?!" Evan shrieked.

The dinosaur lamp was clicked off and the entire room went black. The child stared fearfully into the dark void of the ceiling. "Oh, Evan..," the voice said. "That is *exactly* what I am counting on."

El Rubi, Mexico

25 years prior, Julio laid in bed and stared at the black ceiling. He was eight years old. His bedroom was dirty, sweltering and meager. Nothing decorated the walls and all of his belongings were packed in wooden crates and boxes in the center of a dingy oval rug. Beside his head, a small bible, a rosary and an antique Zippo rested on a tilted stool.

Terror rushed through his veins as he shivered under his thin, orange blanket. He turned his head and glanced quickly at a large, black stain that had formed on his wall, below the ceiling. The blemish was dark like tar and streams from the stigma seemed to drip downward without movement. Julio snapped his gaze back to the ceiling and continued to tremble. He waited—for hours. Just as sleep began to take hold and heavy eyelids became impossible to restrain—*it appeared.*

In the corner of his eye, Julio saw a dark shape move from the direction of the stain like a shadow gliding smoothly across the wall. His body's warrant for sleep vanished and the terror returned in full vigor. He made every mental attempt to keep his eyes on the ceiling but pure impulse forced him to turn his head and point his sights directly in the movement's direction.

From the stain, an apparition emerged. A twisting, nightmarish figure with long, slim arms and a gnarled face floated through the blistered wall with two, nefarious, dead eyes fixated on Julio's fearful gaze. The legless entity drifted silently like a dying birthday balloon, across the room and toward his pillow. Julio looked away as beads of sweat dripped from his forehead and into his eyes. The sweat burned like soap but he did not dare move or react. The ghost brought its ghastly face just centimeters from the boy's cheek and halted its movement. It hovered above the stack of boxes as ebony vapor emitted from its body like smoke from a doused candle. Julio choked back whimpers and moans as he cried in the back of his throat. After what felt like hours, the beast spoke.

"¿Me ves?" The creature asked. Its voice sounded like a corpse brought back to living after centuries of torment in the furnace. Julio did not speak. He did not dare. He had never spoken to it. Not a gasp, not a squeak, not a word. The corpse spoke again, "¿Me ves?" This time the question was more aggressive. Fluid poured from Julio's nose and over his mouth. His hands and feet were ice cold in the heat of the sweltering room. The entity began to quiver. The sound of snapping bone and tearing flesh could be heard clearly as the ghost turned its rotting head and placed its deathly mouth against Julio's right eye.

"¿¡MEEE VEEEEES!?" The monster screamed horrifically with one frozen and hollow breath. The hellish voice shook the room and crashed against the boy's eardrum as he struggled to remain silent. Julio's flesh crawled and his entire body ached. Grueling minutes as the apparition remained.

Suddenly, the ghost huffed, lifted its dangling arms and departed from the bed. With one swift movement, it vanished back into the stain and through the wall, returning to the infierno from which it only could have come.

Julio quickly sat up, gasping and heaving. He grabbed for the Zippo, flipped the top open and lit a flame. Weak light shined upon the mark of death on his wall. The ghost was gone. He took a breath of relief, confident it would not return—at least not tonight. It had come through the stain every night since he could remember and on *truly terrible* nights, it would speak to him—or worse. But not anymore.

Shaking out the flame, he dried his face with his blanket and held the silver lighter in the faint reflection of night light. The words *La valentía se encuentra en el miedo y la oscuridad,* were etched into its side. He gave the stain a final look in the dark. "Me deshice de ti para siempre," he whispered. He would never have to see the demon again, he thought. Not tomorrow. Not ever. He was rid of it for good.

He smiled as he dwelled on the following morning. Tomorrow, mamá was moving him to California where they would both live with her new husband and Julio's new stepfather. He would finally be rid of the ghost that came out of the wall and after tonight, would never have to go to bed in paralyzing and gut-twisting terror again.

In the weeks that passed Julio and his mom had moved to Santa Monica, into the new two-bedroom apartment Nicolas had rented for them. Nicolas was a kind papá. He was friendly, patient and Julio could tell that he loved Mamá very much. By association, Julio as well. Nicolas never lost his temper, he made time for his family and always included Julio when making plans. However, Nicolas *did* have a tendency to curse—a lot. Over a short several weeks, Julio learned an impressive and abundant vocabulary of new words. In Spanish *and* in English.

The new family lived on the fourth floor of a shiny apartment building with a tall security fence. Their windows looked out onto a community playground, a flea market and a bank advertising, *Cash Loans With No Credit*. Julio's room was massive and full of toys. Seventy, carpeted square feet of Matchbox trucks, stuffed animals, video game posters, a beanbag chair and a bed in the shape of a race car. He had clean, running water, dependable electricity and un baño you didn't have to hold your breath to use. Compared to the shack he was used to in Mexico, Julio's new home was a palace. California was truly a blessing. *Moreso* was his mother's online encounter with Nicolas and his devotion and love for them both.

Julio already spoke English. His mother made sure he grew up knowing both languages and all of the channels he had watched on TV were beamed directly from the USA. Now, he had an even *bigger* TV and seventeen more channels to watch. Every evening he would enjoy two reruns of *The Rifleman* along with one episode of *Batman* starring Adam West, nestled snugly between Mamá and Nicolas on their big sofa. Julio preferred heroic dramas to sitcoms. He felt inspired by masked avengers performing selfless deeds to bring justice and protect those who could not protect themselves.

One night, Julio woke to shouting behind his bedroom wall. Out of impulse, his nervousness piqued. The shout came again. The disturbance must have been from a different apartment. His room was right between a separate unit and the edge of the building. Julio wasn't accustomed to this type of disturbance. He had never shared a wall with strangers. A third shout resonated followed by the sound of a door slamming and a child crying, an older child. Julio jumped out of bed and turned on his light.

To be absolutely sure, he checked his walls. No stain, no black, no ghost. He crawled back into bed and reassembled his thoughts. As Julio laid in his warm bed and allowed tiredness to overtake him, he could still hear the boy behind the wall sobbing softly and lonesomely, well into the night.

The next day, Julio made his daily visit to the park in the main courtyard. The sky was blue and the sun was shining. A cool breeze blew through the richly lit palm trees and desert lilies. A bustle of children played on the equipment, crowding the slide, swings and merry-go-round. He noticed a boy sitting on a bench alone. He looked about Julio's age with red hair and freckles. He seemed lonely, even sad. Instead of joining the other children, Julio approached the boy and sat beside him.

"Hi," Julio greeted, making his best attempt to sound like a true, native Californian. Although, he may have added a bit too much of a drawl thanks to the abundance of *Andy Griffith Show* episodes he grew up with.

The boy sighed in response, "Hi."

Awkward silence passed. Julio struggled to find words. "I just moved here with my mom. We're from Mexico," he blurted out. "It's nice here." The red-headed boy sat quietly. His fingers were laced together in his lap and his head hung, woefully. He didn't speak. "How old are you?" Julio asked.

"Seven," the boy said. More silence.

"I'm eight," Julio replied. The dead air began to thicken. There had to be something he could say to begin an engaging conversation. Julio searched his thoughts for anything that might interest an American second-grader who had everything. He quickly conjured the most captivating motion he could come up with. "I know a lot of curse words in Spanish," he spat. "If you'd like to learn any," he added.

The child turned his head and gave Julio an odd smile. The sudden turn in the conversation drew a wide grin across the kid's face. His green eyes reflected the sunlight as he giggled. "Really?" He asked, amused.

"Sí," Julio replied. His ability to speak Spanish felt like a superpower in the company of his new, unofficial friend.

"I know a lot of English ones if you'd like to know those," the new companion attempted to return the offer.

Julio's expression calmed with earnestness. "I'm pretty sure I know most of those too," he stated confidently.

"Oh," the boy said.

"What's your name?" Julio asked. He felt that introductions would be appropriate since the ice was formally broken.

"Cody," he replied. "What's yours?"

"Julio. Julio Becerra." The boys struck an awkward handshake and smiled. Their adolescent attempt at imitating an adult greeting was unrefined but their delight in making the association official was genuine. Their eyes smiled as they sat side by side, watching the other children play.

"Do you know the S-word?" Cody asked. "In Spanish, I mean."

"Yeah," Julio answered. He began to proudly answer, then stopped himself. Introducing his newfound friend to such a dark vocabulary he would *most likely use,* seemed wrong somehow. Julio looked closely at the other children playing. Their dark hair and brown eyes matched his own and most of the street signage, shop windows and advertisements surrounding the complex were Spanish-only or came with Spanish translations. He didn't want Cody to end up in trouble if he decided to begin tossing words around such a robust Latino audience. Julio quickly came up with a replacement word. "Columpios," he said quickly, giving his friend the Spanish word for swing set instead of the bona fide swear.

"Colum-peeos," Cody repeated with a smirk. "Colum-peeos head!" He shouted, adding a noun. "What about the D-word?" Cody asked.

Julio didn't bother asking which D-word curse he meant. "El tobogán," he replied.

Cody laughed. "The F-word?" He inquired.

"Carrusel," Julio lied.

The green-eyed boy roared loudly with glee as if given the ability to magically set fire to anyone who wronged him. He pointed his short finger toward the children playing. "Next time someone pushes me down by the sandbox I'm going to call them a fat, stupid colum-peeos, el tobaggin carasel!" He screeched madly.

Julio's head jerked. "*Who* pushed you by the sandbox?" He asked curiously.

Cody's expression went flat. "*Nobody,*" he said quickly. It was an obvious lie. "But if they *did,* I could call them that! Right to their face!" The boy pointed across the park and to a tall, roguish-looking kid in a white shirt. "Especially him! *He* looks like *he'd* do something like that," Cody snapped.

Julio played along with the ruse. "Well, if he ever *does* do anything like that, there are *two of us* now and we can stand up to him," he said.

Cody smiled warmly. "Ok." His eyes gleamed.

"Ok," Julio repeated with a friendly nod.

The boys took a shine to one another as the day passed and a bond began to form. Cody was the first friend Julio had made since the move and the engagement was pleasing. They played together all day as their individual experiences, likes and cultures mingled and built a promising start to a fruitful friendship. The sun lapsed over the complex as Julio and Cody walked and talked, making laps around the building.

"What curse do you use when you stub your toe? Like, *really hard,* on the coffee table?" Cody asked.

"Ardilla verde," Julio lied.

"Smash your thumb with a hammer?" Cody squeaked. The questions just kept coming.

"Pesticida de malvavisco," Julio droned. He was getting tired of his friend's obsession with profanity. His new superpower had gone from a blessing to a curse in a matter of half a day and coming up with fake swears like *green chipmunk* and *marshmallow pesticide* was getting exhausting.

"What's a bad word you can use for anything? Like all the time, no matter what happens. For good stuff and bad stuff?" Cody inquired.

"Ok, but this is the last one," Julio said firmly. His aggravation was apparent in his tone.

"Oh," Cody whispered apprehensively. He seemed disappointed, even upset.

Julio immediately regretted his outlash. He decided to over-glorify his next and final curse word. "It's a *really* good one," he emphasized. "Probably the best Spanish swear ever."

Cody's face lit up. "Really? What is it?"

"If I tell you, you have to promise to use it responsibly," Julio warned.

"Ok!" Cody was elated. "Tell me, tell me!" He begged.

Julio stopped walking and let the tension build. He cleared his throat and spoke quietly. "Deslplumador," he said clearly.

"Wow," Cody gasped in awe. "Desplumadoor," he repeated with the best tongue he could manage. He said the word again, "Desplumadoor."

Julio gave Cody a commendatory slap on the back. "Use it for good and not evil," he stated. "That's important. That word gives you power."

"I will!" Cody smiled proudly. The boys continued their walk. "What does it mean?"

"What does *what* mean?" Julio deflected the question.

"Desplumadoor. It's a bad word but what does it mean in Spanish?" He asked.

"Um..," Julio hesitated. Cody hadn't asked for translations to his other words and continuing to lie felt impudent if Julio wanted this friendship to continue. "It means plucker," he said. "Like duck plucker or chicken plucker."

"Oh," Cody replied. He looked puzzled. "And that's bad?" He questioned.

"Yeah." Julio wasn't technically lying. He hadn't known anyone who's *wildest dream* was to pluck ducks. It was a chore, and chores were never enjoyed. He elaborated, "In Mexico, everyone hates plucking. It's the most hated job there is." That was more of a lie but still retained somewhat of a gray area. "In Tijuana prisons, they make killers pluck ducks. The killers hate plucking ducks so much, they hate it more than being in prison. So it keeps them from killing and plucking ducks." That was *definitely* a lie.

"Wow!" Cody shouted. "So plucker means you're a killer?"

"Sure," Julio said confidently.

"I like that one! I like that one *a lot*. It's not hard to say, it sounds cool and I like what it means. I think It might be my *favorite* Spanish curse word," Cody nodded.

"Yeah?" Julio squawked.

"Yeah," Cody confirmed. "And I also like it because plucker rhymes with fu—"

"*Cody!*" He was interrupted by an angry woman standing just outside the apartment entryway, shouting to him.

Cody jerked his head back to view her as discontent melted over his expression. Julio noticed the woman as well. "Desplumadoor," Cody cursed under his breath. "I have to go," he sighed. He hurried away and towards the building's entrance.

"See you tomorrow?!" Julio called out.

Cody turned and ran backwards. "Yeah! I'll meet you on the bench. You can teach me more Spanish words! Regular ones!"

Julio laughed. "Ok!" His red-headed friend departed and neared the woman as she threw her arms into the air and reprimanded Cody for some sort of inaudible disarrangement. They disappeared through the silver and glass doors and through the mail vestibule.

The children shouted happily from the playground equipment as Julio smiled to himself. He had made his first friend in this new home and Cody seemed genuinely interested in him. However, he *did* feel guilty about the lies. He didn't know how Cody would feel if another Spanish kid told him that tobogán meant *slide* and carrusel meant *merry-go-round* and that the words Julio had given him were basically verbal placebos. He decided not to worry. If Cody was truly destined to be his friend, it would all work out. Besides, he only lied to protect him from getting into trouble. Julio's lies were used for good and not evil.

Pounding echoes reverberated from the stairwell as Julio ran to the fourth floor. The out-of-service elevator made navigating the building a nuisance for adults, but not for little boys. He ascended the flights like a monkey up a tree without breaking a sweat. Julio made his way to unit 148 and found the door slightly ajar. Mamá and Nicolas always left it open, just a crack, when he was away.

"¡Odio este programa de televisión! ¿Por qué me haces ver esto?" Nicolas shouted from the sofa. He was complaining about something on TV. He held an orange Fanta and his large body was wedged firmly between the cushions. Julio ran up to him, snatched the drink out of his hand and took a long sip. "Not so much, Julio! I only have *two* left after this!" The man growled. "We need to go shopping."

Mom was in the kitchen packing a plastic container of Polvorones she had just baked. "I like that show, they have good recipes!" She responded to her husband's previous gripe.

Julio returned the bottle to Nic's hand. He took a swig. *"Bah!"* He immediately dismissed her answer, lifted the remote and changed the station. "Watch that garbage on your own time," he murmured.

"Mamá! I made a friend today!" Julio announced. "On the playground!" Her face lit up with glee upon hearing the news.

"A girl?" Nic asked. "Is she cute?" He raised his eyebrows in jest.

"No! I met—" Julio answered the first question but was cut off before answering the second.

"She's *not* cute?" Nicolas teased.

"That's ok, papito!" His mom interjected. "As long as she can *cook*, you'll be happy! Ooh, Julio se va a casar!" She sang loudly.

"I'm not getting married!" Julio shouted. "I met a *boy* friend!"

"You have a *boyfriend?!*" Nic opened his mouth widely and cackled wildly. Julio's patience ran dry. He yanked the Fanta bottle from Nic's hand, ran into the kitchen and rested it on the counter. "Hey, that's mine!" Nicolas shouted.

Julio folded his arms contemptuously and shot his stepfather a look of ire, refusing to budge. He knew that it would take an act of God to get Nic off the couch and onto his feet. If a hypothetical fire occurred in one of the rear bedrooms, Nicolas would most likely remain seated until the inferno reached the living room, or the fridge. The man stayed wedged. A large, red frown was plastered across his face. Julio turned to his mom. "My friend's name is Cody! He has red hair and he lives in our building," he continued without interruption.

"Wonderful!" She cheered. "Maybe he can come over for dinner with his family. I'll make my Dulce De Leche!" She glanced toward her husband. "Wouldn't that be *nice,* Nic?" Nicolas remained silent. He pouted, eyes glued to the TV.

"I can ask him tomorrow," Julio said excitedly. "We're meeting on the playground bench."

"Very nice! I'm glad you are making friends, papito. You're a good boy," she praised. "Good boys make good friends." Mamá handed him a pink cookie from the batch. He happily took the treat and ran through the living room and down the hall. "Please clean your room! It's been a mess all week!" She squawked.

Nicolas irritably eyed Julio as he disappeared. "Hey! *My drink! Julio!*" He called desperately. No response came as seconds passed. Nic turned his attention to his wife. "Elena, bring me my drink," he ordered.

She snapped the lid closed on the cookies and dropped them onto the counter. Raising an eyebrow, she brazenly rested her fist on her hip and shot her husband a harsh glare. "I'll bring it to you when you put my show back on," she stated.

Nic threw his head back and slapped the cushion beside him with a large, aggravated hand. "¡Ahh! ¡*Hijo de puta!*" He roared.

Julio entered his room and threw on the lights. He took a bite of his cookie and rested it on a stack of books. Taking a second to observe his space, quickly agreed with his mother. His room truly was a mess. If he was going to have Cody over, he'd have to make it somewhat presentable. After a long sigh, Julio hugged a pile of dirty clothes and pulled them off the bed, dropping them into the hallway. "*Mom! Clothes!*" He screamed. Throwing his dirties into the linoleum hall was the extent of Julio's laundry skills. Mom took care of the rest. He began to tidy up, tossing cars into baskets, placing his books on a shelf and painstakingly making his disheveled car-bed. As Julio worked, something strange caught his eye. He rose from the floor and took a step closer to his wall. Realization, doubt, fear then panic struck rapidly and in that order as he stared. His heart rose into his throat, his skin went cold and his legs began to shake.

On the sandy-beige drywall and between two, colorful posters, a small, black smudge was faded but prominent. It was about the size of a lime and starred outward like a spiderweb. Hastily, Julio ripped down the posters. The rest of the wall was clean. He stepped backward and stared at the smudge as goosebumps danced across his flesh. Julio felt the beginning of a cry at the back of his throat. His mind raced, searching for any excuse for the mark's presence, other than what he feared the very most.

Mamá approached from the kitchen holding a laundry basket. She began tossing undersized shirts and underwear into the receptacle as she began to speak. "Papito, is this all of your socks? I keep finding them all over the hou—" She caught sight of the mark on the wall, stood upright and dropped the basket to the floor.

Julio slowly looked away from the smudge. His tear-covered eyes fell desperately into his mom's mortified stare. "Mamá?" He choked. A tear rolled down his cheek.

Chaos struck the small home as Julio was dragged into the kitchen and subjected to a series of miniature rituals performed by his mother. "¡El diablo ha regresado! ¡El diablo ha regresado!" She repeated the same panicked phrase again and again as Julio stood before her.

Nicolas was wrought with confusion as his questions went unanswered. "What's wrong, what happened?" He asked. Then he asked again, with an amplified vigor. Two eggs were removed from the fridge along with chicken stock and a prayer candle from a bookshelf in the living room. Julio's mom chanted as she pulled a rosary from a junk drawer and placed it around her son's neck. "Someone tell me what happened!" Nic demanded. "¡Lo que está sucediendo!"

Mom was busy touching each egg separately, to Julio's forehead and repeating her phrase. "There's a stain on my wall," Julio sobbed. "The ghost comes out of there at night!" He wept.

Nic gave his famous, dismissive, "Bah!" He waved a careless hand at them and headed down the hall. Mom lit the candle and motioned it in the pattern of a cross in front of Julio's face. Her chants continued. "It's just a stain!" Nic thundered from the bedroom. Magic Eraser will take that right off. Or I can sand it off and repaint it!" He suggested.

"NO!" Mamá shrieked. *"Don't touch it!"* Nicolas didn't reply. She looked into her son's eyes. "You sleep in our room tonight, ok?" Julio nodded and wiped his face. The relief of not having to sleep in his room helped him calm down. His sobbing became sniffling. A sound of running water echoed down the hallway from the bathroom. "NO, NO, NO!" Mom cried out. She stormed down the hall and began shouting at her husband.

An all-out war took place as spanish words of all kinds were hurled, tossed and heaved. Julio was sure the entire building could hear the boisterous quarrel.

Julio nonchalantly looked over his mother's familiar set of anti-demon ingredients as his parents fought. In Mexico, Mamá would perform this sacrament every day and sometimes twice after exceptionally bad nights with the ghost. She was very adamant about it.

Latina moms always seemed to have a holistic cure, defense, remedy and enrichment for just about everything. And, they appeared to be experts in *all* of them. Most mothers and grandmothers Julio knew were devout catholics, but some of their methods seemed a bit eerie, bordering on what *some* would call *witchcraft*. Perceivably, it was hard to tell the difference between a witch casting a spell and an average madre after the devil himself materialized in her living room. When Julio was five, he overheard a woman at a market tell his mom that *poultry* kept evil spirits at bay, *herbs and oils* would bind you to a spirit and *shellfish* could restore a husband's enthusiasm. He had no idea what that third remedy was, but he understood the stuff regarding spirits. In *his* home, it was always *just* poultry.

Julio was invariably patient when mom pulled out her paranormal tool box. He had never objected or raised a fuss about it for her sake. He was sure it did nothing tangible on a magical level, but the spells seemed to make *her* feel better and not completely helpless. When Julio really thought about it, *technically* they had worked. The creature hadn't harmed him —yet. That thought gave him a modicum of comfort.

The hallway war ended, or at least took a hiatus. Mom retrieved a few crucial items from Julio's room and closed the door. She returned to the kitchen as Nicolas dragged his feet to the sofa and sat with a heavy huff. "You are going to stay in the living room with us, then you are sleeping in our bed," she spat. Julio gave a visible acknowledgement, his eyes were red and puffy.

"Estúpido," Nic grumbled.

"*¡¿Qué dijiste?!*" His wife screeched. Nicolas said nothing. If the war *began* a second time he would *lose* a second time.

That night, Julio stayed on the sofa between both of his parents as they watched TV. On a typical night he would be playing in his room or reading a book. Not tonight. Around nine-o-clock, the television was turned off and Julio followed the couple into their bedroom. Just like the sofa, he was snugly pressed between them both. He stared at the ceiling as they fell asleep, imagining what kind of horrors were taking place in his room. The thought made him sick, so he pushed it out of his mind.

Just as Julio closed his eyes, he heard a bang. He would have been more fearful if he hadn't recognized it. The sound came from the next unit. Just like the night before, loud, muffled shouting went on for almost a minute followed by crying. Julio laid awake as the crying slowly faded, once again, into the hours of the night.

The next morning, he woke to the shake of the mattress as Nicolas got out of bed. It was still dark as the man showered, dressed and left for work. Slumber did not return as Julio watched the ceiling become brighter as dawn came and the sun rose. Mamá could sleep until noon on most days. Julio didn't have the patience to lay beside her all day.

His bare feet met the warm, carpeted floor, then the cold linoleum of the hall. The TV called out to him feverishly from the living room but the dark, alluring presence of his closed, bedroom door called his name even louder. He eyed the door and the items placed below it. As precaution, Mom had lined the foot of the door with more ingredients. Bowls of eggs and chicken stuffs were placed neatly and meticulously across the rug. Another useless gesture.

Just a peek, Julio thought. He just had to see if there was anything *to* see. Perhaps, if everything in his bedroom looked the same, he would be able to assume the smudge was just a smudge and he and his mother had overreacted. The more he thought about it, the more probable that thought became. Julio tip-toed to the door, turned the knob and peeked inside.

The dreaded stain was now the size of a monster truck tire. The black tar spread outward as if attempting to swallow his entire room. A sickening, palpable weight filled the room and poured into the hall from the partially-open door. Even the sunlight coming through the window seemed cursed and diseased. Overwrought with hysteria, Julio slammed the door shut. His panicked feet slapped the floor, all the way to the living room.

A dreary overcast loomed over the playground. No children played on the lonesome equipment and the saturated colors that had shone so brightly from the day before were now faded with a shade of somber gray. Cody sat on the bench, hanging his head and staring at the ground. His visage and posture matched the deposition of the cloudy day like a dispiriting oil painting. Julio sat beside him.

"Hi." Julio's voice cracked.

Cody looked up and smiled, but the expression lied. "Hi," he squeaked. He dropped his head back into its previous position. The boy swung his feet to convey sanctity but his shoes lied as well.

Julio began placing pieces of a puzzle together in his head. Cody's sad expression both days and the crying through his bedroom wall both nights seemed too coincidental to be unrelated. Julio wanted confirmation but had to obtain it in a way that didn't embarrass his new friend. "What floor do you live on?" He casually asked.

"Four," Cody mumbled.

Julio lifted his head and nodded to himself. He got his confirmation. "I live on the end of that floor. One forty-eight," he said.

Cody smiled again. This time, the sparkle in his eye was genuine. "I live in one forty-six. We're neighbors," he giggled.

"Cool! I'll bet our rooms are right next to each other!" Julio exclaimed with feigned surprise. He began to imagine what Cody's room looked like, what kind of toys he had and if it was a mess like his own. His thoughts darkened as he remembered the growing stain that cursed his wall. "Did...," Julio began. "Did you hear anything through your wall last night? Like, voices or anything?" He asked. His curiosity went wild, wondering if the ghost had officially returned.

"Oh yeah," Cody said immediately.

Dread gripped Julio's throat. *"You did?"* His flesh crawled.

"I heard a lot of yelling," Cody explained. "Yelling in Spanish. For a long time. During dinner. They were *really* loud, desplumadoor!" He cursed.

The grip on Julio loosened, then dissipated immediately. "Oh," he gasped. "That was just Nicolas and my mom. They had a fight. Nicolas is my stepdad. Sometimes they do that."

"They're loud," Cody said.

"Yup," Julio nodded.

"Did they say swears?" Cody asked.

"Yup," Julio nodded again. "Just Nicolas. Not my mom." Cody chuckled. His green eyes shined.

"What are *your* parents like?" Julio innocently asked. Perhaps Cody would open up about his own troubles with a series of innocuous questions. Nothing that gave away prior knowledge.

Cody dropped his head. His colorful expression evaporated. Julio felt a sting of regret as the dead air returned in full force. He showed patience, giving Cody ample time to think, process and possibly answer. After a long, silent minute, the boy spoke. "My dad died when I was two," he said. "I live with my mom."

"Oh," Julio whispered. "My dad left when I was little. For a long time I lived with my mom too." He attempted to relate but Julio could tell that Cody's mind was occupied.

"She gets really mad," Cody continued. He choked. "Sometimes she hits me," he whispered sadly. His eyes welled up. His voice shook. "I don't even know *what I did wrong!*" Cody's voice went from a mumble to a frenzied shout in just one sentence. Julio jumped in his seat and Cody began to bawl. The red-headed boy's shoulders bounced as he struggled to manage his breaths, moans and cries all at once with little success. He rubbed his fists against his eyes. "She calls me..." He took three, rapid inhales. "She calls me... her little shit stain!" Julio winced. He felt an overwhelming sadness and empathy for his best friend of two days and wanted very badly to take his pain away. Cody continued, "And she calls me that *in front of people!*" His cries became roars as the tension slowly drained from his little body. It was obvious he had never shared what he was sharing now, with anyone. Julio placed a sympathetic hand on Cody's shoulder for long minutes as the pressure was slowly released and the boy could finally come to rest. Moments later, the crying stopped and his shoulders eased. They sat side by side, silent and kindred, a new bond formed between them.

Julio waited for the air to completely clear before speaking. He removed his hand and wrapped his arm around his friend. "Shit stain is *mancha de mierda* in Spanish," he stated bluntly. This time, no placebo was used. That was the *honest to God* translation. Cody laughed through snot and tears, wiping his sleeve against his face. The boys shared a sideways hug as Cody gladly replaced crying with giggling.

"I still like Desplumadoor better," Cody murmured happily.

"Good," Julio replied.

The rest of the day went on with both boys laughing, joking and playing, despite the ominous atmosphere and the blight of their personal affairs. They were free to play on the equipment undisturbed, with no kids to stand up to and no explosive interruptions by Cody's mother. Every several minutes or so, Julio would remember the state of his room and feel a sinking dismay that soured his stomach. He wanted so desperately to share his own affliction with Cody, but kept his lips sealed. He didn't want to seem crazy, drive his friend away or even worse, frighten him. Cody had enough trouble getting sleep already. The stain and the ghost was Julio's problem.

At dusk, Julio pushed his front door open and found Nicolas and Mamá in their usual places. His mother noticed him first. "Papito! Did you have fun with your friend?" She asked as graciously as she could. Her expression was still hazed by the curse on their home.

"Yeah," he replied. Fear still resided in Julio as well.

"Did you enjoy your date with your *boyfriend?!*" Nic jested loudly. He however, was completely impervious to the crisis.

"When is he coming over for dinner?" Mom asked.

"*Oh!*" Julio realized he hadn't remembered to bring it up. "I'll ask him tomorrow. I forgot."

"That's ok," She hummed. "Now is likely not the best time to have anyone here," she cautioned.

Nic shifted his heavy body from side to side, searching under his rear and between the thick cushions of the sofa. "Where's the damn remote?" He barked. "¡¿Elena, lo tomaste?!"

"I didn't take it!" His wife sassed. Nicolas began muttering gnarled curses as his hands moved with an increased vigor as he searched. "Did you take it into the *bathroom* again?" She asked.

With a heaving grunt, Nic stood, faced the couch and scanned his space. *"¡¿A dónde se fue la estupidez?!"* He spat furiously.

Mamá opened the fridge and pulled out a selection of plastic bags and piled them on the counter. She turned and motioned for Julio to approach. "Ven aqui," she snapped. Julio rolled his eyes and shuffled over to the tile. For the thousandth time, Mamá began another sacrament. This time, with fresh chicken feet, hen's blood and pungent livers. Julio was blessed in his scuffed jeans and dirty t-shirt. He did his best to disguise impatience with indebted gratitude.

Nicolas wandered the entire apartment, looking for his coveted remote control. A minute later, he returned from the hall empty-handed. As he turned to search the sofa again, Julio spotted the controller stuck in the waistband of the man's sweatpants. Julio laughed, "¡Está en tus pantalones!" He continued to giggle as his stepdad felt his hips and back, eventually finding it. Nic opened his mouth wide and chuckled uproariously. The floor shook as he embedded his body back into place and surfed through channels.

"Tomorrow, I'm going to talk to the landlord about the leak in the bedroom. It's got to be plumbing or sewage. Something." Nicolas announced.

Julio's mom became irate. "It is not plumbing or sewage! It is that thing that comes for Julio! The same thing that came for him in Mexico! You are not calling anyone!"

Nic muttered more curses. "What are we supposed to do? Keep him in our room forever?!" He exclaimed.

Mamá snapped and went full-on Chola. She stormed over to the sofa and ground the man into dog meat with Latin rage. He sat quietly, staring at the floor as a dead-pan expression of regret and timid submission. The woman finished her rant and returned to the kitchen, placing away her bags. "So, what? We get Julio a dog house?" He joked. Julio's brow furrowed. "Maybe he can go live with his boyfriend!" Cackling laughter erupted from his giant mouth as he continued clicking the remote at the TV.

Julio's mom took his face into her loving hands as Nic snickered. She kissed him on the forehead. "We are going to protect you, Papito. We will figure something out." Her words were comforting but Julio didn't appreciate his stepfather's ignorance or ridicule. The man's ridiculous laughter upon hearing his own jokes was annoying enough. When the joke was on Julio, it became infuriating.

Nic snapped his fingers. "Julio, bring me one of my drinks!" He ordered.

"You were just up, you should have got one then," Mom snipped. Julio just glared at him, Nic noticed the animosity.

"Come on! I was kidding. ¡Tráeme una bebida!" He coughed. A wide grin stretched Julio's lips. He waltzed casually over to the fridge, retrieved the last, remaining Fanta, stood in plain view of his stepfather and held it outward with a playful taunt. "Thank you, Chavo. Give it here," he requested. Julio unscrewed the cap, tilted back the bottle and drank the entire 20 ounces of orange fizz as Nicolas went mad with petulance.

"No! Stop! ¡Deja de beber eso! ¡Es mi ultimo!" He screamed. Mamá smiled to herself as her husband roasted. "Elena! Did you buy more when you went out?" He asked desperately.

His wife shrugged. She shook her head. I didn't buy you more Fantas. You refused to go with me," she shot. Nicolas screamed with a childish rage like a baby who's chupón fell out of its mouth and into a storm drain. Mamá snorted like a pig as explosive laughter forced its way through her dread, through her worry and made her squeal with delight. It had been the first time Julio had seen her smile all day.

It was Julio's second night as a human sandwich. Warm but crushed, he adjusted his posture between them to find comfort. Every now and again, he listened out for Cody or his mother through the wall. Silent tonight. Good, Julio thought. Cody can finally get *one* peaceful night's rest. He buried his face into his pillow and wrapped his body in the 10 inches of blanket he was allotted. Just as he found the perfect level of comfort, he felt a familiar, warm sting in his lower gut. It figured. The urge to pee always came at *precisely,* the most imperfect and inconvenient moment. The soda was a mistake.

Julio dropped his bare feet onto the carpet as his parents snored. He trotted across the room and to the hall. As he quickly glanced in the direction of his bedroom door, terror in the worst form crashed into his heart and seized every muscle in his body. Urine flowed down his leg leaving a black puddle on the dark carpet and his bones chilled like blistering, razor-sharp ice.

There it was.

His bedroom door was wide open. The heinous corpse floated as still as death, staring directly into his eyes from the blackness of his room. Its puss-colored eyes were barely visible in the dark but they hit Julio like noxious spears. The horrid stain lay just beyond it, seething with a hellish energy and framing the demon's starved shoulders and mangled head. It didn't move. Nor did Julio.

A short yelp jumped from Julio's lips. The sound barely impacted the rotting air as he swiftly covered his mouth with bitter hands. The creature reacted. Its head jerked and snapped as it flowed several inches closer—then stopped. It eyed the eggs and chicken innards upon the rug and below the doorframe. It's face twisted with nausea and Julio noticed.

Their sights reconnected. Julio struggled to keep still and quiet for what felt like hours as the ghost's syphoning eyes pulled every degree of heat from the boy's body. An eternity passed.

Suddenly, a shout. Then another shout. A bang. In the next unit, Cody began to cry softly in his room. His voice was clear and mournful. The creature hissed. Its attention was immediately torn from Julio as it curiously examined the wall from which the cries had emerged. Cody moaned loudly then coughed. In a flash, the ghost vanished through the wall and into the next bedroom.

"No!" Julio gasped. He ran into his room, jumped onto his bed and desperately placed his hands on the drywall, terrified for his friend. A scream, an unearthly grunt then running footsteps. The spector returned. Julio felt a deathly chill as the specter passed through the wall, through his body and into the stain. The ghost was gone.

Cody's panicked footsteps faded off towards the main hallway. Julio followed. He jumped from his mattress and raced through the stretch of his apartment. He unlocked his front door and jumped out into the muggy brightness. As Julio's eyes adjusted to the sudden light, he left his door ajar and approached unit 146. The hot concrete was warm on his bare feet. "Cody!" He whispered loudly. No response. He pressed his ear against the door. The crying continued, but not from the unit. The voice echoed and reverberated. Julio curiously pulled his head away from the door. Cody's voice was coming from the stairwell.

Six doors down and past the firehose cabinet, the frightened little boy was cowering in the bare corner with his knees pressed against his chin. His red hair was a mess and his blue pajamas were wrinkled and unwashed. Compared to the stairwell, the hallway was a meat locker. The air was thick with moisture and despair. Julio descended the half-flight and joined Cody by his side. The child was overwrought with fright. His lips shook and his eyes were frozen wide.

Julio took his time, finding the right moment to speak. "I've seen it every night since I was little," he whispered. He *knew* Cody had seen it. No questions were necessary. "Did it talk to you?" Julio asked.

"It talks?!" Cody shouted. Panic struck him. Tears drained down his freckles and his breathing became unruly.

Julio regretted the upset but he had to know for sure. "If it talks to you, *never* say anything to it. No matter what. Ok?" He warned.

Cody's green eyes looked upon Julio in helpless terror. His teeth chattered. "Why?" He cried.

A long moment passed as Julio looked to the floor. The story he was about to tell, had never been told to anyone. Not even his mother. The memory was painful to revisit, but necessary to recount. The words came out with a sour and putrid flavor. "My dad didn't leave when I was little," he squeaked. The words pained him more than he had anticipated. He spoke slowly. "I remember him yelling. Angry yelling. Yelling at the wall. I was in my crib. I don't know where my mom was." He swallowed hard. "Then, he started screaming ...and crying. I saw white eyes in the dark. Then he was gone."

"It took your dad?" Cody asked. His teeth gnashed.

"I think so," Julio whispered.

Cody wiped his nose. "Because he talked to it?"

Julio shrugged. "I don't know."

"Then how do you know it takes you if you talk?" Cody shrieked.

"When I was five, my mom got me a cat. A kitten," Julio began. "It cried all the time. It slept with me in my bed. The ghost came. It talked to me. I didn't say anything. My cat woke up and started crying again. The ghost took him by his paw. I heard a break and my cat cried louder. It took her into the wall. I didn't see her again." Julio trembled. Cody's expression was a wild symphony of terrible emotions. His breaths were scattered and arbitrary. Julio spoke again, "I told my mom the cat ran away. She thinks my dad left too. Or, she just says that to herself." Julio reached into the pocket of his PJ's and pulled out the worn Zippo lighter. He longingly turned it over in his fingers. "This was my dad's," he said. Cody gently took it from his hand and inspected the engraving. "It says, you only find bravery in yourself when things become dark and frightening. —Something like that," Julio shrugged. "I keep it with me to remind me to not be scared." He took the Zippo.

"Does it work?" Cody squeaked.

"Sometimes," Julio replied. He pushed the lighter deep into his pocket. "We can't say anything to it, no matter what, Cody. The ghost will talk to you, but if you stay quiet it will go away."

The red-headed boy's eyes wandered, absorbing the information and the instructions. "Oh," he gasped lightly.

"We need to stand up to it," Julio said. "Just like the kid on the playground. But with the ghost, we need to say nothing and it can't get us." Cody nodded. He was beginning to understand. "We need to be brave," Julio stated strongly. "Nobody will help us but *us*. We need to get mad and stop being scared." Julio's words were as much for himself as they were for Cody. A flicker of inspiration sparked between them.

Cody steadied his shoulders and dried his face. A look of determination and pride hardened like stone across his expression. "I'm tired of being scared," he said. "I'm tired of being scared on the playground, at home and at school. I need to get mad," he repeated Julio's pep talk. Cody ground his teeth and dug his nails into his pajamas.

"Good," Julio encouraged.

Shattering the moment, the sound of a door slamming open and thunderous footsteps shook the building. An angry woman with a rat's-nest hairdo and a mud-colored robe came to an infuriated halt at the entrance to the stairwell. She shook with fury. "Cody! What the hell are you doing out here at this time of night?! Get your ass back in your damn room, now!" Her voice exploded within the concrete percussion.

Inspired by Julio's words, Cody jumped to his feet and misdirected his anger. His expression hardened. He pointed a strong finger in his mom's direction. "I'm not going to be afraid anymore and you can't tell me what to do!" He scolded. Cody's seven-year-old voice yapped like a fearless chihuahua in the face of certain death.

¡Dios mío! Julio thought. He had just finished amping up his friend's nerve but there was a time and a place for courageous insurrection. *This* situation was not applicable.

Mom looked as though she had been slapped in the face with a cold fish. Her eyes narrowed. "You will *march* up these steps and into your room or I'm painting your ass red you *little shit!*" She roared.

Cody's demeanor did not change. Julio stood, reached over and tugged on his friend's PJ's in an attempt to shut him up. "You're never touching me again you... you... *¡Mancha de mierda!*" Cody pronounced the curse flawlessly. It was the first time Julio had ever heard him repeat a *single word* in Spanish without an accent out of place, let alone an entire phrase. Julio slapped a hand against his forehead with mortification.

"*What did you just say to me?!*" She gasped with outrage. She snapped her fingers and pointed at Julio. "Hey! *You!* Brown kid! *What* did he just say?" Cody's mom demanded an answer.

Julio spat, "Mancha de mierda means mother of mine!" He lied. "It's not anything bad," he assured her. "It means he loves his mother and she loves him."

Mom just stood in place. Tired confusion danced across her eyes as she glared at the boys. Her voice calmed but the anger was still thick. "It's late," she said. "Get to bed." She turned and thundered back to her unit, closing the door.

Julio lightly slapped Cody in the back of the head. "You shouldn't have done that, Cody! You almost got into serious trouble!" He whined.

Cody grinned widely. "Desploomadoor! Did you see that?! I stood up to her and she left! Just like you said the ghost does. I'm going to do that all the time!" He cheered.

"No!" Julio barked. "That's not smart to do with your parents. You have to do what your parents tell you! It's *not* the same."

"Thanks, Julio. I couldn't have done it without you." Cody hugged his friend tightly, completely ignoring his warnings and advice.

"Ugh," Julio grunted. He gave up the fight and impassively returned the hug, patting Cody on the back.

Cody took a deep breath. His face went sour, he sniffed the air strangely and searched the stairwell. "Why does it smell like pee in here?" He asked. Julio's face went red with embarrassment.

The boys returned to their separate units. The hour was late and dead silence loomed over the building. Julio sat on the sofa in the dark living room and listened. If any kind of disturbance, argument or beating took place in Cody's apartment, Julio would never forgive himself. Silence for ten long minutes now. His eyes became heavy and exhaustion settled in. He leaned his back against the cushions of Nic's spot and felt a warming shroud of comfort engulf him. Before he fell to sleep, the putrid scent of his wet pants jerked him back into a wakeful alertness. Julio slid off the sofa and headed for his room. Clean, dry pajamas would be in his dresser. He could change and finally sleep in his own bed. The beast had never returned twice in one night and Julio wasn't looking forward to his cramped, overheated crevasse between Nic and Mamá.

Just as Julio passed the bathroom and rounded the corner to his room—there it was again. He froze. This time, the wretched phantom seemed disinterested in Julio. It hung menacingly, four feet from the carpet and stared at the wall against Julio's bed as if contemplating or waiting. It didn't even seem to notice he was there. His pep talk to Cody about being brave resounded in his head. Julio knew he couldn't speak but the ghost didn't seem to react to movement. An hour prior, Cody had jumped out of his bed and ran from it and all the demon had done was retreat. Julio took a step closer. It didn't budge. He crept towards the open door and noticed the eggs, innards and chicken feet. *Why had it looked upon them with disgust?* Julio thought. *Was there some kind of truth behind Mom's paranormal toolbox?* His thoughts churned. He had to know.

Julio slowly kneeled. He took one, brown egg from the wooden bowl and held it between his thumb and forefinger. He held it outward, making it as visible as possible. The creature was still fixated on the wall to Cody's room. He took a step towards the room, then another. As soon as the egg passed the threshold, the ghost's head jerked and its eyes met Julio's. It grunted and hissed as the egg neared. Its neck snapped with agitation and its body vibrated and seized.

A rush of courage swelled in Julio. After years of torment and oppression by the beast, he finally felt a sense of control—a sense of reprisal—a sense of *power.* Julio's expression narrowed as he looked upon the ghost. The pent-up fury of a thousand sleepless nights roasted in his indignant stare and fearless heart. Julio stepped over the boundary and snatched two more eggs as he passed into the room. The demon drew backward as the furious boy and his arsenal of poultry neared. It was cornered like an agitated cat as it spat, growled and hissed.

Just for a second, Julio wondered what the entity would do if he spoke to the ghost in its current state of restraint. He discarded the idea. Discovering what the spector was afraid of was one small step towards ridding himself of it completely. He didn't allow the high of one victory lead him into making a deadly error.

Unexpectedly, voices erupted in the bedroom behind the wall. Julio stood before the spirit holding his eggs as Cody and his mother shared an uproarious confrontation. Cries, curses and physical violence shook the building as Cody's bedroom door was slammed shut and the boy's pain-induced sobs reverberated from the next unit. Over the course of an entire minute, the sobs eased into familiar and silent whimpers.

The creature twitched, rose, made a wide circle around Julo and vanished into Cody's room. "No!" Julio cried. He dropped the eggs onto the carpet and jumped onto his bed. *"Don't talk to it, Cody!"* He shouted. Silence.

"Don't talk to it, don't talk to it, don't talk to it..," he repeated again and again in tearful whispers. Julio listened intensely as his friend's voice became more prevalent. No words, just fearful, audible moans. He could hear the ghost as well. Its horrible words were too quiet to make out but Julio was all too familiar with the monster's string of questions.

After Julio counted five times the creature had spoke, the squeak of a mattress met his ears. *Cody is standing up,* Julio morbidly thought. His heart raced with panic. In the same manner Cody had bravely confronted his mother earlier that night, he rose to his feet, gathered his nerve and spoke without hindrance. *"Leave me alone you ugly shit stain! Desploomadoor!"* The little red-headed boy's words resounded perfectly through the boundary.

Julio slapped the wall as tears streamed and his voice cracked, *"Cody! No!"* A nightmarish howl struck the building's foundation like an earthquake and Cody's screams sent a helpless chill through Julio's body. In a span of just under a second, The ghost passed directly through the wall and straight through Julio. It dragged Cody by his bare foot and blue pajamas as the boy cried out like an infant in the cold grip of agony and apathetic death. In the brief tick of a single moment, Julio met eyes with his friend. Before he had a chance to connect thought with sight, the wraith disappeared along with Cody, through the wall and into the stain.

Silence again. Julio was left a quivering heap upon his floor, retching and heaving with anguish. Mamá and Nocolas rushed into the room. Julio's bedroom light was illuminated as his mother dropped to her knees. She embraced her son, spouting prayers and comforting words that fell deaf. Julio's bloodshot eyes rose to the stain as it retreated into the wall like hot tar down a rust-covered floor-drain. All at once, the blemish was gone.

In the following years, the dark mark never appeared for Julio again, nor the spector or any sign that they had ever existed. As Julio grew, a dark vengeance grew with him. A vengeance that pulsed and boiled with a dark detestment, just like the blemish itself. It drove him, pushed him and formed him. He interpreted the glance he had shared with Cody, just before his disappearance, as a solemn promise. A promise to one day find his friend, find his father and put an end to the ghost that comes out of the stain *forever.*

El Paso, Texas

Evan stared at the ceiling. It had been over thirty minutes since he had heard even a whisper from the strange man. The boy wondered if he was still seated in the corner. The darkness made it hard to tell. The time that had passed began hazing his memory of the visitor and the short conversation they had shared. Evan wondered if the man had been a dream. He desperately hoped not. He sighed and grew impatient. "Hello?" He whispered. Silence. "Are you still there?" Nothing. Slowly and carefully, Evan sat up.

With the same deathly hiss as it had for several months, the twisted wretch emerged from the portal. Evan collapsed onto his mattress and covered his face. The phantom floated like a dying birthday balloon and drifted toward Evan's pillow. Evan shook and cowered as the creature jerked and clicked above his comforter. Beneath the linens, Evan prayed the man hadn't been a dream. He prayed hard and begged for it all to be real in the silence of his mind. With a quick spark of faith, Evan decided to follow the man's instructions all the same. Real or not, dream or no dream.

Before the spirit could speak. Evan threw off the blanket and popped up from under his sheet. Quickly he spat the words, *"I can see you!"* The monster's white eyes widened and an otherworldly grin crept across its mangled face. No man, no voice. Evan panicked. He drew his back against the wall as the ghost brought its rotten gaze inches from Evan's cheek. Regret congealed in Evan's veins as the ghost roared with a monstrous fury and grabbed him by his trembling arm. Its frozen grip was painful and Evan could feel his very life draining through his flesh and into the monster's embrace. The helpless boy shut his eyes tightly and waited for the worst.

From behind the ghost and out of the darkness, a strong arm seized the demon's throat and squeezed. The echo of snapping flesh and cracking bones added to the creature's gags and choking gasps. Evan was released. The pain ceased.

The flick of a Zippo lighter cast a warm glow onto the ghost and onto the visitor holding it captive. "¿Me recuerdas? ¡*Maldito hijo de puta!*" The man growled as he shook the helpless monster in his fist. The sleeve of his jacket was rolled up and a thick coat of olive oil and fresh basil flakes dripped from his fingers all the way to his elbow. Evan gasped with desperate relief. The man turned a kind eye in his direction. "Gracias, Evan. I wouldn't have been able to trap your little friend here without it first, grabbing onto *you*. I appreciate your bravery. And I apologize for the language. My stepfather cursed like a sailor. I still haven't shaken the habit." He held the lighter close to the ghost's horrible face. Evan shuddered as its horrible details were made clear in the flickering light. "Take a good look at your friend, Evan. You won't be seeing *him* again," he said with confidence.

Evan's young body rushed with a mixture of emotions and adrenaline he couldn't handle. "Never?" Evan asked. He trembled with excitement.

"Never," The man spoke. "And I'm afraid you won't be seeing *me* again either," he said softly. Evan's face flattened with a hint of disappointment. "Because seeing *me*, means you are in *trouble,*" he added.

"What if another ghost comes?" The boy's voice shook.

The vigilante snapped the lighter closed and tossed it onto the bed before Evan. "You'll have that," he said. "It gives you power, makes you brave." Evan grabbed the antique and held it close to his chest. The man winked. "Use it for good and not evil," he warned with a smile.

The demon jerked and attempted to free itself. The intruder tightened his grip and shook it again. "¡No te muevas o te parto la cabeza, pendejo!" He barked. The man took one last look at Evan's thankful face. "I left twenty dollars on the fridge. That should cover the sandwich." He glanced at the quilt on the floor and pointed around Evan's bedroom. "And tell your mom to hang her ugly blanket someplace else. It doesn't match the colors in here. You can keep the chair."

He turned on his heel, faced the black portal and whispered to the ghost, "Ahora llévame a donde llevaste el resto de ellos." In a quick flash, the spirit took Julio off of his feet, into the air, through the wall and into the stain. Blue sparks and violet arcs reflected in Evan's eyes as he beheld the spectacle. The flashes doused and the stain faded, leaving behind a bare wall and a clean coat of paint. The man and the ghost were gone, as was the boy's fear.

Evan collapsed onto his back and onto his pillow. His body tingled with inspiration and wild admiration. He would never forget the brave man with the funny accent who saved him from his ghost. And he would go on forever with a selfless drive to help others as the man did for him.

Evan smiled as he looked upon the strange inscription on the magic lighter. "Zorro," he whispered.

FUN RUN
A Disgusting Yet Horrifying Trot

Lucy's feet pounded the belt of the treadmill as she ran in her athletic socks. Her worn, black running shoes were placed neatly beside the machine while she took calculated breaths. Three steps to inhale and three steps to exhale, just as she had taught herself. Her blonde ponytail spun like a propeller behind her head as the equipment whirred. Her gray and white sweats matched the drabness of her colorless shoes. A heavy-set man holding a tablet analyzed her running pattern, step angle and arch impact. "Ok, you can step off now," he instructed kindly. Lucy punched the red, *Stop* button on the control pad before the belt slowed to a halt. She stepped onto the cold tile. The man tapped his device a few times and opened a gridded chart of shoe types, styles and sizes. "Looks like you're a C-eleven," he said.

"C-eleven?" Lucy asked. Her breaths were relaxed. The short, twenty-second jog had absolutely no effect on her current stamina.

"Yep," he replied. "You have high arches and your toes point outward when you meet the ground. That puts a lot of strain on your femoral joints when you impact. I'm guessing you've had femoral pain since you started running?" He asked.

"Femoral?" She questioned. Lucy couldn't help but notice the man's beer gut hanging just past the hem of his white, collared shirt. She rolled her eyes with disgust.

"Hips," he clarified. "Have you had *hip* pain?"

Lucy firmly pressed her fist against her right hip and nodded. "I have," she said. "Ever since I started."

He turned his attention back to the tablet. "Well, a C-eleven shoe will greatly help with that, among other things. It'll feel like you're running on a cloud," he assured.

Lucy raised her eyebrows with relief and took her tired shoes from the floor. "Sounds heavenly," she said not too enthusiastically. She felt a sharp pain in her calf as she leaned to retrieve her trainers. Lucy stood, bent her knee and massaged the ache with her thumb.

"How often do you run?" The man asked. "Once a week? A few times a week?"

"Every day," she said proudly. "Every night after work."

"Every day?" He asked concerningly.

Her tail bounced with a nod. "That's right."

His eyes wandered. "Umm ...typically you want to run *every other day*. Every time you exercise you damage muscle. You need to give your body time to heal and build more muscle to progress," he explained.

Lucy's tone became sharp, "Yeah, well I didn't lose forty-six pounds in *one year* doing the bare minimum. When I set a goal, I go for it. No breaks."

He argued, "I'm *just saying* it because any professional trainer is going to advise you to—"

Lucy cut him off. "And *I'm just saying* that if you *were* a professional trainer maybe I'd listen to your advisement. But until then, keep selling shoes and stop giving me advice," she snapped.

He nodded his head, dropping the issue. "Ok," he said. He turned and pointed toward the corner of the store. "The C-elevens are going to be on *that wall,* blue tags. Anything marked with a blue tag is a C-eleven."

She eyed the three columns and six rows of blue-labeled trainers. Every shoe on display emitted at least one blinding hue of neon orange, yellow or pink. They almost glowed from across the sales floor. Lucy winced with dissatisfaction. "Do you have anything a little less ...*obnoxious?*" She asked.

"Those are the styles!" He happily replied. "People love the colors, the brighter the better! Our new *sports car* line of running shoes license pantone colors from Bugatti, Lamborghini and Aston Martin. It's like a luxury car for your feet! Nice for showing off," he smiled.

Lucy ground her teeth in protest. "I'm more of a *winter colors* kind of girl," she growled.

He ignored her gripe. "Take your time. When you cash out, tell them Gary helped you out. I'd really appreciate it," he requested. The salesman stepped away and headed towards the front.

With a sigh, Lucy approached the wall of blazing colors. She stood in her ankle socks examining the damaged rubber of her current pair. They wouldn't last another mile and the thought of *running on a cloud* was intriguing. She decided that yellow was the best choice when compared to hellfire-orange or 1980's-prom-dress pink.

Lucy took a yellow and dark-blue shoe labeled *Ocean Sunrise,* from the rack and was legitimately surprised when she felt its weight in her hand. It felt light like foam and the construction, stitching and design was flawless. Her brow raised with fascination. Although, her optimism quickly vanished when she read the price tag. She whispered harshly through her teeth, "Holy crap, Lamborghini is right! These things cost a fortune!" She yanked her gaze away from the wall to see the fat salesman assisting another customer near the far end of the store. Groaning with defeat, Lucy took one last look at her exhausted, black trainers and dropped them into a nearby trash bin. "Ocean Sunrise it is," she sighed to herself. Lucy returned the display shoe and grabbed a box from below, marked with her size. Dragging her socked feet to the checkout counter, she tossed the shoebox before the energetic clerk.

"Did you find everything you were looking for today?!" The woman asked wildly. Her immense smile took up most of the real estate of her face and the brightness of her expression matched the tint of the shoes. The clerk was short, portly and displayed signs of middle-age.

"I sure did!" Lucy matched her enthusiasm sarcastically, out of resentment. She unzipped the athletic pouch at her waist and retrieved a brand-new credit card, tapping it on the counter.

The oblivious cashier nodded. "Wonderful!" She opened the shoebox. The trainers were unlaced and the tissue-wrapped fitters were still wedged into the shoes. Her smile faded slightly. "Oh. Did you try this pair on before you decided on them? We do fittings as well, just to be certain the size is correct," she explained.

Lucy blushed with irritation. "I know my shoe size," she bit.

"Of course you do," the woman agreed politely. "But, we *strongly advise* that you try the pair on to be sure."

Slapping her card flat onto the laminated surface, Lucy leaned forward and hissed like a serpent, "I'm a twenty-six-year-old blonde living in L.A. *Nobody* knows more about *shoes* than me. *These* are my size!"

The cashier's smile drifted into a concerned frown. "By store policy, we can't actually sell an unfitted pair of—"

Lucy interrupted explosively, pointing the corner of her card directly at the clerk's face. "If *I want information* regarding fitness and fitness-related products, I'm going to speak to someone with *personal experience* in that arena. Not you and not your crew of sales jerks," she spat. She leaned in even closer, her soft tone twisted into cruelty. "And I refuse to learn anything about running shoes from someone who looks like the only marathon they've ever ran is to the *refrigerator and back.* Sell me the shoes." Lucy's glare drilled into the woman as she rang up the pair. The cashier handed over the receipt and the shoebox bagged in plastic. Lucy snatched the bag from the clerk's hand and stuffed the card with the receipt into her pouch. *"You and your team* can take your advisements and shove them up your overfed asses," she whispered firmly.

The cashier just stared, hurt and speechless. A cold wave of immediate regret washed over Lucy. She awkwardly stood before the woman she had just torn apart.

Lucy hated her impulses. Her first thought when the cashier argued with her was to attack and attack fast. Hit her where it hurts. She had read somewhere that your first thought and reaction was the *correct* thought and reaction. If that was true, Lucy *truly was* a terrible human being. In the face of a confrontation, her first thoughts were often selfish, judgemental and mean. The reaction that followed was a similar ugliness. She hated that about herself. Her attitude towards others had always been sour, but it was only until just recently that the sourness became monstrous. Just like she had displayed today. She frantically attempted to think of one, kind thing she could say before departing. Even if it was dishonest.

Lucy's demeanor reversed as she pointed cordially toward the back of the shoe store. "Oh, and *Gary* was the associate who helped me out today," she said kindly. Her smile lied and only advanced the awkwardness. The cashier's eyes flashed with unabashed confusion as she nodded with compliance.

Water from the wet pavement soaked into Lucy's socks moments after leaving the store. She threw her head back and growled audibly. It would have probably been a good idea to slip the shoes on before leaving, but after the fuss she had made about the fitting, placing them on and lacing them up in front of the staff would have looked ridiculous. More ridiculous than walking out into the rain-drenched street in polyester socks? She didn't bother to compare.

Lucy carried her purchase to the nearest bench and sat on the sopping wood. More wet clothing. She pulled the box out of the bag and unwrapped the brand-new pair of overpriced trainers. The yellow sole reflected every lumen of the daylight and almost burned her eyes. The deep, royal blue however, looked gorgeous in natural light. She discarded the packing materials and laced the shoes tightly around her feet. Wiggling her toes, she noticed there was a little bit of extra room between the tip of her foot and the outsole. Admitting to herself that she should have listened to the clerk's advice made her sick, so she refrained from doing so. Lucy stood and lifted her feet off the sidewalk individually. Her feet felt ventilated and almost weightless. Her arches felt better supported and cooling relief made its way from her ankles to her hips. Lucy smiled and hopped on her toes. It *did indeed* feel as though she was walking on a cloud.

The Ocean Sunrise trainers took her down Baker Street, through Calgary Park and onward, to her condo in Gables Village. Alternative rock pumped into her ears as her ponytail spun and her steps bounced. The air was cool after the rain from that morning. Icy droplets from the breeze felt refreshing against her face and the moist air lubricated her breathing pattern.

One year prior, Lucy had been invited to be maid of honor at her best friend Audrey's wedding. She happily obliged. She and Audrey had been friends since middle school and rarely separated. At 17, Audrey was in a near-fatal car accident that left her with a broken leg and a shattered pelvis. Four surgeries and a titanium hip-replacement later, Audrey was confined to a bed for 14 weeks. During that time, Lucy had rarely left her side.

The dress fitting for the wedding was held in Olla Bella's, a prestigious boutique in Beverly Crest on the northwest side of L.A. Lucy was heavier then. In her opinion, *grotesquely heavier.* To embarrass her further, the boutique had to special-order her a dress because of her size. Mortified, Lucy almost dropped out of the bridal party and avoided the wedding altogether. But, after a kind pep-talk by Audrey, Lucy was convinced to stick to her commitment.

Two weeks *after* the wedding, Audrey threw a party for the women who stood with her at the altar. She gifted each woman in the bridal party a framed picture of them together, beside the four-tier wedding cake. Lucy had almost vomited when she saw herself in the photo. Four, thin, athletic beauties and *her—a hog* in a special-order, barely-fitting, off-the-shoulder slit. Upon receiving the photos, one of the women made a snide comment regarding the fact that Lucy was the closest of the group to the cake. A second woman followed up the comment with, "How appropriate." The group laughed. All except for Lucy and Audrey.

Lucy snapped, shouting at her best friend and cursing her for convincing her to stay on as maid of honor, resulting in the disgusting photograph and embarrassment. She smashed her photo on the kitchen floor and stormed out of the house. The incident was never spoken of again and *that night* had been the last time she had spoken to Audrey.

The wedding, the party and the loss of Audrey lead to Lucy's under-eating, running regime and her increasing temperament. The health change was a step in the right direction, as long as she didn't eventually take it too far. But, her mental health was declining. She needed her friend. After all this time, Lucy had no idea how to *even begin* to reconnect.

She jogged down Handes Boulevard, passed the dog park and through the gate, into Gables Village Condos. Removing her ear pods, Lucy slowed to a stop, caught her breath and stretched. She ascended the two flights of stairs with ease, unlocked her door and entered her home. The sunlight fell below the horizon to the west, ending the day.

Hills Electric rested on a short cliffside, overlooking a large, commercial district in western L.A. The building was a marvel of silver and glass, standing five stories above the lot filled with rows of service vans and employee vehicles. Lucy's new, white Volkswagen purred past the structure. It eased into a front parking space marked with her full name. She exited the shiny bug dressed to impress, in a tweed, slim dress, charcoal pumps and a cashmere scarf. The ensemble was exceedingly different from her gray sweats, white socks and black trainers, but retained the exact same color scheme. She gripped a tall latte as she carefully closed the door, straightened her dress and made her way to the wide, welcoming entrance.

Inside, her heels knocked at the thin carpet adding to the ambient sound of copy machines, key tapping and soft chatter. A young, chubby receptionist greeted her as she passed, "Morning, Lucy!"

Lucy barely looked at her. "Morning," she replied with as little effort as possible. She approached her office door, took a proud look at her name etched in bronze and entered. Lucy tossed her purse onto an extra chair, rounded her desk and sat in the large, leather seat, sighing with satisfaction. A small, yellow post-it note on her monitor read, *Go For The Goal*, written in pen.

Raising her latte to her lips, Lucy almost choked when a knock came at her door. Tammy cracked the door and leaned inside. She was tall, slender and commanded the presence of a fourteenth-century dictator. She was in her early sixties and wore a striking, ruby-red skirt with a leopard-print top. Although beautiful, Tammy's powerful aura and charismatic presence was frightening. "Nine-o-clock, conference room B," she announced.

Before Lucy could answer, the door snapped closed. "On my way," Lucy said to no one but herself. Tammy's stomping heels faded from the door. The handsome clock on Lucy's wall indicated seven-minutes-to-nine. She woke her computer, opened her email and glanced through about sixty messages that had poured in over the weekend.

One message in particular caught her attention. She didn't recognize the address and the message was not sent from a Hills employee. Lucy never received mail from outside the company and she had never given her work email to anyone. She eyed it curiously. The subject simply read, "Hey." Upon opening the email, Lucy's eyes went wide. Her cup slipped from her hand, bounced off her knee and slapped against the floor. With a jerk, Lucy moved away from the spill, avoiding a stain on her shoes or dress. Brown coffee and white foam oozed onto the carpet as Lucy impatiently read the message. Her heart pounded in her chest as her eyes moved quickly, reading the short email again and again.

Hi Lucy. It's Audrey. I hope you don't mind, but I reached out to your Mom and she told me where you're working now. Dale works for Cottage Springs, he said they often do work with your company. Your mom also told me that you got a promotion recently and took up running. Congrats :) Dale and I just did the Hollywood Hustle last month, you should join us for a run sometime! I miss you. Call me. We don't have to talk about what happened. I just want my BFF back. Love you. Audrey.

A rush of conflicting emotions raced through Lucy's entire body, making her ache with fear, excitement, sadness and joy all at once. After several seconds, relief washed over her like ice water. It was cooling but made her shiver with anxiety. She took a long, calming breath. *Thank God,* she thought. She didn't have to wonder anymore how Audrey felt and thankfully, no longer carried the burden of making the first move. The wait was over. The stress was over. Now, all she had to do was respond. However, the thought of picking the *time to respond* made her shiver again.

Lucy glanced at her clock. Four minutes past nine. "Oh crap!" She exclaimed. She jumped from her seat, rushed through her door and headed down the hall.

Conference room B was spacious and opulent. A large, glass table, art deco light fixtures and full windows overlooking the cliff. However, the elegance of the room was thwarted by the atmosphere. Unamused frowns and despondent gazes filled the chairs on both sides of the table. Lucy sat upright and attentive in her seat. Tammy, sat at the head of the group. A stack of colored folders rested beside her oversized coffee mug. "Edmond," Tammy said sharply. A man in a yellow tie looked up from his phone. "Have we heard anything regarding the bid on Del Rey Convention Center?" She asked.

Edmond looked stressed. He wiped a sleeve against his shiny forehead. "I called last week and left them a message. Cottage Springs is being flaky. The decision is between us and Wagon Electric. That I know." Lucy's ears perked up at the mention of Cottage Springs.

"Have you paid them a visit?" Tammy asked. "Showed your face? Talked to anyone in person? I can't stress how *important* that is. That's how Hills has always done it and how I used to do it back in the day. A good face-to-face relationship can win a bid far more effectively than a number can." Edmond didn't respond. Tammy grew irate. "That job is forty million and the *only* job you should be concerned with. Westside school district can take a seat for now. I'd love to see Del Rey Convention Center on the front page of our website next year. Please, please land us that contract!"

Edmond nodded, making no eye contact. "I'll do it," he said quietly.

"Please see that you do!" Tammy took a long breath. She pulled a violet folder from the top of her pile and tossed it to the center of the table. Her voice softened, changing the tone of the room. "Safety committee. Who wants it?" She asked. "David retired last month and it's up for grabs." Several voices around the table groaned painfully. Tammy eyed a man in a tan suit and brown tie. "Paul, I'm looking at *you*. You were an Osha inspector in Seattle, were you not?" She asked him.

"For three days as a fill-in." Paul moaned. "Officially I was an administrator. I was never an inspector on paper."

"You just volunteered. Take it," Tammy ordered. Paul dropped his hand dramatically, onto the reflective surface and fussed under his breath as he took the folder. "Download my outline for managing safety committee correctly. I don't need you mucking it up with your own useless ideas," she ordered. A second, green folder was tossed in. This file was thicker, brimming with contents. "Permits." Tammy snapped. "Cad department is overloaded with work, we need extra hands to drop off and pick up permits. Who wants it?" The groans repeated.

One man in a vest and button-up shirt clicked his tongue and claimed the folder. "I've got sitters waiting for Saint Joseph's Hospital to start. They won't mind gophering for a bit, at least until March," he said.

Tammy nodded. "Very good, Thomas. Thank you. Remember to only send your men for pick up and drop off when I tell you to. Not before and not after." Thomas looked irritated but complied with a nod. Tammy took a blue folder in the pads of her fingers and rolled her eyes upon reading the label. She dropped it onto the glass and laid an open hand on the manilla file. She sighed, "I'm going to say two words that will make you all sick. If you favor vomiting, go right ahead. But..." She shook her head heavily. "Lemar *insists* on a stronger social structure in our branch and who am I to argue?"

Paul threw back his head and dropped his hand to the table with a smack. "Oh, God no!" He griped. Another man wretched with disgust.

"You guessed it," Tammy murmured. *"Team Building."*

Everyone but Lucy snorted, gagged, moaned or made a jerking gesture, in objection to the proposition.

A woman in a lavender pantsuit laughed, "God help whoever gets stuck with *that one.*"

Tammy slid the file to the center of the conference table. Everyone leaned backward, as if avoiding a terminal disease. "I know nobody *wants it,*" she said. "But who's going to take it?" She searched the rows of eyes. None looked in her direction. "Team building events aren't mandatory for all employees, *but* whomever takes charge of this had *damn better* be sure they get at least twenty percent of our branch to attend. Ausin had an attendance of fifteen percent, New York had seventeen and Chicago had nineteen." Her eyes narrowed. *"We* will have twenty percent or more. I will *not* be outmatched by that prick, Donnivan in Chicago a second time," Tammy spat. Everyone pretended to be distracted. Lucy's eyes fixated on the blue file. Gears in her mind turned. "Who thinks they can do this?" Tammy asked.

Lucy remembered the words that had kept her going for the past year. The words she constantly repeated to herself and she had posted on her desktop. *Go for the goal.* She wouldn't climb to the top of the mountain by avoiding responsibilities and she had to prove she was worthy of the promotion she had just received. Without taking another second to think, Lucy stood, leaned over the table and took the file. "I'll take it on," she said boldly. The tension in the conference room released and so did the breaths of everyone present.

Paul clapped his hands together. "I think Lucy would be *perfect* for it. She's the same age as seventy percent of our staff. She's the demographic. She knows what's in. Good show, Luc," he praised with a sharp smile.

Tammy glared in Paul's direction. "You would have said that to *anyone,* Paul. You're just glad it didn't end up in *your* lap."

He gave a quick, agreeable nod. "You're absolutely right," he laughed. "Still, I was right about her age. I would have arranged a golf outing but only about five men in our office would have gone."

The head of the table had no reason to disagree. She turned her overbearing eyes to Lucy. "This is important, Luc. We're not in competition with other branches on this—*but* as far as I'm concerned, we are *absolutely* in competition with other branches on this. Find something everyone will want to do on a Saturday or Sunday. I'm not pulling anyone away from a workday for this. *Ideally,* something for charity. That would look *fantastic* in corporate's eyes ...and mine. Chicago did a scavenger hunt in a park district for heaven's sake," she sneered. "If you can somehow combine a *team-building day* with a *fundraiser,* you'll have my praise but it's not a requirement. Make it happen."

"I will!" Lucy's ponytail bounced. Her terrified lips lied with a grin. "You can count on me," she said confidently, feeling no modicum of confidence at all.

The meeting continued as Lucy dwelled on her sudden, self-inflicted commitment. Volunteering was easy. Having the creativity to generate an idea, following it through and *making it happen* was a completely different challenge altogether.

The California daylight began to fade over Gables Village. Lucy stretched in her sweats as a muted news cast reporting sudden earthquakes on the westside of the city flashed on her TV. She clicked the television off, grabbed her phone and stepped out the front door. Descending the concrete steps, she pressed her ear pods in and took a few hops in her new, cloud shoes. The burn in her calf still ached and was becoming increasingly painful. After a quick thumb-massage, she started along her normal route.

One, fortunate side-effect of running she did not expect when she began, was the time to process. To live in her own head for an hour each day and to think deeply with minimal distractions. Tonight, all she could think about was the team-building assignment. She had spent the rest of the day researching *team building for offices* online and the same ten suggestions had popped up however she worded the search. Bingo, escape rooms, trivia nights and virtual murder mysteries were the typical go-to's. Her choice had to be something fun, but also involve working together as a team to achieve some kind of objective. Also, something familiar. Nobody would want to attend an activity on a day off if it was weird, unusual or had to be explained to them. Frustration burned in Lucy's chest. She teetered back and forth between cursing herself for taking it on and beefing up her confidence to deliver.

That night, Lucy took one last look at Audrey's email on her phone. She had forwarded it to herself from the office. The anxiety returned. Reaching out to her best friend would definitely happen but she decided that tonight was not the time. Not under the pressure of her current predicament. *One bridge at a time,* she thought. She closed the app, clicked off her screen and crawled into bed. She did her best not to allow the pressures of life to keep her from much-needed sleep.

Lucy paced quickly from the elevator lobby to her office. Different outfit, same color combination. "Morning Lucy!" The receptionist called out, as she did every day. Dodging the only greeting she received on a daily basis, Lucy passed the front desk, rigid and sleep-deprived. As she neared the break room, Lucy faintly heard her name mentioned by a colleague, buried between coughs of laughter. She paused and listened. The voices continued, reflecting from the open, breakroom door.

"Well, if Tammy were a man I'd be convinced that Lucy *slept* her way to the top. She's been here, what? Seven months?"

"We don't know *for sure* Tammy isn't a man."
Laughter.

"Come on guys, we need to be a little more open-minded here. Especially in the world we live in today. Tammy *could* be a lesbian. *That's* how Lucy made assistant branch!"

Harder laughter.

"She won't last. Nobody has any respect for her. She's a twenty-five-year-old kid. She probably took pics of herself naked in her shiny office on her first day to show off to her social media friends."

"I wouldn't mind seeing those!"
Chuckling.

Lucy seethed. She swung around the corner and stood in the open doorway. She glared at the group of three men. Upon seeing her, their smiles remained but their eyes displayed shock and surprise. "You assholes have somewhere to be?!" Lucy thundered. "Or does someone need to get down on their knees and unzip your pants to get you to do some damn work around here?" The men took their coffee mugs into their fists and filed out of the room. "I swear, if your small peckers weren't constantly telling you to be dumbasses, the world would be a much better place! Hills should pay you in blowjobs, our stock would go up forty percent!" Lucy roasted with fury. The men dispersed and returned to their desks. Every pair of eyes in the giant room peeked over cubicle walls and in her direction. The entire office had heard Lucy's outlash. Humiliation poured over her flesh like vinegar. She marched into her office and slammed the door.

Lucy roared behind her clenched teeth and kicked the wall. Once again, her first thought and reaction had betrayed her. She could have handled the situation differently. Far differently. Instead, she responded to sexual harassment with more sexual harassment and showed no guidance or leadership whatsoever, the way a supervisor would—the way a *leader* would. How was she supposed to get twenty percent of her branch to attend an office event on a *day off* if nobody respected her? Now, they'd certainly avoid team-building day altogether out of spite and resentment. She dropped her purse onto the extra chair and collapsed into her seat. Dark circles showed heavily below her eyes. Her tired body groaned from exhaustion.

She jumped when her door snapped open. Tammy entered and shut the boundary behind her. "October seventeenth and eighteenth," she snapped. Quickly, Lucy rubbed her eyes and tucked her disheveled hair behind her ears, attempting to hide signs of fatigue. "Did you hear me?" Tammy asked.

"Yes," Lucy responded. "October seventeenth and eighteenth. I heard."

"We are *losing* those days," Tammy said sternly. A hint of aggravation scratched in her throat.

"Losing?" She asked.

Tammy gripped her large mug of caffeine with polished fingernails "It's a Thursday and a Friday. Timber Property Management is kicking us out of the building for some sprinkler-code, violation inspection. No one is allowed on the property but we still have to pay everyone," she huffed. "I need you to send out an email informing everyone that they are off. If they need to get any work done, it will have to be from home."

"Oh," Lucy said, surprised. She opened her digital calendar and observed the days to confirm.

Tammy turned on her heel. "Let everyone know by the end of the week."

"I will," Lucy assured.

"This is going to kill us," Tammy exaggerated under her breath. She left the office. The door knocked closed.

Lucy took a large, drawn-out breath, collecting her thoughts. She opened her email. More junk notices. She scrolled through them and stopped, staring stoically at Audrey's message. Opening it again, she read it for the hundredth time. However, this time a little bell went off in her head when she read the words, *Hollywood Hustle.*

Curiously, Lucy searched *Los Angeles fun runs* and was presented with a rich and abundant list. Schedules filled her screen with sprints, runs, trots and walks with dates ranging from the upcoming weekend, all the way to December of the following year. She scrolled up the list to mid-October and found a thought-provoking listing, *October 17th, Culver City Race To Feed The Hungry. Admission price: Free entry. Locally sponsored.*

Lucy threw open her file cabinet, pulled the blue folder, laid it flat on her desk and stared at the label, *Team Building.* Questions and ideas churned in her head. Finishing off her coffee, she stood, left her office and made her way to the break room. It was welcoming and empty. No obnoxious men. Lucy brewed a fresh cup, stepped through the doorway and looked out over the sea of cubicles. She observed her colleagues closely. Specifically, their physical fitness. Most of the team appeared healthy enough to take part in an athletic venture. All except for the receptionist. Lucy glanced over at the front desk from across the office floor and took a swig of hot coffee. Brimming with inquiry, she approached the reception desk. "Barb?" Lucy addressed her quietly and attentively.

Barbara was startled, almost dropping her bundle of shipping labels. "Lucy! Hi! What can I do for you?" Her beaming smile resembled the clerk's at the shoe store.

Lucy rested her coffee on the high edge of the desk and rested her elbows. "I want to apologize for earlier," Lucy lied. "You said good morning to me but I don't think I responded. I swear I said *Good morning* back, but it may not have come out verbally." Her grin was as fake as cardboard.

"Oh," Barbara exclaimed. She nervously fumbled with the labels, fastening them together with a binder clip and setting them aside. "Not a problem at all! It's my job to meet, greet and repeat but it's not a requirement for others to greet back!" Her voice was bubbly and almost sickeningly effervescent.

"I have kind of a personal question for you, if that's ok." Lucy inquired.

"Oh? Shoot!" Barbara encouraged.

Leaning in closely, Lucy asked, "Have you ever done a fun run, a walk or any kind of race for a cause, or even just for recreation?"

Barbara's face lit up even brighter. "Oh, absolutely! I did the Seaside Stroll last April with my choir group and earlier this year, Tracy, Justine and I did the Baldwin Bustle at the scenic overlook!"

"Tracy and Justine from our billing department?" Lucy asked.

"Oh yes!" She replied. "The run was a benefit for cats with muscular dystrophy." Her brow narrowed. "Can you believe nobody gives money to causes like that?! Poor things." Barbara's beam returned. "But, Tracy, Justine and I did our part ...despite all the aches and pains. *Nothing* compared to what those poor little kitties go through, though."

Lucy ignored the nauseating cause. "So, would you say ...*hypothetically,* that most of our office would participate in a run if something like that were arranged?" She asked.

"Why?" Barb's expression emitted rays of sunshine. "Are we going to do one?!"

"Not quite yet, *officially.*" Lucy said. "I'm just gathering information for the possibility." Barbara nodded excitedly. "But you *are sure* that most of the office would be capable of a run? A short one?" She asked.

Barb cocked her head to the side with a grin. "Lucy, this is L.A. Everybody runs."

Lucy nodded, thanked Barbara for her time and returned to her office. She now had all the information she needed. Unable to help herself, she read through Audrey's email again. Another name snatched her attention. *Cottage Springs,* she thought. A second idea presented itself. Grabbing her phone, Lucy unblocked Audrey, unlocking a never-ending stream of texts that had accumulated over the past year. She ignored them, opened a new message field and drafted a text. Her thumbs moved like lightning. *Audrey, I miss you too. Everything is water under the bridge at this point. Listen, would you and Dale be interested in a fun run coming up? October 17 Culver City Race To Feed The Hungry. Dale can invite anyone from his office to go. My company is hosting.* She read through every word carefully and tapped *send.* Lucy placed the phone on her desk with the screen left on, hoping for a quick response.

After two anxious minutes, a text appeared. *Sounds great! Dale says yes. He will send the word out.*

In her excitement, Lucy scribed another message, pushing her plan even further. *Does Dale know anything about the Del Ray Convention Center account? Is he involved in it at all?* She sent the text without hesitation and waited. Immediately, Audrey responded.

Oh yeah. He talks about it all the time. Why?

Lucy sat back in her leather chair and a crooked smile crept across her lips . She took a sinister sip of coffee. A plan formulated in the depths of her mind. A disgustingly-wonderful, terrible plan.

One week later, Lucy entered her building with a confidence and attitude she had not before possessed as assistant branch manager of Hills Electric. She stepped off the elevator and beamed as she passed the reception desk. "Morning Barbara!" She hailed before Barb could open her large mouth.

"Good Morning, Lucy!" Barbara clamored happily.

Lucy passed her office and approached the tall, oak door leading into Tammy's dungeon. Under her arm, she held two files, the team-building folder and a second, red file stuffed thickly with documents and drawings. Without knocking, she snapped open the door and announced "Meeting. Conference room B. As soon as you can." Before Tammy could speak, Lucy shut the door and made her way to the meeting room. She readied her presentation, at the head of the table. She sat, placed the files meticulously before her and rested her tall, double latte on the spotless glass.

Flustered, Tammy entered the room and approached the table. "What's happening? What's wrong?" She barked with disgruntled panic.

"Absolutely nothing," Lucy said brightly. Her supervisor just stared at her, bewildered. "This will only take a minute." Lucy gestured to a nearby chair.

Tammy ignored the invitation. "I have a lot going on today, what's the problem?" She snapped.

Lucy lifted her coffee. "No problem at all, Tammy. In fact, I'd say we have the *opposite* of a problem." The titan just stared. "Would you like to hear *why?*" Lucy asked. She realized she was displaying hefty doses of smug complacency but was ignorant to her appearance due to searing confidence. Tammy crossed her arms and lifted her brow, humoring her assistant.

Opening the blue folder, Lucy read from a leaflet. The flier for the fun run was colorful and eye-catching. She began, "Our team-building day will be October seventeenth in Culver City." She placed the flier before Tammy. "It is a fun run and it is a charity event. It's a 15k. Roughly nine miles."

Tammy took a step closer and looked down her nose at the leaflet, displaying flat indifference. She almost scoffed. "Nobody will go for this," she complained. "You think everyone is going to want to run nine miles when they could be at home, beginning a four-day weekend? You'll never get twenty percent of our branch to attend." She looked up from the leaflet. Her patience grew even thinner. "I have matters to attend to. Is that all?"

"You *are* right about that," Lucy said. "I did *not* get twenty percent of our branch to attend."

"Then why are you wasting my time?!" Tammy barked.

"I got *eighty-nine* percent of our branch to attend," Lucy announced.

"Eighty nine?" Tammy asked. Her pencil-thin eyebrows rose.

Lucy pulled a stack of papers from the blue folder and tapped them on the glass table. "Fifty-two employees of Hills Electric L.A. branch, signed up, processed and confirmed through the event website itself," she glowed.

"How did you get fifty-two to sign up?" Tammy asked.

Lucy shrugged and laid the stack flat on the table. "I just ...*made it happen,*" she whispered matter-of-factly. "Oh, and the event is *free* so there is no cost to the company, with the exception of paying the staff for that day and Friday, which was happening anyway." She slid the stack in Tammy's direction. "Everyone will show up to the event on Thursday morning and pose for a photo in their running gear. A showy post for our social media. Show Chicago a thing or two, huh?"

Tammy took it all in. Frustration returned to her expression. "Ok, fine. You arranged team-building day. Congratulations," she spat sarcastically. "But I have bigger things going on today, bigger than office social structure. So, if you'll excuse me..." Tammy started for the door.

Lucy called out as Tammy departed, "Bigger things like Hills losing the Del Rey Convention Center bid?"

Tammy stopped in her tracks, spun around and approached her assistant furiously. "How the *hell* did you know that?" She bellowed.

"*Hills* didn't lose the convention center bid. *Edmond* lost the convention center bid," Lucy said.

Confusion danced across Tammy's face. "I don't understand."

Lucy gestured to the seat a second time. "I wasn't finished with my presentation. It'll just be another minute," she said with conviction. Tammy sat slowly and folded her long fingers. Her full attention was focused on the head of the table. Lucy dropped her index finger on the stack of registration sheets. "Not *only* will fifty-two employees of Hills be attending the event, but twenty-seven employees of Cottage Springs Construction will be attending as well." Tammy's face went red with arousal. Lucy continued, "*Of those* twenty-seven, a Dale Matthews will be there, assistant to Jeff McAlroy, their branch head. You may know him?"

Tammy was paralyzed with astonishment. She nodded slightly. "Yes. Jeff and I go way back. *He's* with Cottage Springs now?" She asked.

"He is," Lucy beamed. "And he still remembers *you*. In fact, Dale said he spoke very fondly of you when they spoke." She leaned forward. "Hills had the lowest bid by under a million for the convention center. They don't want Wagon Electric, but on the other hand they don't want our boy, Edmond either."

"Why not?" Tammy asked.

"You said it yourself last week," Lucy explained. "He doesn't show face, he barely called, he never took anyone from Cottage out to lunch... Jeff wants to decide on us but he wants someone to handle this job that he's dealt with before. Someone he *knows*. They're almost considering going with an out of state contractor." Lucy looked Tammy closely, in the eye. "If you show face at *this event* and mingle with Jeff, Dale and the rest of Cottage, I'd say we have a damn good shot at landing that job, *same day*. Just tell them that *you personally, have* taken over Edmond's bid and will oversee the job as project manager. After that, you can hand the project off to anyone here you trust to get it done."

Tammy just stared, awestruck.

"So," Lucy said. She took the heavy, red folder into her hands. "This is the bid for Del Rey Convention Center. The job is likely ours if the right person is interested." Lucy slapped it onto the table in front of Tammy and smiled. "Who wants it?"

Lucy floated back to her office across the carpeted floor like a Goddess with her coffee in hand and the blue folder under her arm. She had not only hit a hole-in-one with the team-building assignment, she had potentially landed the biggest job Hills Electric had ever placed a bid on. Sending that response to Audrey had been the best move she had ever made, socially and professionally.

Audrey's husband, Dale awarded Lucy contacts with Cottage Springs nobody in her company could have ever dreamed of.

However, her current silver lining did come with a stormcloud. In her gut, she knew that she had *used* her friend for professional gain. And the process by which she convinced her fifty-two colleagues to sign up for the fun run, was based on a horrid and barbarous lie.

Days ago, instead of telling her branch they had the two days off as she was instructed to, she told them the company agreed to give them Friday off if they attended the event on Thursday. She also told them to sign up for the run themselves and to submit a confirmation that they had done so—or work from home both days as an alternative because of the inspection.

The move made Lucy sick with regret if she thought about it too much, so she pushed it out of her head. She was sure nobody would find out about the lie and Lucy's actions were done for the good of the company. It didn't matter if she had to pull some shady strings to get it done. She *went for the goal* and made it happen, just as she had promised to herself and to Tammy.

End of day neared. Lucy began wrapping up, placing files away and going through the last of her emails. She looked forward to her afternoon run. The worried and stress-filled thoughts that bustled through her mind while out on her trail all week would today, be replaced by assurance and accomplishment. She smiled as she locked her file cabinet and closed the digital windows of her desktop. As she did, she noticed a flashy news report pop up on the blog of her search engine. The image showed police setting up blockades in a rural district of the city. The caption read, *Mini Earthquakes Continue On Southwest Side.*

Unexpectedly, Lucy's door opened. This time, it opened slowly. Tammy sauntered into the room with the race leaflet in her fingers and her arms crossed. Lucy tore her attention away from the earthquake report and focused on her supervisor. "Yes?" She responded attentively. Tammy did not speak. She waltzed slowly over to the chair across from Lucy, dusted off her skirt and took a seat. She crossed her legs and subjectively examined the details of Lucy's face. The assistant grew nervous, tension danced in the air.

Tammy spoke, "Months ago, before your ascension to management, I overheard you speaking to one of your fellow employees. The employee, whom I will leave nameless, wanted to blame company guidelines for an injury to one of our electricians on an incident report. Do you remember this instance?"

Lucy's face went white. "Yes," she choked.

Tammy continued, "If we're being truthful, that injury *was* a direct result of poor policy and was later changed. *You,* on the other hand, ignored the *honest decision* and filed the mishap under, *Misuse of materials by company installer,* resulting in the termination of that electrician." Lucy was cold with angst. She swallowed hard in her throat. "You used the words, *I'd let a hundred people go before I allow an investigation to shit-tank this branch."*

The tension thickened as Tammy brushed her hands across the fabric of her skirt and rested her elbows on the arms of her chair. "Now, I didn't let something like that hinder my decision to promote you. In fact, it became the very reason you're sitting in that chair today." Lucy remained silent, the pressure in her chest eased. "I get it," Tammy said. "This business is dog-eat-dog and women in positions such as ours do not have the advantages most *men* have. We need to keep a few cards hidden under the table to stay in the game." She tapped a finger against her head. "We have to use our *brains.* Something I haven't seen a *man in this business* do in four decades," she laughed. Lucy thought of the three idiots in the breakroom. She couldn't help but agree. Tammy's amusement faded. "God knows I've performed some ...unethical tasks to get ahead. Tasks I did not regret and I do not regret now. Hills Electric is better for it and *I'm still standing.*" Her brow raised. "You *do* know what I'm saying, do you not?" Tammy asked.

Lucy swallowed again. "I do."

Tammy shot an icy stare of omnipotence. "I know what you did, Luc." Her words were soft but felt like a hammer. "I know that you didn't tell the staff about the closed days and I know how you got a *staggering* eighty-nine percent of our staff to agree to attend on October seventeenth."

Lucy's mouth opened. An excuse began to roll off her tongue, "I didn't think you—"

"Oh, come now, Lucy," she interrupted with a dark chuckle. "You sent the emails out to the entire team, you *really didn't* think I would intercept *one* of them?" Lucy sighed, conceding. "Your mind was in the right place but you forgot about *one* imposing variable that could bring your elaborate ruse to the ground," Tammy explained.

"What variable?" Lucy asked.

"Me," Tammy said. "Pulling a hat-trick you can get away with is one thing ...getting caught is a *completely different* matter altogether. And the heat from it falls on *both of us.*" Lucy didn't move but her eyes conveyed crystal-clear understanding. Tammy continued, "Corporate doesn't know about the closed days and I'm going to leave it that way. We will go about October seventeenth and the eighteenth as you presented to me today and no one will be the wiser." Lucy eased with the calming warmth of relief. *"But,"* Tammy stipulated. She pointed the pamphlet directly at Lucy's nose. "...the *next time* you decide to pull another scheme and drape the wool over the eyes of our branch and our superiors ...you be *damn sure* to let *me* in on it first!" She ordered.

Lucy's tail bounced. "Yes ma'am," she complied.

Tammy nodded upon the agreement and eased back into the seat. She glanced at the race flier. "Question about the race," she changed the subject.

"Question?" Lucy chirped.

"Culver City Race For The Hungry," she read out loud, lifting her eyes. "Whom is the race benefiting and why is there no admission donation?" Tammy questioned.

Lucy shrugged and remembered the description from the listing. "It's *locally* sponsored," she cited.

Awkward silence drifted. "Hm," Tammy snorted. "Well, as long as it alludes to charity on the header, our team-building activity is still miles ahead of a dreadfully poor-conceived scavenger hunt." She tossed the leaflet on Lucy's desk. The subject shifted again. "Jeff McAlroy will be attending the event as well," Tammy announced. "But, not to run. He and I will be at Lumetti's, a coffee club a block away from the starting line of the race. We will catch up, mingle, perhaps he'll mention any further work he plans to send down the pipeline, after the convention center."

"Sounds great," Lucy concurred.

Tammy extended a strong finger. "I want *you* to stay glued to Dale Matthews. Talk with him, get to know him. I want you side-by-side with him during the entire run." She cracked a smirk. "If you can keep up," she added.

"Oh, I can keep up," Lucy said confidently.

"Good." Tammy stood. "Start training. I want Dale to see you go nine miles without breaking a sweat. A metaphorical example regarding the integrity of this company," she said sternly. "Oh, and email me your bib number before the race so I can track your progress from the coffee bar. Meet us there after you cross the finish line with Dale." Tammy turned, knocked her heels against the floor on the way to the door and yanked it open. Lucy dropped her limbs to her sides, flopped her head against the back of the leather chair and melted with reprieve. "Oh, and Lucy," Tammy squawked suddenly.

Lucy jerked her head forward and corrected her posture. "Yes, ma'am."

Tammy's eyes moved over Lucy's face again. She gave a miniscule but satisfying smile. "Good show, girl," she said with a hidden dash of praise. Tammy stepped out of the office. The door shut behind her with a hollow thud.

Lucy's head returned to the leather and she exhaled for what seemed like minutes. The stress oozed from her body and a tingling excitement swelled from the back of her mind. The lie was out, at least to her supervisor. To Lucy, her supervisor's opinion was the only one that mattered. Now, the lie was on Tammy, alleviating Lucy from guilt and accountability. It was over, and Lucy would be sure not to underestimate her boss again. Nor her infidelity. Still, Tammy didn't know the *whole truth*. She didn't know that she had known Dale for seven years and even attended his wedding as maid of honor. She was relieved Tammy didn't know that. Lucy wanted her to think she had made those contacts herself, without a pre-existing relationship. *Get to know him,* Lucy thought, mocking Tammy with a laugh. Already done. Now all she had to do was train for nine miles without stopping, keep everyone in line during the event and let Tammy reel in the convention center. Culver City's Race To Feed The Hungry would be the greatest thing to happen to Lucy and to Hills Electric for a long, long time.

The morning of the race, Lucy woke sore and stiff. She had pushed herself to the max over the last seven weeks without a day to rest. *No breaks,* she thought, twisting from side to side and bending over to touch her toes without bending her knees. She took her phone from the nightstand and noticed a missed text from Audrey. The line simply read, *I have news. Tell you at the race :)* Lucy's lips twisted with inquiry but the smiley face assured her the news was nothing adverse.

She shot a message back, *See you there!* Dropping the phone to the bed, Lucy undressed and jumped in the shower.

Her footsteps made the path of a pinball as she rushed from the bedroom, the living room, the bathroom and back to the bedroom, frantic not to forget anything she needed or had to do before she left. She pinned on her bib, laced her progress chip tightly to her shoes, fastened her pouch and stood in front of the mirror. Her bright trainers contrasted the thin, white tank top and tight, black leggings. During the past several weeks of being reunited with Audrey, Lucy was encouraged to add more color to her wardrobe. The advice fell on deaf ears. *The shoes are enough,* Lucy thought. She grabbed her keys, stuffed her wallet into her pouch and left the condo. Her white bug purred to life, sped out of the lot and bounded south, headed for the event.

Culver City was a bustle of activity. Runners from every corner of L.A. were massed into groups, meeting up with friends and taking leave from loved ones who dropped them off or accompanied them to the start. Every coffee house, bar and restaurant was filled with spouses, family members and friends who would track their athlete's progress from their phones as they ate, drank and visited. The crew members running the event stood at attention near street-dividers, rows of traffic cones and the giant, inflatable starting arch colored loudly in blue and red.

Lucy found her coworkers and joined the group. Barbara was the first to greet her, just like at the office. Edmond, Paul, Thomas, Tracy and Justine were there, along with the three obnoxious men Lucy had cursed out. Everyone who had signed up had shown and Lucy found it difficult to think of anyone working for her branch that wasn't bibbed, laced up and accounted for. After a quick head count, Lucy gathered the group and snapped a photo. Barbara and an intern from billing held a banner stretched across the smiling faces reading, *Hills Electric* printed in gold lettering. Lucy grinned as she texted the image to Tammy with an attached message, *Take that, Chicago!* Lucy beamed with pride. She checked the time. 24 minutes until start.

Her phone chimed as a text was returned from Tammy, *Fantastic. Have you located Dale and his team yet?* Lucy felt a tinge of anxiety as she lifted her eyes from her screen and searched the crowds for Audrey and her husband.

Suddenly, in the height of the commotion, the ground began to vibrate as a low hum resonated from below the street. Car alarms from every surrounding lot began to chirp, howl and honk. Surprised cries erupted from the thousands of people, followed by a frightening silence. The ground steadied and the rumbling stopped. Every runner stood awkwardly with eyes on the crew who showed absolutely no reaction to the disturbance and continued to man their posts. The chatter swelled, several laughs rang out and the noise from the crowds returned to normal volume.

"I guess that was one of the quakes we've been hearing about all month! Talk about kicking off with a bang, huh?!" Paul said jovially.

"Is *that* going to happen during the race?" Barbara asked concerningly. Unease loomed in the eyes of several colleagues.

"I'm sure the function staff have a safety procedure for if that happens. It was most likely just a tremor!" Lucy assured her team. She had no idea what she was talking about. Who knew if the staff had a contingency plan for earthquakes. And Lucy didn't know a tremor from a tremble. Distress lingered on Barbara's face as the rest of the Hills employees went back to bright conversation and cackling laughter.

Lucy's phone dinged again, *Tell me they are not canceling the race. I will be absolutely livid if today is canceled or postponed!* The text from Tammy made Lucy shiver. She stared at her phone, praying the seismic activity stayed dormant and the day went on, as planned. She checked her last message from Audrey and glanced around the crowd, searching for her face.

Abruptly, her heart jumped into her throat as a pair of strong hands grabbed her shoulders from behind and shook her playfully. "Bla! It's another earthquake! Get under a doorway!" A familiar voice shouted in jest. Lucy spun around and saw Dale in a white athletic shirt, bib and running shorts. His group from Cottage Springs had followed him. They poured into Lucy's already sizable gang. "What's up, Luc?!" Dale greeted her excitedly. "I barely recognized you. You look fantastic! —*Er,*" he choked. Dale suddenly remembered he was in front of the Hills staff and glanced around for Tammy. He quickly changed his tone from genial to formal, offering his hand. "I mean, It's a pleasure to meet you, Lucy. It's wonderful to finally speak in person."

Lucy shook his hand, smiling from ear to ear. "It's a pleasure to meet you too, Dale." She almost laughed from the charade.

Dale was in on Lucy's predicament and attempted to play along as best as he could. He gave her an impartial wink. Giving in to the excitement and tugged her close, wrapping his arms around her. "It's so good to see you again," he whispered. His voice was kind and genuine.

"You too," Lucy returned the affection. "Where's Audrey?" She asked.

He jerked his head around and searched behind him. "She was just with me a minute ago."

From an unexpected direction, Audrey came running toward them in a floral, crew neck blouse, yellow yoga pants and hot pink wedges that clacked against the pavement. A striped tote bag hung from her shoulder. Hardly the attire for running a race. "I'm so sorry! I ran into a woman I know from my gym!" She exclaimed. Audrey threw her arms out and opened her mouth wide with elation upon seeing Lucy. "Aaahh! You look so thin!" She screamed excitedly. The reunited pair hugged long and hard, tilting the embrace from side to side. "I missed you so much," Audrey growled. Dale gave Lucy a pat on the back and moved into the group of Hills employees, introducing himself and shaking hands.

"I missed you too," Lucy said to her best friend. She sighed, "I'm so sorry."

Audrey released the hug and gave Lucy a stern but affable eye. "No! No. *I'm sorry.* And we'll leave it at that. Ok?"

Lucy nodded and the pair hugged again. Audrey brought her lips to Lucy's ear and whispered softly, "I'm pregnant." They both leaned backward and shared a look of frenzied thrill. Audrey glowed wildly and hopped up and down, her wedges slapping the street. "We knew eight weeks ago but just couldn't wait until the twelfth 'mester to tell you!" She exclaimed. Dale returned and stood beside his wife, grinning with the pride of a future father.

"That's wonderful!" Lucy feigned jubilation. She was happy for Audrey but when applied personally, the idea of having a baby was career and social suicide. In addition, Lucy hated kids. She had always felt awkward around them. She continued her act, "I'm so happy for you! I guess that explains the outfit." She gestured to Audrey's getup.

Acrimony fell upon Audrey's expression. "*I* wanted to run the race today!" She slapped the back of her hand against her husband's chest. "*This one* said it would be too much strain on the baby!" She shouted bitterly.

Dale placed an easing hand on Audrey's shoulder and addressed Lucy, "*We* decided not to take any chances.

There'll be plenty of time for running after the birth," he said calmly.

"Like hell!" His wife barked. "I'll be home with the baby all day while *you work!*"

He smirked. "You can run with the baby. We'll get you one of those jogging strollers with the monster truck wheels," he half-joked.

Audrey contended, "I've been a fitness junkie my whole life! You can't expect me to just sit and *bloat* for nine months!" They continued to lightly argue.

Lucy's ringtone sounded furiously. The name Tammy flashed across the screen of her phone. "Oh shit!" She coughed. Lucy answered, covering her opposite ear to block out additional noise. "Tammy, sorry I—," she started.

"When I text you, you answer! Right then and then! Do you understand?!" Tammy's voice scratched through the speaker like rusty nails.

"Yes, ma'am," Lucy replied.

"Now, is the race still on and have you met up with Dale?" She asked.

"Everything is taken care of. As far as I know the race is still a go and Dale and his team are here," Lucy assured.

"Good! Remember, Lumetti's after the race. You and Dale. Got it?" Tammy asked.

"Got it." Lucy heard the call-ended toll and dropped her phone to her side, exhaling through pursed lips and puffed cheeks.

Audrey remarked on the minimal event signage and lack of local business logos, "So this is strange, huh?"

"What's strange?" Lucy asked.

"No entry fee, no cause. I thought this was a race to feed the needy? What's the charity?" Audrey wondered loudly.

Lucy repeated, "It's locally sponsored."

"By who?" Audrey chuckled with sincerity. "Usually sponsors print their names all over these damn things." Now that the issue was dragged so vigorously out into the open, Lucy began to wonder the same thing. They both stared up at one, large banner that simply read, *Culver City Race To Feed The Hungry* with no tagline, benefit, organization or sponsorship. The discovery was baffling and inescapably daunting.

From the starting line, the sound of an ear-piercing horn reverberated through the crowded streets. Dale clapped his hands together and turned to the group. "That's our cue to move to the start, everyone! *Let's go!*" He howled.

His wife gave him a warm hug. "Have fun," she said to him. "I'll be at Shakers, at the bar." She pointed to a nearby tavern.

"No wine," he ordered. Raising his brow.

Audrey ignored him. "And don't get competitive!" She added. "Remember, you have to stay with Lucy the whole run," she implored. Another stipulation they graciously stuck to for Lucy's sake. Dale smiled, nodded and kissed his wife.

"Audrey, you're ok with Dale and I doing this without you?" Lucy inquired. "It's not too awkward, just the two of us?" She was surprised to find herself expressing actual empathy. But she also knew Audrey wouldn't raise an objection.

"Nah!" Audrey gave a dismissive wave. "Dale's cheated on me lots of times," she said. Dale's face hardened with vexation, glaring at his wife.

Shocked and disturbed, Lucy's eyes shifted between the couple. "Seriously?" She asked honestly.

"No!" Audrey laughed. She glanced at Dale. "I'd *kill* him!" Raising her hand, she pressed a firm finger against his chin. "...Slowly," she growled.

Lucy and Audrey hugged and the crowd of 79 contractors herded through the streets to the starting post. Lucy and Dale stood side-by-side, packed together among thousands of sprinters, runners, trotters and walkers as the timer counted down from 60 seconds. Competitors were lined up twenty-bodies-thick from the post, stretching back a full, five, city blocks. Dale turned to Lucy and flashed a judgemental eye. "Did you train for this? If you didn't, It's too late now!" He bantered.

Lucy scoffed, *"Did I train for this?"* She returned the trash-talk. "We'll just see if you can keep up. I'll slow down for you when you straggle behind after the second mile."

"Oh, I can keep up," he cracked. They both laughed.

The horn erupted and the runners poured from under the nylon arch and down the blocked-off street. A sea of colorful polyester, white bibs and beating shoes flowed down the gray pavement as cheers rang out from onlookers and supporters from the sidelines. Lucy kept up her pace, thoughtfully managing her breaths. Three steps to inhale and three steps to exhale, just as she had done for over a year. Dale looked as though he was putting in no effort at all. His breathing during cardio looked the same as when he was rested. He grinned and picked up his pace playfully, leaving Lucy several feet behind. Lucy's competitive nature kicked into high gear. She pushed herself into a sprint to pass him.

Suddenly, Lucy felt a dagger drive deep into her calf and twist. She screamed, fell forward and plummeted into Dale. His ankle twisted, his tibia buckled and his knee dislocated, sending the core of his weight straight to the ground. Lucy hit the pavement, helplessly massaging her calf with her fingers. The pain only amplified. Dale turned to a seated position and straightened his leg, popping his knee back into place with a yelp of agony followed by a soothing breath of relief. Racers attempted to dodge the injured couple as some of them tripped and staggered over them. The pair dragged themselves off the street, over the curb and onto the sidewalk as the thick flow of runners continued their normal traffic pattern.

"Are you ok?!" Dale asked with alarm.

"Shit!" Lucy shouted, pressing the corner of her fist into her muscle, attempting to rub the pain away. "Shit, shit shit!"

"Feels like a corkscrew?" Dale inquired.

"Yeah." She gasped with pain, "Dammit!"

"It's a muscle strain. You won't be able to finish the race," he said.

Lucy exploded, *"I have to!* My boss is tracking me with the *stupid app!"* She dropped her face into her hands, crushed by discouragement. Dale leaned back, resting his hands on the concrete and his legs extended, inhaling and exhaling deeply. His knee throbbed. Lucy lifted her head and dropped her hands to her lap, glancing at Dale's injured leg. "What about you?" She asked.

"Knee dislocation," he said. "I can't finish the race either. My leg is going to swell up like a melon. Happens every few years or so. Ortho says I have high kneecaps. They shift if I turn funny, twist my ankle..." Dale looked directly at Lucy. "Or if someone slams into me." He smiled.

"I'm sorry!" Lucy shouted, irate.

"I'm kidding!" He shouted back. "Well ...I'm kidding about the *blaming you for intentionally ruining the race* part but in all seriousness, this was definitely *your fault."* He grinned again.

Lucy's face went red with enmity. She seethed with outrage. "You have *no idea* what's riding on *this race* today for me, Dale! My supervisor is going to *have my ass* if I don't—"

Dale lifted a settling hand, stopping her. "Whoa, whoa, whoa. I'm not your enemy, Luc. The *situation* is, and that cannot be controlled. And you're supposed to be getting on *my good side* today, *remember?* Stay with Dale? Feel him out? *Get to know him,"* he reminded her.

Lucy growled through her teeth, forced into reasonability. "I *already* know you," she said stubbornly.

He nodded dramatically. "That you do!"

Her face twisted. "How is it that you can be so laid back about this? You hold the same title as mine. Isn't your boss up your butt about today, too?" She asked.

Dale spoke coolly, "I'm so laid back because I know that when tonight comes, you and I are going to walk away from today in *fantastic* shape. Not physically, of course." He referred to their injuries. Lucy wondered if that was a clue regarding the convention center bid. She felt a hint of excitement. Dale spoke again. "And *no*, my boss is *never* up my butt," he answered. "I wouldn't work for him if he was."

Lucy's mental train shifted tracks. "Isn't Jeff tracking you, too?"

He scoffed, "No. He's my supervisor, not a dictator."

Lucy's forehead wrinkled. "What happens when he finds out you fell out of the run?"

"You act like I should be *afraid* of him, Luc," Dale said. "I run my branch as assistant head and Jeff trusts me to do so. Let alone a company outing." He noticed the look of internal struggle on her face. "Don't you?"

Lucy found herself opening up. "Aren't you worried about screwing up? Making a mistake? Making a decision *he* wouldn't make?" She asked, painfully honestly. Her strife with Tammy was now bare naked in front of him.

"Making mistakes is part of growth," he said. "And my boss didn't promote a clone of himself, he promoted *me*. I run my office with Jeff's *guidance*. If he doesn't like the way I do things he'll replace me and if he promoted the wrong person, that's on him," Dale explained. "A manager's job is to train, teach and guide. Their branch should function so well that it continues to succeed and earn a profit in their inevitable disappearance. Tammy is going to retire one day and it's likely that *you* will be her predecessor."

Lucy's mind processed. She had never once thought about becoming head of her own branch. The idea drew her to panic. She spoke quietly and earnestly, "If Tammy disappeared, the whole L.A. branch of Hills Electric would come crashing down."

"Then she has done you all a *terrible* disservice," Dale said. Lucy just stared between her legs and to the surface of the sidewalk, pondering. He gave her a few long seconds to process what he had just told her before pointing toward a street corner, two blocks away. "You think you can limp all the way to Shaker's?" he asked. "Audrey is probably on her second glass of *I'm going to kill her with my bare hands* by now."

"Yeah," Lucy groaned. She leaned forward and steadied herself on one leg, standing. Dale did the same. They braced against one another and the two runners hobbled on two uninjured legs, down the crowded sidewalk and to the tavern. They hopped through the entrance.

Audrey noticed them from the bar. "Oh my God!" She exclaimed. She ran over and helped them to two, empty stools, giving up her stool in the process. "What happened?" She asked as they sat.

"Oh." Dale answered, "Lucy pushed me down, trying to cross the finish line first and I blew my kneecap out." Audrey slapped him on the shoulder, in light of his tasteless joke. Quickly, Dale noticed a wide margarita glass filled with dark red liquid and a thin straw. It rested beside Lucy and the stool Audrey had been sitting in. He pointed at it, the pitch of his voice heightened, "What's that?"

"It's pomegranate juice," Audrey answered flatly.

"Oh yeah?" He interrogated, "You sure there's no rum in that?"

She took the glass and teased him with it, keeping it away from slow, playful minimal-effort swipes with his grabbing hand. His suspicion grew into irritation. "Seriously, Audrey. Is that alcohol?"

Audrey slapped the glass in front of him and slid it under his nose. "It's pomegranate juice, asshole. Drink it!" She demanded, annoyed with his distrust.

Dale took a sip. "Oh wow. It *is* pomegranate juice. I'm proud of you, hun." She rolled her eyes. He sipped again, then chugged it right from the glass.

She asked Lucy, "So, are you both ok?

Lucy moaned, "I pulled a muscle and knocked him over thirty seconds into the race."

"Isn't your boss tracking your chip?" Audrey questioned with concern.

"Yeah, but ...I'll deal with that when the time comes," she answered.

Audrey kicked off her wedges and slid them against the foot of the bar. "Give me your shoes," she ordered, motioning to Lucy's feet.

"What do you mean?" Lucy asked, confused.

Dale knew exactly what his wife meant. "Uh, yeah. What the hell *do* you mean?" He asked angrily.

"I'm running the race for Lucy," she said boldly. She whipped off her blouse, exposing a bright, yellow sports bra. "I *want* to do this. I *can* do this and there is noth—"

Dale stood and raised his voice, cutting her sentence short, "No you're not!"

Audrey continued, pointing a finger at his face, "...And there is *nothing* you can do to stop me! My OB-GYN told me that running is *perfectly healthy* during the first trimester and *you* are just being paranoid! I want to do this and I owe it to Lucy for what happened at my bridal party last year."

Lucy shook her head. "Audrey, you don't owe me anything."

"Please, Luc. I want to do this for you," she begged. "I'll carry your chip the whole loop so your boss can see that you completed it." Audrey held a hand out. "And, when my child is seven, I can tell all the lazy moms at soccer practice that I ran a fifteen kilometer race while pregnant."

"Or ballerina practice," Dale suggested.

Audrey shot a sharp eye at her husband. "We are *not* having that debate again, not here," she shouted. She turned back to Lucy. "Please, Luc? I know they'll fit, we used to trade shoes all the time." Lucy turned her eyes to Dale. He threw his hands up and returned his butt to the stool, surrendering from the battle. Painful seconds passed.

Lucy's phone broke the silence. A chime sounded from her pouch. She unzipped it, pulled her device and read the text from Tammy, *Have you started yet? I don't see that you've moved. You had better not have lost Dale!* Lucy looked back and forth between her phone and Audrey's face.

Lucy could have said no. She could have taken the heat from Tammy and been the only force that kept her pregnant best friend from possibly overexerting herself, causing some kind of damage and losing her child. Dale didn't have the power to stop Audrey, but Lucy did. All she had to do was keep her shoes on.

With a long sigh, Lucy pulled her shoes from her heels with the tips of her toes and slid them towards Audrey. The progress chip dangled from the tight laces. Work, Tammy, the assistant manager position and all she had worked so hard for, just meant far too much to her. Lucy drafted a response to Tammy, *We just passed the start. Long queue.*

Audrey jumped up and down, clapping her hands excitedly. She untied the new, blue and yellow trainers and relaced them tightly around her feet. "Damn, these are nice, Luc. How much did these set you back?" She asked.

"Don't ask," Lucy groaned.

Pushing on the toe of the shoes, Audrey noticed extra space. "Are these a little big on you?" She inquired.

Lucy groaned again, "Don't ask that either."

Double knotting the laces, Audrey stood. "Give me your bib." She wiggled her fingers eagerly in front of Lucy's chest.

"Oh, right," Lucy gasped. She unpinned her number and fastened it to her best friend's athletic bra, very carefully.

Audrey hugged both of them at the same time, impatiently. "Love you! See you after I finish!" She erupted. Audrey ran out of the tavern, around the corner, up to the street, passed the starting line and kept on going.

Lucy and Dale turned on their stools and faced the bar. The bartender approached after Dale waved her over. "I'll just get a Coke, please," he requested. He turned to Lucy. "You want anything? Cottage Springs is picking up the tab today." He pulled a company credit card from his wallet and handed it to the server. Lucy's phone chimed.

"Diet Coke," Lucy said as she unlocked her screen.

The message read, *I see you moving now. Let me know if Dale says anything about the convention center.*

The text reminded Lucy she could now track Audrey. She downloaded the app, entered her bib number and a map of the area filled her screen. A small, blue dot appeared approximately five percent into the race. She grinned. "Wow, I'm really hauling," she joked.

Two beverages were placed before them as Dale observed the map as well. "That you are. And you'll probably stop to use the bathroom about nine times as well, *during* the haul," he said. "Audrey has a small bladder," he whispered. "She's going to be a fountain during the third trimester," he laughed. They both chuckled.

Lucy placed the phone on the bar and took a sip of fake sugar and fizz. She tapped her nails on the hard oak. "So...," she began.

"So?" Dale inquired curiously.

"...speaking of Cottage Springs..." Lucy alluded.

He smirked, "Ohhhh, I see. You want some inside information." Lucy's brow raised high and wide, she nodded slowly and dramatically. "You want to know if you won the Del Rey job, don't you?" Dale asked. He took a sip and said nothing. His eyes sparkled and his cheeks went red.

Lucy gasped so hard she snorted, "We did?!" She grabbed his arm hard, digging her nails in.

"Ah!" He winced with pain. "Easy, easy!"

She released him and started pushing on his arm, rocking him back and forth. "Did we?! Did we get the convention center?!" Lucy begged the question. Dale gave her the slightest of nods, his face still flush. "Oh my God! Thank you, thank you!" She wrapped her arms around him.

"Don't thank me! It wasn't me," he said strongly. She stopped abusing him and listened intently. "Jeff decided on Hills as soon as Tammy's name was dropped.

The decision was made weeks ago. I had nothing to do with it," Dale said.

"Wait." Lucy's excitement narrowed. "Then why did you let Audrey run for me? I could have told Tammy we won the bid and she wouldn't have given a damn if I raced or not!" She shouted.

"*You* aren't supposed to know about it yet and that goes for *Tammy* as well," Dale said sternly. He pointed at Lucy's phone. She leaned back, indicating she wouldn't spill the beans. He continued, "Jeff is taking the three of us out to dinner tonight to make the announcement. So act surprised," he said. Lucy bounced up and down on her stool, swelling with delight. Dale sighed with a grin, "And... Audrey wanted *nothing more* than to run this race today. We were arguing about it all morning. She wants to be one of those *power moms.*" He pumped his fist in the air. "She definitely *will* be." He took another sip. Lucy noticed the look in his eyes when he mentioned his wife. "May as well let *everyone's* dreams come true today, right?" He added benevolently.

"You really *do* love her, don't you?" Lucy asked. Her elbow rested on the bar and her cheek rested against her fist.

"Of course I do. That's why I married her," He said honestly.

"No, I mean you *really* love her. Like in movies," Lucy clarified.

Dale nodded with all the confidence in the world. "You could say that," he said as he pondered her comparison. "You could *absolutely* say that."

Lucy examined Dale's face. Her attitude towards men softened a tad from the incident in the breakroom, from the sluff-off anti-action of Edmond and from Tammy's derogatory words spoken weeks ago in her office. She still had no desire to meet a man and fall in love, but perhaps her interaction with Dale would help her be a little less prejudiced when dealing with testosterone on a daily basis. Maybe. If she didn't let her initial thoughts and reactions get the better of her. And, if the men she dealt with deserved it.

Dale yanked her from her thoughts, *"You're* Audrey's best friend, What do *you* love about her?" He asked curiously.

"Umm," she stammered. Lucy took a second to change gears. "I guess..." She was surprised to find that she had never asked herself that question before. She sifted through memories and emotions. Easily and quickly, she realized the *exact* reason she loved her best friend. And it had only taken her 15 years to do it. "I followed Audrey everywhere when we were kids," she began. "I saw how she interacted with others, how she helped people and how she always assumed the best in people until they proved otherwise. Even then, she was always there for them. She never judged or turned her back on anyone." Lucy couldn't believe she was saying the following phrase out loud. "I love Audrey ...because she is the person that I *always wanted to be,"* she said. Lucy's face reddened. She felt a choke of emotion in her throat. "And all this time we've been friends, I *never once* told her that."

Dale bobbed his head up and down, understanding completely. "You should tell her," he suggested.

She turned her head and looked him in the eye. "I will." Her ponytail bounced.

Murmurs and yells from outside swelled as the last of the racers crossed the starting line. Event crew members were rushing quickly past the windows. Dale noticed. His brow furrowed. "What the *hell* is going on now?" He mumbled. Lucy turned her head and watched the commotion from her stool. A black van pulled up and parked beside the tavern blocking one, large picture window. Nearby voices grew louder, shouting directions and commanding instructions like sergeants administering orders.

Dale rose and curiously approached the window. Lucy followed closely behind him. She stood in her socks, she wouldn't be caught dead in Audrey's pink wedges. Teams outside were gathering cones, collapsing canopies and loading barricades into the parked, nearby van at a hurried pace. Identical vehicles pulled up along every curb. Their doors opened wide and their cabins filled quickly with event materials. The starting arch was deflated, rolled up and stuffed heedlessly into the side of an ebony, sprinter van. Crew members climbed into the cargo hold with the deflated arch and slid the door closed. Dale leaned his elbow against the frame of the window and watched in dismay. "Do they think there's going to be another earthquake?" He speculated out loud.

"I'm guessing this isn't typical of an organized race?" Lucy asked.

"No," he replied, still baffled. "It's not." They watched each crew load up the last of the vans, pile in, slam the doors and speed off, leaving the entire intersection as unrestricted and clear as it had been the day before. Normal foot traffic resumed and vehicles were now free to use the streets. The only evidence left behind that there had been an event at all was the banner left carelessly strewn upon the sidewalk. "You know...," Dale began. "I hadn't wondered this until *just now.*" He turned his nose to Lucy. An expression of unease and troubled confusion lingered in his eyes. "Where the hell is the finish line?"

Lucy lifted her phone and observed Audrey's dot approaching the third mile mark. She scribed a text, asking her if she was ok. Dale watched her thumbs tap the screen. They hovered over the device, waiting for a reply.

The phone chimed. Her words appeared, *Barely breaking a sweat! Tell asshole to have a bottle of Pino ready for me when I finish!*

"Sounds like everythings going normally on *her end,*" Dale said after reading the text. He turned his head back to the window. "Why in God's name did they clean up so fast?"

Lucy shrugged. "Maybe these things are getting more efficient," she guessed. "L.A. has the highest vehicle traffic rate in the country. Have you seen how quickly they clean up after a parade downtown?"

He teetered his head from side to side. "That's true," he agreed. In the middle of Dale's reply, another rumble struck their feet. A pitcher of beer slid off the bar and smashed upon the floor. Hanging, light fixtures swung vigorously. Dale and Lucy braced themselves against the window as patrons gasped and shouted. Cars slammed on their breaks outside and more alarms bleeped. After five, intense seconds of hysteria, the motion settled and the ground steadied.

Dale forced his hand into his pocket and retrieved his phone. He dialed Audrey and brought the device to his ear. He waited a long moment before she finally picked up. "Audrey!" He said loudly. "Did you feel that? …Yeah, that means you're *done.* Turn around and come back the other way." Lucy could hear Audrey's voice but couldn't make out any words. "Then stay there and I'll *drive to you,*" Dale argued. *"No you're not!* You're done, do you hear me?! *Turn around!"* Dale heard his wife hang up and yanked the phone from his ear. "Ah, for God's sake!" He squawked angrily.

"What did she say?" Lucy asked.

"What do you *think* she said?! He snapped. "She wants to finish." Dale jammed the phone back into the pocket of his running shorts.

"She's always been stubborn," Lucy commented.

He sighed heavily. "No kidding. Try being married to her." He rested his hands on his hips and stared at the ceiling as if wondering how to handle the situation.

Lucy's phone hailed another Tammy message, *How's it going?*

She tapped back, *Good. Six miles to go. Keeping up with Dale.*

Lucy placed a reassuring hand on Dale's shoulder and shook him blithely. "She'll finish the race, you'll get her home and everything will be fine," she said warmly. He shot her a look of cold conjecture. "I'm *not* saying that because her finishing the run makes me look good in front of my boss," she clarified. "I just think you might be being a little..." She hesitated.

"Smart?" He said firmly. "Prudent? Safe?" He added.

"Overbearing," Lucy stated. "Think about the advice you gave me earlier," she said calmly. "Your boss promoted you based on your integrity just like you married Audrey because of hers. You can't expect her to make all the same decisions you would."

Dale fussed, "I said I married her because I loved her. I could write an *entire book* about her integrity." He alluded to his wife's faults. Lucy tugged his arm in the direction of the bar and reclaimed her stool. He reluctantly sat beside her. The bartender was mopping up the mess as glasses were replaced and new drinks were distributed. Placing her phone back onto the bar, the screen showed Lucy's dot closing in on the fourth mile.

Dale eyed it. "She'll be done in about a half hour," he said. "Audrey runs six-minute miles, average. When she's competing."

"Holy shit," Lucy exclaimed. "I'm eight or nine minutes, tops."

"Tell me about it. I run a seven-point-five. If we do a ten mile loop, sometimes she'll lap me," Dale said.

"How long have *you* been hitting the pavement?" He asked her.

Lucy dithered awkwardly. "Ever since I threw that fit in your kitchen," she admitted.

He laughed. "That was quite a spectacle. I *told* Audrey you'd hate that photo. But, I didn't know you were going to react like *that,*" he said.

She almost choked on her Coke. *"You did?"* She asked with surprise.

"Well, you looked so uncomfortable that day and I could see the relief on your face when the wedding was over," he explained. "I told Audrey not to gift you that picture but she wouldn't listen. Her excitement about the day made her naive to how uncomfortable you clearly seemed with yourself in that dress."

Lucy's tone sharpened. "And exactly why would I be uncomfortable with myself in that dress?" She asked.

Dale defended himself, "I didn't say you *were* uncomfortable, I said you *looked* uncomfortable. It's called intuition. I figured the photo would just remind you of how much you hated that day and I was trying to protect you."

She eased. "I guess seeing the good in everyone can blind you from seeing the faults people are uncomfortable with in themselves," Lucy said.

"More of Audrey's integrity at work," Dale joked. His eyes smiled. "I'm glad it happened."

"You're glad what happened?" She asked.

"Your freak out. The fight. The separation," he admitted. "Audrey needed a wake up call and to choose her friendships more carefully. When you left the party, those three bitches had nothing but shitty things to say about you. Audrey kicked them out and hasn't spoken to them since. You're the only one she rekindled a relationship with."

"Really?" Lucy asked.

Dale nodded. "And look at you," he said brightly, gesturing to her. "Clearly it did *you* some good, too. You took charge of yourself, took charge of your health, furthered your career. It shows that you've finally accepted yourself. You're more confident, poised, certain. You've bettered yourself inside and out and you're a better person for it," he congratulated.

Lucy stared at her drink and drifted into thought. Within herself, she could only see the way she had treated everyone in the past year and prior. Cashiers, wait staff, clerks, strangers and her colleagues at work. She saw the looks on their faces when they had responded to her sarcasm, complaints, reprimands and flat-out meanness. Acting on her first, initial thoughts had made her impatient, bitter and callous and her attempts to show kindness had been too little, too late. She *had* changed in the past year, but for the better? She wasn't sure.

Lucy's phone beeped. Audrey's dot vanished and a window appeared displaying the status, *Location Out Of Range*. "What does *that* mean?" Dale said nervously. Other phones in the bar buzzed with similar notifications.

"I don't know," she said. Lucy pulled up her contact list and tapped on Audrey's name. The phone dialed. Rhythmic hums pulsed from the tiny speaker.

"...ucy," Audrey answered. Her voice was a digital mess of electrical interference.

"Audrey, where are you?" Lucy asked. She put the call on speaker so Dale could listen in.

"I'm ...ing in ...ong tunnel," Her voice was cutting out.

"Tunnel? What tunnel?" Lucy questioned.

Dale became annoyed and irritable. "Tunnel? No. These runs don't take you into any tunnels!" He spoke loudly into the phone, "Turn around and come back! Exit the tunnel!"

The speaker spat and clicked, "I ....an't. All closed. ...an't find a way out!" The audible portions of Audrey's voice were panicked and unsettling. Abruptly, the call ended.

"Shit!" Dale cursed. He pulled his phone and dialed only to get a busy signal with each attempt. Lucy's calls gave the same results. Dale ran out of the tavern and into the street, trying to find the most open area to get a strong signal. Lucy followed in her athletic socks. He called again. Busy signal. "Where the hell is she?" Dale shouted. He looked in the direction where the racers had initially started. Other groups looked as though they were making the same attempt. Calls to loved ones that failed to connect.

Dale and Lucy ran up to a couple who were also attempting to make a call. The woman held a large, green sign at her side reading, *Run Like You're Being Paid To!* Dale frantically asked the man, "Are you able to contact anyone in the race?"

The man replied, "No, his location dropped out and we've been calling with no answer."

"Do you know where this race finishes?" Dale asked. The couple just shook their heads. He asked two more athlete supporters the same two questions but received similar answers. Stopping in front of a corner drugstore, He dialed Audrey's phone again. Lucy kept the map open, in the event that the signal strengthened and Audrey's location dot appeared. Dale paced, listening to silence. Suddenly, he threw up his hand, indicating he may have succeeded in connecting. The call picked up. Lucy could hear Audrey's high-pitched voice, faintly emanating from Dale's phone. "Audrey!" Dale shouted. "Where are you?" The digital voice squealed madly over the line, repeating the same indistinguishable phrase again and again. *"What?!"* Dale screamed. "That doesn't make any sense, baby!" His eyes glazed as he descended into a saddening desperation. *"Just tell me where you are!"* He shrieked with hysteria. What Dale heard next drew his eyes wide open with horror.

He pulled the phone away from his ear and stared at it in shock, seized by distress. "What is it?" Lucy asked. Her voice shook. "What's going on?!" She shrieked. Dale tapped on the screen, placing the call on speaker.

Loudly, thousands of ear-splitting voices emitted from his device. The ghastly sound was similar to that of a worked-up crowd at a concert or sporting event. However, these were not shouts of jubilation or excitement. They were screams of terror. The call ended.

Dale and Lucy's breaths trembled. "What did she say?" Lucy asked. "What did Audrey say to you?" Dale continued to stare at his phone, paralyzed by dejection. Lucy grabbed his arm and shook him hard, demanding an answer. "What did Audrey say, Dale!"

He turned his head toward Lucy but his focus wandered. Redness formed around his eyes and a tear rolled down his cheek. "She said...," he started. He sniffed and wiped the tear away. "She said ...*It's eating us.*"

Lucy's face went white. "That doesn't make any sense," she said. She released his arm and checked her phone. Still no Audrey dot.

The sound of a giant crack rang out from down the street. Debris from a nearby, five-story building fell to the pavement as a flock of birds burst from its roof and into the air. Shouts erupted from onlookers and short trees surrounding the structure shook. Another gargantuan snap from behind them sent a large break in the street directly between Dale and Lucy and continued to the center of the intersection. Other cracks from separate locations met at the same point as the road began to cave. Considerable chunks of freshly-finished pavement fell, piece-by-piece as a sinkhole formed and widened.

The hole grew as vehicles, people, trees and traffic lights were swallowed up by the immense mouth as it yawned and spread, nearing the drug store. Fleeing the collapsing man-made landscape, Dale and Lucy did their best to ignore their afflictions and sprint from the expanding destruction. Dale's shoes and Lucy's socks pounded the hot asphalt. Although injured, the pair moved at a slightly quicker pace than the pedestrians accompanying them as the crowds escaped the chaos.

Buildings crumbled into the sinkhole and dense, yellow dust rose into the blue sky, dimming the California sunlight. The cries from the frightened horde sounded dismally familiar to the screams from the last call to Audrey. All at once, the ruination stopped. The sinkhole stilled as the last, loose pieces of street, dirt and sidewalk fell into the smoking pit. The crowd settled, the voices faded and the fleeing seized.

A deep rumble reverberated from the hole, shaking the ground. People, bleached by dust stared curiously and unnervingly into the void. Minutes passed as the tension grew. Sunlight broke through the thinning dust and visibility cleared. Another deep rumble emerged as people gasped and shrieked. Within the pit, the jagged concrete and twisted debris began to rise.

An enormous mass covered in scales and mucus-covered skin, rose from the hole and through the smoldering cloud. As though weightless, the bulbous object passed the edge of the broken street and ascended into the sky above them. The bulging, circular body resembled that of a toad with four limbs that hung heavily at its sides. It hovered over the destruction emitting another deep growl, forcefully impacting the air surrounding it. Its eyes were wide and amphibian-like and the lips of its gargantuan mouth ran from one side of its body to the next. Grotesque rolls of blubber bulged from under its thick hide. The beast was the size of a football stadium and the shadow it projected covered six city blocks. Faintly, the sound of hundreds of panicked screams could be heard from its gripping fists.

It lifted its thick arm and opened its stocky fingers revealing a crying handful of blood-covered runners, stuck to its slimy flesh. The monster opened its mouth. From the back of its throat, an armlike tongue rolled out and slapped against its open palm. The tongue pulled away as strands of ooze and crushed bodies were pulled into its gaping, toothless jaws. It lifted its opposite hand and did the same with a second helping of mangled athletes. Its mouth closed and so did its eyes. The toad's colossal eyeballs deepened into its head as a deep bellow and a gut-wrenching smell waved across the onlooking crowds.

From between its hanging legs, an explosion of steaming excrement erupted onto the city below. White foam and crimson mucus filled the sinkhole, crashed into buildings and flowed down every street. Dale and Lucy ducked into the doorway of a nearby bank to dodge the wave of noxious waste. Other civilians attempted similar escapes as some were thickly covered in the atrocious substance. Lucy fearfully observed the street from the doorway as the excrement spread and thinned. Scattered across the drenched roadway, running shoes, clothing and human bones laid eroded and burned, left by the wake. Terror rushed through her veins as she locked her eyes on a smoking, human rib cage draped in polyester and pinned with a racing bib. Lucy shook with revulsion.

The beast had eaten and digested every participant in the race and purged their remains in one massive bowel movement, painting Culver City in a mammoth blanket of feces and blood. All of a sudden, Lucy's phone chimed.

Unlocking her screen, Lucy opened the map. Audrey's dot appeared around a corner and two blocks down from Lucy's location. It did not move. She turned to Dale. He sat in the concrete corner, his knees to his chest and his eyes wide with insanity. He trembled and rocked himself, maddened by what he and everyone else had just witnessed. Dale was lost.

Lucy stepped onto the wet street in her socks. The liquid soaked into the fabric but the substance did not burn her feet. She leaned out of the doorway and looked above the sinkhole. The colossal amphibian still hovered, final remnants of waste dropping from its haunches. Phone in hand and her calf aching painfully, Lucy ran across the road, around the corner and two blocks down.

She slowed as she limped across the fallen banner and blood-soaked words, *Culver City Race To Feed The Hungry* and neared Audrey's location. Searching the mass of skulls, bones and running accessories, she noticed the bright yellow sole of one of her Ocean Sunrise trainers. Approaching the sight, her heart deflated with irredeemable loss. The shoe laid on its side, the progress chip tied tightly in its laces. A steaming tibia protruded from the trainer's collar attached to a long femur. At the joint of the femur was Audrey's titanium hip replacement. The reflective, metal joint gleamed portentously in the sunlight.

Another impactful rumble emitted from the beast. Lucy looked to the sky. The monster opened its eyes, pulled its limbs closely to its body and rose. It ascended into the California sky, sped towards the wispy clouds and vanished into the upper atmosphere. Silence fell over the city, the horrid musk of filth still lingering in the air. Lucy stood over Audrey's remains, her socks soaked in muck and ruby-red blood splashed across her clothing. Finally some color was added to her array.

Lucy knew once and for all and at that very moment, she *was in fact,* a terrible human being. Her first thought when everything was over wasn't for the thousands of lives lost, for Audrey, for her widowed husband or for their unborn baby.

Her very first thought when the massacre stopped, the destruction ended and the beast disappeared ...was simply, *Is this going to get me a demotion?*

SEA MONSTER
Imprisoned By Madness

It was a bleak and solemn afternoon on Brighton Beach. Charcoal clouds and a stiff breeze made south Brooklyn feel like late November in early June. A million footprints and cigarette butts haunted the sand like ghosts of a sunnier and more agreeable day. The gray ocean was still and condos lined the coast with dingy brick and vacant-black windows. Today, Brighton Beach made little effort to live up to its own radiant and optimistic name.

Despite the forlornness, one man limped along the tide. His dirty, white T-shirt and cargo shorts did little to fight the cold, but his somber expression conveyed indifference to the weather. Ormy Greene was in his early 40's. He held a brand new metal detector in his oversized fist. He was a tall man, with hulking shoulders and a blunt, hairless head. The silent giant carried a long tote bag over his arm and searched the beach with small, shifting eyes. Over thousands of walks, his feet had developed a thick callus from corrosive seawater and the occasional slice and puncture of shells and stones. He made a mile-wide zig-zag from the New York Aquarium to Little Stone Pier. He moved slowly from the tide to the boardwalk, until the path was completed or until the beach closed.

Every few yards, he felt a sharp sting in his heel as he bent and snatched an aluminum can or foam scrap from the sand and placed it into his bag, ridding the beach of litter. The sting had always been present but he did very little to resolve it. To Ormy, the pain was worth the effort. He hated litter, especially on the beach. The millions of tons of trash that found its way to the oceans every year, perfectly portrayed humanity's cruelty, apathy and true integrity. Every once in a while, the digital hum of his detector would peak and so would the chance of discovering a new treasure. The tote was for trash and his many cargo-pockets were for keepable finds. With treasures becoming more scarce, his standards had fallen to a radical low. Nowadays, Ormy found it difficult to decide what to keep and what to discard, in order to preserve his treasure-to-trash ratio.

Far ahead and moving in his direction, a couple happily made their way up the beach. Ormy eyed them for a short second, then dropped his eyes to the sand. They were *obviously* tourists. When one lives in a large city like New York for most of their life, country mice are easy to spot. Their eyes constantly look up to the skyscrapers or out towards the ocean. Their expressions often convey excitement and wonder. *City mice* are disinterested, unamused and keep their eyes down; numb to the miracles and architectural feats surrounding them. Ormy became nervous as the couple approached. They would be only twenty feet from him when they passed and a local on the beach holding a metal detector was a prime target for light conversation, as was a Great Lakes fisherman holding a fifteen-foot pole with his line in the water.

Ormy cringed as the man raised his arm and greeted him. "Finding anything good today?!" He shouted. Ormy kept his head down as he moved. The stress of human interaction, especially with strangers, was almost unbearable. He found social situations extremely difficult to tolerate. All he *really* had to do to make the passers move on was wave back or possibly smile. The giant lacked the cognitive intelligence or experience to be aware of such an option. Ormy seldom had to deal with others until just recently.

The couple halted and the man spoke again, "I said, are you finding anything good today?!" Ormy's feet stopped moving as well. He lifted his head and met eyes with the interrogator. The tourist chuckled and made an inaudible comment to his companion. Most likely something rude or insulting. Giving into the man's crass persistence, Ormy reached into one of his pockets and pulled out a corroded, iron rivet. A remnant from bridge construction he had dug up earlier that morning. The man jogged across the beach as Ormy presented it between two fingers. "Nice!" He praised. "You found that today?" Ormy nodded. "I always wondered what kind of junk washes up on the beach but I've never gone detecting myself. What's the best thing you've ever found out here?" He asked. Silence. "Or anywhere?" The man generalized. Ormy just wanted the man to go away. He turned his eyes to the beach and searched the sands and his thoughts. Looking back at the man, he shrugged. Perhaps *that* would be enough of an answer to convey reclusion and a strong disinterest in the present intercourse. The tourist caught onto the hint and quickly wrapped up the meeting. "Well, you keep at it, big guy. Hopefully, one day you can find something you can take to the bank!" He slapped Ormy on the shoulder and ran back to his wife or girlfriend. The man made another muffled comment that sent them both into laughter, as they continued down the coast. Another insulting jab. Ormy dropped his chin and hastily moved along his path.

The sun was sinking and the hour was aging as Ormy's detector bit something under the sand. Its digital moan deepened and choked. He waved the coil over the spot to find the precise location of the item and began to dig. His large hands scooped like a plastic bucket as he sifted through the sediment. The glint of white metal reflected the remaining daylight as Ormy plucked a piece of jewelry from a handful of sand. He smiled as the thick, high school ring was dusted off and picked clean. The hollow, centerstone was fractured but the feature that made Ormy tremble with delight was an engraving of a barracuda in the item's side. The aquatic creature was most likely a school mascot or displayed the owner's love of fishing. Either way, Ormy had found a treasure on the beach that represented his love of the ocean—and *that* made it all the more valuable.

Ormy pushed the find deep into his pocket as his watch buzzed. He silenced the alarm and looked toward the beach patrol shack. His shoulders sank as he noticed a parked Ford pickup. The guard shack lights were illuminated and the door was cracked open. Brighton Beach security wasn't managed or appointed by the state, nor the city of New York. It was run by a charity and staffed by volunteers. This meant that on some weeknights, the beach would be free of guards and patrols all evening, leaving Ormy free to continue searching after the beach had closed. As of twenty seconds ago, Brighton Beach was no longer open to the public and bodies were on guard to enforce the restriction. His search was over, at least for the day.

Ormy dragged his feet to the nearest set of refuse receptacles and pulled the sack from his shoulder. One by one, he retrieved dented cans, plastic cutlery, paper bags and water bottles, tossing them into the corresponding bins for proper processing. He felt the pockets of his cargo shorts for any trinkets he had decided to keep and reconsidered them. He discarded four bottle caps, a fishing weight and a pair of tweezers. Furthering his search, he found a cylindrical bulge in his back pocket. He pulled an orange prescription bottle from his shorts and looked it over. One single pill rattled inside and Ormy couldn't remember when he had found it or why he hadn't placed it in the tote with the other litter. The name on the pills was long and unpronounceable. Aware of the dangers that came with taking unprescribed medications, Ormy dropped the bottle into the receptacle for plastic refuse.

In the dark parking lot, he threw open the passenger door of his white Geo Metro and tossed his equipment onto the broken, leather seat. He climbed behind the steering wheel, fastened his seatbelt and finally started the engine on his fourth attempt. The barely-operable vehicle pulled out of the empty lot. Its one, working tail light, dented bumper and handicap plates disappeared down Coney Island Avenue and north towards the center of Brooklyn.

On the sixth story of an amiable Williamsburg condominium, Ormy unlocked his door and arrived home. He smiled as he beheld his new residence. The quiet and comfort of finally having a place of his own was gratifying. He swore that his loft became more luxurious and extravagant every time he arrived. Saltwater fish tanks lined the walls with treasures, trinkets and oddly-shaped stones decorating the home's interior. Fifteen-foot windows, a cathedral ceiling, a california-king mattress and a 35-inch TV filled the space with illustriousness and personal character.

Locking the door firmly behind him, he approached a dresser topped with his smallest and more delicate finds. He added the class ring and the rivet to the display, adjusting their positions and facings for the most copacetic presentation possible. Ormy removed his sandy flip flops and checked his mailbox. Delighted, he found a letter from his brother, enclosed with an American Express Platinum card. He quickly unfolded the note and read the hand-written words.

Ormy,

I hope this letter finds you well. As you get settled into your new place, I thought I'd lend another helping hand until you fully get onto your feet. I've sent you an expenses card to help with food, clothing and anything else you may need. Don't worry, you won't have to pay me back for its use. I'm always here to help you. As for the car, I'll do what I can to find you something dependable.

I'm proud of you, brother. You're finally out and on your own, tackling the world, finding yourself. It took you twenty years to do it, but the point is, you did it. Mom would have kept you prisoner in that house forever and I'm glad that didn't happen. I'll take care of her for now, you need to focus on yourself. It's best that you keep your distance from Mom for now, anyway. She wasn't exactly in the best of spirits after you left. As matters progress, I will keep you posted.

Love, Hayden.

Ormy returned the letter to the envelope as glee shined in his small eyes upon receiving the credit card. Throughout the years, Hayden was often far away but remained close through letters and an intimate, brotherly bond. He pulled his wallet from his pocket and added the card to his driver's license, Pets Pro member card and large collection of saltwater-enthusiast coupons.

That night, Ormy laid in bed. Two weeks now, without sleep. He hadn't slept since the move and slumber was his happiest time. Despite his mother's constant nagging, abuse and torment, her singing throughout the night always helped him sleep. It seemed ironic now, he had pined for independent freedom his entire life. Upon gaining it, he had traded captivity for insomnia. The only sound that echoed against the tall walls was the growl of the aquarium pump motors and the TV was too obnoxious and distracting to gain him any rest. He stared at the shadows of fish as they slipped across the dull light. Ormy sighed. If only he could be a fish and swim as he pleased and slept as he pleased, *without the awareness* of captivity.

Shadow after shadow drifted across the walls with jerking fins and wading tails. Cardinalfish, royal grammas and angelfish made graceful shadow puppets as he watched the entrancing show.

Suddenly, the outline of a woman joined their dance. Her arms were drawn back and her hair flowed behind her majestically. A long, fishlike tail propelled her quickly past the projection of light. All at once, her shadow vanished from the wall. Ormy sat up and snapped his gaze to the tanks. He sharply examined the aquariums. Only fish populated the luminous enclosures. He dropped his head to his pillow. Ormy couldn't help but ponder the anomaly as night hours gave birth to morning light.

Days later, Brighton Beach was sunny but the shivering chill continued to nip at the air. Doing his best to avoid contact with rude tourists, Ormy made his path tight to the tide and lapping water. Foam brushed against his toes as he moved his coil along the beach, listening intensely and focus sharpened. He checked his watch. Four hours and nineteen minutes until close. He lifted his sights to the guard shack. No truck, door closed and no sign of life. Ormy didn't allow optimism to make him any promises. On some evenings, the guards would arrive as late as five-minutes-to-close. He kept along his route, zigging and zagging.

The first hour turned up nothing but litter. Typical for a start. Treasures were seldom found so close to the tide. Although, upon his second hour, luck seemed to smile. Four, vintage bottle caps, a silver bracelet with an anchor pendant and another class ring. This time, the ring's centerstone was solid amethyst, Ormy's birthstone. Astonishingly, the engraved graduation year matched his own. He beamed. The chances of coming across such a coincidental find was staggeringly monumental. Ormy trembled with delectation as he pocketed the ring and moved on. His steps eager and anxious.

On his third zag and sixth guardshack pass, Ormy heard an eruption of seawater followed by a shrieking wail. A cold mist brushed against his bare arm and face. Jerking his attention to the lazy waves, he noticed the wake of a disturbance in the water, about twenty yards out. He rested the coil on the sand and watched the surface return to normal. Intrigued, he continued to watch the water. A seagull cried out in the distant cold as his eyes darted. Nothing for almost a minute.

Ormy flipped through his mental checklist of native, North Atlantic sea life. Harbor seals were more present during the winter and Humpback whales wouldn't be this close to the coast. He had been in the presence of both at specific times of the year, but none of them were known to make sounds like the one he had heard. He turned to search for any other witnesses. Presently, Ormy was the only soul on the beach. He gave the water a final glance, lifted his coil and resumed his pattern.

Almost immediately, his finding device clicked with an electronic growl. Ormy pin-pointed the source, dropped to his knees and dug. His hands shook and his heart raced. Seized with an even balance of remarkable awe and confused amazement, the silent giant pulled a gleaming, yellow coin from the sand. His panicked fingers wiped the trinket clean as he clumsily got to his feet. He cringed with pain upon putting pressure on his heel but ignored the discomfort out of excitement. The 15th-century piece was stamped with the image of a ship upon a cross-cut crest. An Old English inscription circled the relief surrounded by an elegantly-detailed rim. Tempted to bite the coin to confirm its authenticity, Ormy withdrew from doing so. He'd only seen that method of appraisal done in films. He did not dare take the chance of damaging something so precious. He smiled widely as a single, audible choke clicked from the back of his throat. Never in his thirty years of hunting, had he turned up a find so inestimable. He snapped his head and searched up and down Brighton. No tourists, no locals, no guards. An hour and twenty-two minutes until close and a lot more path to cover.

Not wasting a second, Ormy sped as quickly as he could limp, along the beach. He efficiently waved his coil from left to right, listening for that delicious, electrical moan as his feverish elation tingled. He felt like a midnight slots player, surfing along an isolated winning streak in an empty casino. An hour passed. Still nothing. Ormy stayed vigilant with his remaining time.

On his eleventh patrol shack pass and six minutes until close, the roar of a motor entered the beach. Ormy halted. Expecting to see the Ford pickup filled with volunteers, he was surprised as he watched a substantially-sized recreational vehicle pull through the guard entrance. A strange symbol was painted across the vehicle's side, like a large, violent letter X over searing flames. The RV carefully puttered along the beach and came to a stop near Little Stone Pier. Much like the discovery of the coin and his current, incredible luck, activity such as this on Brighton Beach was *also* unusual. After a long minute, the RV's brakelights vanished and the engine silenced. Ormy watched curiously as a group of suspiciously-dressed individuals deboarded and gathered together. The sun had just set and visibility was below adequate. The strangers were dressed in black shrouds and came in a variety of odd heights and weights. Some were as tall as basketball players and some were as small as children. In the darkness, Ormy could not see what they were up to. Fear began to slowly grip his throat and a heavy weight pained his chest as he watched the cult busy themselves. They moved back and forth from the RV to a spot they had chosen near the pier. He swallowed hard in his throat and felt an uncomfortable chill. Abruptly, his wristwatch alarmed. Panicked, Ormy silenced the buzz, then focused intimately on the group. His disturbance hadn't seemed to distract or draw attention. He turned to the guard shack. No truck and no light. No security tonight.

Ormy was now stuck at a crossroads. Should he walk away from a hot streak with his winnings—or, press on and risk being seen by the sinister group? Resolute to proceed, he quickly chose the latter. He could still complete his final zigs and zags while avoiding them, but he *would* have to come uncomfortably close.

With his head down and his steps swift, Ormy turned the volume down on his detector and made the first pass without detection. Then, another. A campfire was lit near the pier as the shady cult stood in a circle around the blaze. Loud chants and strange, otherworldly tunes resonated from the site. The sound was frightening, eerie and bizarre.

As the summoning chants grew louder, *another* musical piece joined in. Up the beach and near the water, a miniscule, siren lullaby began. The heavenly piece seized Ormy on an emotional level and gripped directly onto his heart. In the same way a long forgotten song on the radio could conjure joy, sadness or remembrance, *this song* brought him an instant and familiar feeling of sympathy and affection. Smitten by sentiment, Ormy attempted to overcome his fear and follow the voice.

Meters ahead, he found the source. He dropped his metal detector to the sand and went white with revelation. The gold coin he had found hours ago was *nothing* compared to the treasure he presently beheld. Reason, logic and common sense vanished as he stood over a miniature mermaid waist-deep in the tide and crying out towards the chanting cult. Her body was the size of his hand and her hair was long and golden. Her musical shouts danced in the air above her and brought tears to Ormy's astonished stare. She seemed deeply disturbed by the activity by the pier and she reached out toward the group with an expression of anguishing objection. Her aquamarine tail was knotted tightly around the razor-sharp plastic of aluminum can rings, cruelly left behind by apathetic humans.

Without hesitation, Ormy attempted to free her. His large fingers made it difficult to perform such an intricate task, but his determination made up for hindrance. He loosened the ring, undid the knot and pulled the hazard from her tail, tearing one of her fins in the process. She screeched in pain and fought against his giant hands. Ormy cringed upon injuring the mermaid and the guilt hit him like poison.

Suddenly, the crack of an explosion emitted from the clan's fire. A horrible spectacle ignited Brighton Beach with a demonic energy. The hot, licking flames of their blaze took the form of monstrous tentacles and rose towards the night sky. The twisting, curling limbs writhed and flexed with a searing, hellish conflagration as Ormy watched in terror.

Upon witnessing what the group had summoned, the mermaid screamed again. The pulse from her banshee-cry boomed across the beach, disrupting dry sand, twigs and trash. Ormy looked up to see the horrible group turn in his direction as the tentacles slammed into the fire and vanished. Intense panic, sadness and remorse thundered in Ormy's chest.

He came to a *second* crossroad. He could leave the injured beauty to the mercy of the cloaked demons—or, attempt to save her. He had everything he would need to mend her at home and Ormy trusted *himself* far more than he trusted them. Swiftly making a decision, he dumped his collected trash onto the beach and put the mermaid in his tote.

Thick callus feet pounding the sand and his pain almost intolerable, Ormy ran to the parking lot. He did not dare take a second to look back, but he imagined the cult was not far behind. He got to his car, swung open the door and leapt inside. The tires of the old Metro jerked him forward and out of the lot. Not a soul could be seen in his rearview mirror as he sped down Coney Island Avenue and headed home.

Ormy unlocked his tall, oak door and entered with haste. He never left a light burning after vacating, but the beautiful skyline of Manhattan Island cast a magical glow through his stained-glass windows. Without wasting any time, he pulled a bucket from the kitchen and syphoned water from one of his aquariums to fill it. Laying the tote onto the cashmere comforter of his bed, he opened it wide, exposing his precious rescue. She was pale white and appeared to be suffocating. She coughed and gagged as blood dripped from her injured tail. Ormy took her gently into his hands and placed her into the bucket. The mermaid took to the water like an infant taking her first breath. Unscrewing a bottle of MelaZyme, he dosed the bucket with ten drops of fin regrowth and damaged-tissue treatment for fish. He turned up the lights as her color returned and her activity and energy normalized.

Ormy cleared off his cherrywood nightstand and placed the bucket on its treated surface. He sat on his mattress and let the events of the last several hours sink in. Happiness, amazement, wonderment and disbelief flooded him with the fall of adrenaline. Questions upon questions came to mind. *Were mermaids common? Were they always this small? What was that demonic sect doing on the beach? And, what would they have done to the mermaid if they got their hands on her?* He didn't bother tormenting himself with that *last* inquiry. What happened, had happened and Ormy was sure he had made the right decision. He let out a long sigh as his drum returned to a normal beat.

He felt a metallic bulge in the pocket of his cargo shorts. His attention shifted. Standing quickly, Ormy pulled the coin, anchor bracelet, amethyst ring and bottle caps from his shorts and displayed them with his other trinkets, on the titanium, lighted display stand in the corner of his loft. He smiled as he watched each of his remarkable finds sparkle like diamonds in a jewelry-store window. However, *none of them* held a candle to his treasure in the bucket. What would his brother think? Upon that thought, Ormy removed his sandals, placed them neatly by the door and checked his mailbox. Another envelope. Eagerly he broke the seal and unfolded the letter.

Ormy,

I hope this letter finds you well. I trust you are getting use out of the card I sent and I've almost found you a trustworthy vehicle. Hopefully that bucket of bolts hasn't broken down on you yet. I finally found a place for Mom in Highland Park with a nice view of the water and a good reputation regarding her needs and our expectations. She always preferred lakes to New York's ugly ocean and other residents there don't complain about the conditions. I still strongly advise you to remain distant. I'll let you know when it's safe to pay her a visit. Write me back as soon as you can. I want to know how you are doing. As matters here progress, I will keep you posted.

Love, Hayden.

Ormy smiled. He sharpened a pencil, sat on his bed and excitedly drafted a response. He joyously told Hayden all about the coin he had found, the coincidental ring and with hesitation, the mermaid. In detail, he explained what had happened that day, how he felt about it and what he had brought home. He figured, the details matter when explaining something true that seems so unbelievable. After filling out an entire page, he folded up the letter, sealed it tight and mailed it. Ormy had never looked so forward to a response from Hayden. He sat on his bed, clicked on a lamp above the bucket, and watched his treasure.

The mermaid peeked her head above the surface. Her long, wavy hair flattened against her head and fanned out across the water as her gorgeous eyes watched him curiously. She was nude with the exception of her tail and the magic in her stare exhibited a childlike innocence. Ormy marveled over her. He could not believe his luck. She was absolutely beautiful and the silent giant felt a jealous admiration for the mythical creature as he watched her swim and dance.

Slowly and magically, she began to sing. Within his cathedral walls, her voice reverberated with an ethereal and alluring intoxication. Ormy felt his heart sing right along with her as a wave of tingling emotion cascaded over his body. Completely taken by her lullaby, his breaths deepened and his eyelids began to close. Within a matter of minutes, Ormy succumbed to slumber, fell backward onto the bed and fell fast asleep. It had been the first time in weeks he had gained any kind of rest. The mermaid's soothing song kept him in a dreamy state of tranquility, into the evening, through the night and beyond.

Ormy woke. He woke in the same position he had passed out in. His arms were sprawled outward and his body laid horizontally on the bed. His legs were bent and his feet touched the floor. Ormy had almost forgotten what waking up felt like. At first, he had no idea *where* he was or what *day* it was. The sun shined through the windows and rays of light stretched across his loft and to the floor. He sat up. The mermaid peered at him from the water in the bucket. *The mermaid,* he thought. The events from his last visit to Brighton Beach rushed back into his sleep-fogged memory. Ormy went through every detail of the night in his head, however long ago the night had been.

He stretched, yawned and shifted his weight to his feet. The bite of pain throbbed in his foot and up his leg. A raw tenderness was beginning to form that hadn't been present in the past weeks. As usual, he ignored the affliction. A small shriek resonated from the bucket. The mermaid began splashing and flailing, making irate expressions directed at her savior. Ormy acknowledged her and examined the rusty bucket he had placed her in. He didn't blame her for objecting. His *fish* were swimming in luxury compared to the dingy home he had made for *her*. A swell of eager exhilaration filled his chest as he remembered the credit card. He grabbed his wallet, his keys and his neatly-placed footwear. Ormy flashed the mermaid a look of assurance as he opened his door and departed from the regal, Brooklyn condo.

The silent giant opened the driver-side door of his Metro and paused as he glanced at the back seat. It was empty. He melted with regret as the realization hit him. In the stir of the madness and upon rushing off of Brighton Beach, he had left his metal detector by the shore. He examined all of the negative consequences that mistake would possibly incur. To his thoughts, there weren't many. The cult couldn't find where he lived upon discovering it and security was on site before the beach opened. Any items left behind would go into their lost-and-found. For a second, Ormy considered purchasing a new device, then quickly decided against it. That metal detector was now his *lucky* metal detector and his streak could be cursed if he simply replaced it. The best chance at getting it back would be to return to Brighton Beach now, and speak with the volunteers. He cringed. More unwanted, human interaction—but necessary.

The white metro crawled slowly onto the lot. Emergency vehicles, news vans and people swarmed the coast from Steeplechase Pier to Manhattan Beach. Ormy could tell immediately that something was wrong. *Had the cult harmed someone? Or possibly worse?* All manner of possibilities rushed through his head. Parking in a far, empty space, he stepped out of the vehicle and beheld the commotion. A helicopter circled above, making passes over Little Stone Pier and camera-mounts atop reporter vans were extended high. Ormy closed his door and carefully approached the beach. Pushing through the crowds, he was stopped at a police barrier. What he saw sent chills down his spine and a salty lump into his throat.

N.Y.P.D. officers were stationed around an overturned ocean-tanker. The immense ship was half way onto the sand and extended almost a mile into the North Atlantic. Two, large gashes were left in the tanker's hull like claw marks and parts of it had been crushed or chewed. Police were measuring a large hole in the sand like a footprint or a gouge. Immediately, Ormy remembered the disturbance he had seen in the water before finding the mermaid. *Had that sighting been connected to this?* He thought. *Did the cult conjure something?* Ormy wondered if any members of the sect had been apprehended or questioned by police. He turned his eyes to the security shack. The door was closed and no volunteers were present. He would not be going home with his lucky detector today, and for good reason. If it was safely collected and placed in the patrol shack, he could come back another day to claim it. Ormy happily left the intolerable group of reporters and on-lookers.

Limping across the lot, he felt a tinge of regret. He wondered if he could have helped authorities in any way. Perhaps he could have given a description of what he saw or made the police aware of the cult's presence on the beach. The thought of returning to the crowd made him sick, and the overturned tanker was a bigger issue than anything *he* had witnessed. Answering questions would also be difficult. When Ormy told a story, he told the *whole truth.* He wouldn't put himself in a position that would compromise the safety of his treasured mermaid. The hole and the ship was the city's problem. He had his own concerns to worry about. The excitement returned as Ormy realized why he had left his loft to begin with. He eagerly jumped into his car and departed from the chaos of Brighton Beach.

Pets Pro Supplies was located in South Williamsburg and just off of Flushing Avenue. It sat comfortably between a dry cleaners and an empty establishment with a wide sign displaying *For Lease* across the front windows. Ormy pulled into an empty space and killed the engine. Armed with his new credit card and Pets Pro membership, he crawled out of the Metro and rushed inside.

The smell of dog food and chlorine wafted against Ormy's face as he stepped into his personal heaven. The shop was large for a New York supply store and tall racks lined the space with every kind of pet need and habitat mock-up imaginable. He made a line straight for the saltwater-fish department and took his pick of an abundant selection. Every item his mermaid would need was presented before him and he was filled with enough knowledge and experience to give her the perfect home.

Ormy approached the front of the store with a cart filled with a mythical-creature-friendly assortment. The familiar cashier greeted him as he arrived. "Big fish! How's it going my man?!" He shouted. Ormy nodded with a slight grin and began unloading the cart onto a short conveyor belt. The cashier eyed the stock as he rang it up. "You get something new that you didn't get from us?" He asked. Ormy shrugged. The man took a scan-gun from the register, leaned forward and scanned an oversized fishbowl in Ormy's cart. "Let me guess, It's a bulldog?" Ormy didn't respond. "I'm just teasing you, man! They say people get pets that look like themselves, so I was just speculating!" The man finished adding up the total and helped Ormy reload his cart. High above the register, a television was broadcasting coverage of Brighton Beach. Ormy watched it intimately as aerial shots of the tanker and hole flashed on the screen. The cashier noticed it as well. "Can you believe that?" He commented. "I've got kids that play on that beach." He turned to Ormy. "Some people are monsters." He spat.

The broadcast didn't give any information Ormy didn't already gather from his earlier visit. Only speculations were reported by the caster. Ormy took his cart, nodded to the gentleman and headed for the exit. "Take care, Big Fish! Bring me pictures of your new dog!"

He called out. Ormy smiled as he lifted a friendly hand to the jesting cashier and made his way to the car.

In his loft, Ormy syphoned more water from one of his tanks and filled the bowl. He didn't want to put her in an existing habitat. They were too far from his bed and the mermaid's songs helped him get to sleep. She was also *more* than just a fish. In Ormy's mind she was half human and putting her with pets seemed wrong somehow. Placing her beside his bed felt like better treatment for a guest. He filled the new enclosure half way, rested it on the nightstand and carefully poured the bucket into the bowl, filling it the rest of the way. The mermaid was transferred during the pour and seemed to enjoy the new home. Ormy placed a large stone at the bottom of the bowl and treated the water with a few drops of Quick Start and additional drops of MelaZyme. When it came to food, all he could do was guess. He dropped three seaweed rods into her water and sprinkled the top with traditional fish food. She hadn't taken an interest. Perhaps she wasn't hungry. Ormy finished the project, cleaned up his items and wiped down the nightstand. The mermaid smiled as he polished her fishbowl from top to bottom. Ormy smiled as well.

Spending the rest of the day staring at his mermaid and watching her swim and sit upon the stone, Ormy grew tired. The sun had set and the evening was deepening into the passing hours. He doused the lights, crawled under his blanket and laid his head upon the pillow. The air in his loft remained silent. The mermaid was not singing. Ormy turned his head to see the creature's silhouette sitting quietly upon her stone. He lifted his hand and tapped on the bowl. Not a peep.

Frustrated, Ormy threw off the blanket, approached his collection of stones and returned to his bed. He gave the bowl three, forceful taps with a sizeable, star-shaped rock. She jumped at the disturbance, rose from her seat and brought her head to the surface. Her siren song began, just as it had on the first night. Ormy smiled as he sank into his mattress and drifted pleasantly into dreams.

Over the next several weeks, Ormy and his new guest got along swimmingly. She would sleep during the day and would sing to him each night, and throughout the night. He was finally on track with a proper sleeping schedule and living with a companion that didn't nag, abuse or torment him at all hours of the day was freeing. His move out of Mom's and his decision to take his own life into his hands was now justified. He hadn't been sure at first, but things were all coming together now. His independence and his lucky find on Brighton Beach were steps to a happy and successful life on his own. Ormy couldn't wait to see what came next if *this* was just the beginning. However, two problems had emerged.

Hayden hadn't written back since the letter about the mermaid and the growing time had made him worry. Typically, he would receive a letter no later than seven days after a response. This time, 23 days had lapsed. His brother's silence was unnerving. Ormy had sent two more letters to follow up. Both were met with no return mail.

The second problem was the mermaid's diet. She hadn't touched the flakes, nor did she eat anything else he had tried to feed her. Rods, dried seaweed, pellets and frozen cubes all went to waste. In desperation, Ormy had also resorted to feeder fish, but was extremely hesitant due to the chance of introducing disease and bacteria into her habitat. She *still* hadn't eaten. The issue was causing Ormy to feel distress. If she didn't eat, she would die, unless there was some exception for fantasy mer-life.

He grabbed his wallet and sifted through his thick wad of coupons, desperate for an answer. Maybe there was a food he hadn't tried. Aquarium items of all sorts met his eyes as he thumbed through the stack. He saw air-pump tubes, gravel, thermometers, tank decorations and replacement light bulbs. The list was endless. But, nothing that provided a solution. Evidently, he had used up all of his fish food discounts. Although, one coupon in particular grabbed his interest. *20% Off All Books,* gleamed across the shiny paper. *A Book,* Ormy thought. It was possible that a book on the subject of finicky fish could be found at Pro Pets. He once possessed books on taking care of fish but he hadn't used them in years. He also hadn't brought them with him when he recently moved. Ormy stuffed the coupons into his wallet and headed for the pet store.

Night had fallen and Pro Pets book selection was smaller than he had expected. Fortunately, there was one title regarding the feeding of rare, tropical fish. Ormy grabbed the book and made the long walk to the register.

The cashier's eyes were glued to the TV as he approached and dropped the book onto the belt. He opened his wallet and plucked out the coupon. The man motioned to the television and turned his attention to Ormy. "What's up, big fish? Are you seeing this?" He asked. Ormy glanced at the screen and felt a stiffening numbness seize him almost immediately.

An aerial view of Brighton Beach captured the hellish image of a titanic creature rising out of the North Atlantic. Its blood-red and royal-blue scales reflected the light of the helicopter spotlights as it dragged its massive body onto the shore. The kaiju's mouth looked large enough to swallow a sky-scraper and its glowing, red eyes seared with an abominable rage. Countless tentacles and immense, gnashing teeth made the horrid spectacle a vision to behold as it roared with a terrible and other-worldly boom. The shop's windows rattled as the wave of the roar hit Flushing Avenue, reminding them of just how close they were to the event. The cashier scoffed, "I hope that monster gets what he deserves." With no time for the man's commentary and the book no longer a priority, Ormy ran out of the store and unlocked his car.

He bolted into his loft and slammed the door behind him, locking it securely. Ormy threw on the lights, grabbed his TV remote and illuminated the screen. It had been the first time he had used his television since the move, but he was damn glad he had decided to take it with him. Panicked, Ormy flipped through the stations to find the report.

There it was. The creature looked larger and even more terrifying on his oversized flatscreen. Now, the broadcast showed multiple views of the demon from different angles. It roared again. Three seconds later, the shockwave hit the stained glass of his loft and sent his heart into spasms. Ormy collapsed into a seated position onto his bed, remote in hand, staring at the screen and breathing heavily. He glanced at his mermaid. She was asleep on her stone. The disturbance hadn't woken her and he had no reason to disturb her sleep.

An hour passed. Then two hours. The kaiju hadn't moved from its location on Brighton Beach but it remained lively and active. Ormy thought of the cultists he had seen and the tentacles he had witnessed in their campfire. *Had they conjured this ...thing?* He thought. Questions crowded his mental track. All he could do was watch and speculate as the creature roared, flailed, growled and continued its threatening display of catastrophic fury. He stood and sat beside the mermaid, eyes still glued on the frightening image. The evening had reached the hour when she would typically wake. But Ormy was in no mood for sleep.

He stared at the demon on his screen and pondered. *One would think that a man so obsessed with the ocean would revel in such a sight. Would this not be the crown-jewel discovery for any thalassophile or saltwater-creature obsessor?* Ormy thought about that. Why wasn't he excited? He was absolutely ecstatic when he found the mermaid but *this* had induced nothing but fear and anxiety. Ormy did his best to think rationally about the situation and clear his head of any emotional interference. For a brief, fraction of a second, the TV flashed with the image of police interviewing a sobbing woman on the beach, then back to the creature. The sight only confused him further. His dread returned and his heart raced again.

In the corner of Ormy's eye, he detected movement. The mermaid was waking up. She sat slowly upward, rubbed her eyes and drew her slender arms outward in a long stretch. She spotted the image on the TV and reacted. Swimming to the top of the bowl, she reached one hand toward the television and let out a screech that nearly shattered his windows. The mermaid writhed with trepidation and screamed as she seemed to be reaching for the creature. Another painful howl emitted from her, scrambling Ormy's thoughts and causing his head to pound in agony.

He stood, approached his collection and lifted a large, wide sandstone. On his way to the bowl, he noticed the beast on his screen. It jerked its massive head north and roared in response. His windows shook again. Ormy examined the mermaid and then the demon. *Was it looking for her?* He thought. *Could it hear her somehow?* The kaiju used its muscular tentacles to pull itself from the ocean and began to move—north—towards Brooklyn.

Ormy rested the sandstone on his shoulder and used a free hand to push the mermaid back into her bowl and into the water. He laid the stone flat, on top of her enclosure and sealed her inside under its weight. Her screams were muffled and all she could do was helplessly strike the inside of the fish bowl with her tiny fists. Ormy sat on the bed and watched the leviathan leave a path of destruction through Gravesend, Homecrest and down Ocean Parkway. The helicopters followed the beast as it traveled. Reporter commentary only described what the creature was doing and where it was. No military involvement or federal action was mentioned. *Was the country going to do nothing about this?* Ormy screamed inside his head. It had emerged almost three hours ago and no shots were fired, nor was there any military presence whatsoever. His confusion grew as his terror escalated. Over the next thirty minutes, the kaiju rampaged through Midwood, Kensington and finally came to a stop in Prospect Park. Without the cover of manmade structures, the creature's entire anatomy was visible.

It stood on four long limbs like a dog with a maine of waving tentacles around its head. Its eyes cast red and blue light onto the grass, trees and surrounding neighborhoods. The beast's howl sounded like a raid siren. It just stood in place, staring north with a terrible expression of determination and outrage. Ormy ran to his windows. He couldn't see the creature, but the helicopters surrounding it from above were as clear as daylight.

All night, Ormy stood at his windows. He felt as though days had passed, possibly weeks. The only sense of time he possessed was the dark sky and the absence of a rising sun. Over the excruciating hours, the kaiju had not moved a step out of Prospect Park. He turned his eyes to the covered bowl. The mermaid had run out of steam hours ago and had fallen back to sleep. Ormy's head thundered like a storm. The anxiety, the fear and the rush that had gone on forever, finally took its toll. He stumbled backward, fell to his knees and hit the carpet.

Ormy woke up. He woke up in the same position he had fallen. Sunlight shined brightly from his windows and onto the bed and carpet. His head still pounded and the pain was still prominent. He got to his feet and glanced at the bowl. The sandstone had been removed and the mermaid was sitting peacefully on her rocky seat. Painstakingly, Ormy attempted to piece his thoughts together. Memories, rational thought and understanding blended together in an unfamiliar haze and became hard to decipher or distinguish. *The demon!* He realized. The TV was turned off and the remote was resting on his bed. He sprinted for the window. No creature, no helicopters. Wild bewilderment made him dizzy again. He sat on the bed and stared towards the floor. *Had it all been a dream? Had the beast been real?* If he was hallucinating creatures, it would be reasonable that he had dreamed up the mermaid as well. But, there she was, in her bowl just as she had been for weeks. Hesitantly, he took the remote and activated the TV. Every channel he clicked through seemed typical. No news reports, no demon, no destruction. He found nothing but average, daytime, New York television.

He clicked the TV off and dropped the remote to the floor. Ormy rubbed his face with his large hands and shook his head. He would just have to accept that what he experienced was a fabrication and carry on. If the broadcast had been real, it would still be found on the news the day after and even weeks after the event occurred. He took a long, calming breath and accepted the delusion.

His stomach growled. Hunger nagged at his throat. Quickly, Ormy remembered the book. He had left it at the pet store. If *he* was hungry, he couldn't imagine how starved the poor thing in the bowl must have been. He jumped to his feet, snatched his wallet, retrieved his keys and headed for the door. All at once the terror returned.

In one swift motion, the entire southeastern corner of his loft was stripped away. Glass, debris, bricks and dust exploded from the disturbance as harsh sunlight poured into his condo. Ormy shielded his eyes from the light and gazed up at the monstrosity peering down at him from the outside. Red and blue scales, hulking limbs and gnashing teeth. It roared with a terrible frenzy and reached into his loft with one, enormous tentacle. The silent giant screamed helplessly as the kaiju grabbed him by his ankle and lifted him into the air and above the building. A flock of birds passed fearfully, as he dangled from its horrible grip and over its hungry, gaping jaws. Terror and anguish crushed him like a vice as he was released, and sent howling with formidable horror, down the beast's cavernous and damning throat.

"Mister Greene?" A voice asked. All he could see was white. "Mister Greene, can you hear me?" She asked again. The room came into focus and his surroundings became clear. Ormy sat in a chair facing a stern-looking woman at a desk, holding an open file. He was in some kind of office. Dark wood, potted plants and the familiar hum of a pump motor met his senses. He spotted a small aquarium in the corner of the room. His eyes smiled as a school of neon tetras danced inside. Ormy was dressed in white scrubs and an armed guard stood near the only door. She spoke again, "Mister Greene, can you tell me your first name?" His eyes shifted to her condescending glare. Like the sharp scent from a deceased flame, ascertainment engulfed him. For once, all became clear. Memories, rational thought and understanding unfolded behind his eyes. The events leading up to this moment became perfectly aligned and distinct. Ormy's eyes narrowed to a perfunctory grimace. "Let's try something less complicated," she said. "Nod if you can hear me." He gave her nothing. His stare drove through her like a cold spike. The woman noticed his shift in presence. "There he is," she said quietly. She closed the file and laid it on the polished wood. "What were you planning to do with her, Mister Greene?" A marble statue would have twitched or blinked at the question. Ormy did not. "Kill her? You almost succeeded." She pulled a photo from the file and presented it. He did not look at it. "Cynthia Williams, age eight. Taken from a church function near Coney Island on June eleventh." She examined his face then laid the photo beside the file. "During the raid, police found her *and you* on the sixth story of an abandoned hotel on Lee Avenue. She had a broken femur and a fractured skull—starved, beaten and covered in household chemicals. Her blood was found on a large brick beside the dog kennel you were keeping her in." Ormy didn't budge. "The TV in your room was turned to channel nine," she stated. "Were you watching the investigation on the news?" The interrogator shifted in her seat and folded her fingers below her chin. Only the high-pitched sting of perfect silence drifted between them. She continued, "Your medical records state that you've been on Risperidone since childhood with frequent, short-term lapses in the dosage over the past several years. I'd tell you that you are currently *back on* the medication, but I'm sure you are well aware of that now." She took a moment, then cleared her throat. "On April seventeenth, you and your mother disappeared from your home at fourteen thirty-two River. Her vehicle was found parked at your hotel." An expression of frustrated inquiry grazed her lips. "Mister Greene? *Where* is your mother?" She asked. Ormy looked away for just a second. He dwelled on his brother and the letters they had shared. His heart grinned with an inauspicious delight. *That* was evidence neither her nor the police would *ever* find. The woman sat back in her leather chair and waved her fingers dismissively. "I guess that's enough for today," she sighed. Her eyes focused sharply on his. "I want you to think long and hard about what we talked about today. We will talk again very soon." She signaled for the guard. He softly approached and helped Ormy from his seat. They walked slowly towards the door. "Mister Greene," she said again. He and the guard turned. "Can you at least say your first name for me?" She asked. A pinch of desperation shone in her eye. Ormy coldly looked away and continued for the door. He and his armed escort departed from the office.

In a comfortable cell, Ormy laid on a twin mattress, staring at the ceiling. Day came to a darkening close and night fell. The dim glow of a hall light loomed in his enclosure as he gave one last listen for guards or patrols. Only silence. Slowly, Ormy sat up and lifted his sore foot, resting it on his knee. With a worn thumbnail, he scratched the flesh away from his callus heel. Chunks of white skin and droplets of blood fell to the tile floor as he pulled a small, plastic bag out of his foot. He opened the bag and removed a roll of paper, a golf pencil and his mother's weathered credit card. Ormy unrolled the paper and read the last several messages addressed to Hayden. He turned a page over and sharpened the pencil against the painted brick beside the bed. He drafted a letter back.

Ormy,

I hope this letter finds you well. I'm sorry it took me so long to respond. I heard about your mermaid and I'm so sorry she was taken from you. I'm sure you will find another very soon. I'll make sure of it. I have enclosed an expenses card to help get you on your feet and to replace your metal detector. I will find you a car as soon as I can but stay clear of Brighton Beach. I hear that Rockaway Beach is beautiful this time of year. I'm proud of you for standing up to Mom. She got what she deserved. If you'd like to visit her, she is buried in Highland Park near the old fountain, beside a tree marked with a seahorse-shaped stone. As matters progress, I will keep you posted.

Love, Hayden.

He rolled up the letter and placed it into the bag, along with the pencil and card. Clenching his teeth and wincing in pain, he pushed the bag back into his foot and cleaned up the blood and flesh.

Abruptly, a door down the hall opened as a patient was brought inside. She cried and screamed as she was led to a cell and sealed inside. Her escort's footsteps faded off and the door was slammed closed. The inmate continued to cry, beg and weep into the long hours of the night.

The silent giant smiled. He laid in his bed, pulled the thin blanket over his hulking shoulder and rested his head upon the soft pillow. Singing *always* helped him get to sleep.

FOREVERGREEN
Plantlife Long After You're Gone

Earl K. Pike was an angry man. Likely, this was due to the fact that he was balding at the age of thirty-five, his favorite pair of athletic-fit khakis no longer fit and his cat no longer found him interesting. Even more likely, his anger could have derived from the fact that after a decade of loveless marriage, his wife Maggie, refused to send him a returning text message.

Earl stood just outside the busy restrooms of Wellsave Warehouse. The oversized store was a membership-based supply club that sprawled out over twenty acres of used-to-be desert in southern Arizona. He looked out into the sea of bargain-hungry faces as he searched for his wife, with no immediate triumph. Two women fought over the last vegan-friendly air fryer in the home goods department, a man was using his child's agility to reach a can of weight-loss powder, and a Wellsave associate manning the service desk was retaking a member's photo that developed out of focus for the seventh time. Alas, no Maggie.

Grunting in his throat, Earl reached into the pocket of his draw-string stretch pants and pulled his phone. His fatty thumb tapped a where-are-you message to his spouse in frustration-laden vain. He knew she wouldn't respond. Earl wondered if his number still held residence in her contact list at all. Recent history gave strong credit to that suspicion.

Commencing the long tour he always took when searching for Maggie in Wellsave, he started through the pharmacy. After eleven minutes and a shortening emotional fuse, he found her long, red braid and green tank top in the floral department. Earl's fuse burned down to a nub. *Typical,* he thought. Maggie was and always had been, an anthophile.

Earl approached his wife and stood beside her. A group of women surrounding them eagerly watched a wide-eyed sales rep demonstrate a new useless product. Above her, a wide banner displayed the words, *Forevergreen Growth Booster.* In a tight, emerald apron, the rep spoke loudly and fulgently, "Your flora-babies deserve only the best and Forevergreen's new life-extending formula will keep your begonia's, bee balms and bulbs flourishing, fit and fabulous *long after* you're planted in the ground *with* them!" Earl stewed with agitation. The rep was obviously regurgitating from a corporate script she had committed to memory. And like every woman Earl had ever known, his wife Maggie was a sucker for new product pitches delivered in this fashion. Especially when relating to plants. He could feel his bank account draining as the pitch went on, "Just one teaspoon a day of Forevergreen's growth booster hormone is all it takes to empower the only family member in your household who lacks the ability to bark, hiss or squawk when things get ruff!" The group of women sickeningly laughed at the pun, including Maggie. The words, Plant Mama showed prominently in white across her lime-green chest.

Earl turned his nose to his wife and spoke quietly, "Water and dirt. That's all your plants need. You dash them with enough chemicals to cause another Chernobyl."

Abruptly, the sales rep pointed at him directly. She must have somehow heard his gripe. "That, is a common misconception, sir!" She smiled. "The garden of Eden was crawling with every species of animal, defecating their individual and unique enzymes into the soil, optimal and crucial for perfect vegetation health!" The miniature crowd nodded in agreement and fascination. The woman smiled again. "We all know what happened after that, don't we?" She asked rhetorically. Laughter once again erupted from the group.

Earl cringed at the irony. The biblical event the sales rep had referred to involved a *woman* causing the fall of mankind and humanity's expulsion from grace. He didn't bother to comment on the observation. He was vastly outnumbered and had already tarnished his reputation. "How much is this going to cost us?" He asked Maggie.

"Quiet," she hushed. "She's getting to that."

He winced. A price revealed in closing was never a good sign. His hypothetical bank balance circled the metaphorical drain. Earl handled the finances in their home. Since his marriage to Maggie, she was left out of the stress and responsibility of balancing a checkbook as a mercy. Earl figured it was his duty as a husband to take on the burden of money distribution himself. Over time, her obliviousness and carefree spending had become a problem.

The saleswoman retrieved a tube the size of silicone caulk and presented it with the label facing outward. "A ten-ounce supply of Forevergreen's growth booster will last thirty days for medium sized potted plants.." A green, star-shaped tag on the tube read, *$79.95 plus the cost of application gun.* Earl rolled his eyes and groaned. She set the tube aside, reached under the folding table and hoisted a white bucket with the same label, onto the polyethylene surface. "However, we *strongly recommend* the economy size for shrubs, gardens and all of the in-ground family members you're lovingly responsible for and helping to reach their full potential!" The bucket was not marked with a price. Earl dropped his nose, slapped a palm against his forehead and died with despondency.

The woman continued, "Before I open up the floor for sales, I *am obligated* by Forevergreen Co. and our agreement with the EPA to warn and urge you *not* to combine Forevergreen Growth Booster with *any other* branded or non-branded supplement, stimulant or additive." She paused oddly. "This is a *strict instruction* that *must be* adhered to!" She added.

"That's one way to weed out the competition," Earl mumbled.

"Enough," Maggie spat.

The rep bloomed with a sunbeam grin. "Now, who's ready for forever-life with healthy, long-lasting, forever-green?!" She announced. Immediately, excitement erupted from the crowd as women pulled out purses, wallets and credit cards. An avid line formed before the saleswoman as Maggie and her sisterhood of anthophiles ravenously purchased armfulls, cartfulls and pallets of Forevergreen's fresh-off-the-market, growth-boosting, hormone supplement.

Earl stood in his kitchen. Same tie-string sweats and same worn-out clogs. The room smelled of fresh dirt and mineral-growth formula. He sliced a piece of coffee cake from a clear, plastic clamshell. The coffee maker coughed and bubbled as a new pot was brewed. Steps away, Maggie stood diligently over what used to be their kitchen table and her ever-growing collection of potted flowers. She emptied old soil and repotted daffodils, primroses and orchids, whispering kind words and supportive phrases to them as her hands moved. The brewer finished. Earl took a semi-clean mug from a nearby cupboard and filled it with steaming coffee.

He watched her work and talk to her plants. Maggie was seldom clear of dirt smudges and earth-covered hands. Her clothes resembled a child's who had just come inside after making mud cakes in a rainy yard all day. She smelled of wet grass, musty earthworms and ammonia. Her swift pace and work ethic was similar to a chemical engineer's, industriously working on an end-all cure for Alzheimer's and earning her a Nobel Prize. Her focused expression matched.

Maggie treated every plant as equal to herself and cared for them all with the same delicate attention. Her crown jewel was a sunspot, dwarf sunflower. It sat at the center of the table and commanded the most attention after winning her a gardening award, issued by an online magazine. The sunflower was her most coveted possession and its needs were tended to on an hourly basis. It stood at the top of Maggie's priority list in any situation, with her husband left arbitrarily at the bottom.

Maggie hadn't always been obsessed with plants. There was a time long ago, when *Earl* held top precedence in her life and all kind words would be whispered to *him*. Back when he had all of his hair and his clothes fit. Over time, Maggie's attention shifted to lovers who didn't complain, judge or criticize. In their twelve years of marriage, he had lost his wife to younger, thinner and more agreeable suitors. Lovers that didn't bark, hiss or squawk.

"Why do you have to re-pot them *all?*" Earl squawked.

Maggie stood and shook her long, crimson bangs out of her face. "Weren't you listening?" She snapped. "We can't mix Forevergreen with any other additives."

Earl bobbed his head, remembering the instructions — and the odd look on the rep's face when she had given them. "They wanna' own the monopoly on what you keep in your chemical collection, huh? Tactical move," he remarked.

She ignored his sarcasm. "We're getting more Forevergreen some time this week," she commanded. "I want to plant oleanders in the yard. The ones I saw at Kipley's."

Before Earl could object to additional spending, he noticed movement in the corner of his view. In the sink, a cockroach climbed out of the drain and approached a previously-used cake plate and crusty fork. "Gah!" He shrieked. Earl took a brand-new bottle of drain cleaner from below and doused it into the sink. The roach slipped down the pipe as he ran hot, scalding water as a chaser. Noxious steam plumed into the air. "Does that new, magic formula keep bugs from infesting the kitchen, too?! Our house is turning into a roach commune!" He complained. His hatred for unwelcome insects was almost as strong as his disdain for her unwelcome plants. Maggie continued to work and whisper affectionate words. Earl's temperature rose. "You know, It doesn't matter what you say to them!" He clamored. "It's carbon dioxide either way. And we breathe all the time in the house, talking to them directly isn't some kind of adrenaline boost for weeds!"

Maggie's dirt-covered fists clenched. She swung her head around as her long braid slapped against the table. "I told you to *never* use that word around them! They're *not weeds* and I'd thank you kindly to *please* use some respect when referring to my petal-babies!"

Earl slapped the water to a stop beside the open bottle of cleaner. He petulantly took a sip of coffee and a bite of cake from a clean fork. "Petal babies," he repeated. "Unbelievable." He marveled at her stupidity, then took another bite. Earl often wondered if his wife's detachment from reality would one day drive him to the end of his rope and plunge him headlong into mental instability. It seemed inevitable.

The tension in the room was jerked into panicked alarm as Maggie gasped at the sight of something on the table. "Oh my God!" Her voice shook. Earl almost choked on his cake. Shaking loose dirt from her hands, she carefully took a fallen leaf from beside a pot and eyed it with disdain.

"What? What's wrong now?" He belted.

Maggie turned on her heel, stepped to her husband's feet and held the miniature leaf inches from his nose. He chewed like a disinterested cow. "What does that look like to you?!" She growled.

He examined it carelessly. "Mulch?" He dismissively guessed.

Maggie stomped her ankle-socked foot onto the linoleum floor with a clap. *"Teeth marks!"* She shouted. Earl noticed small bite holes in the green leaf. He shook his head with vexation. "Your stupid cat is *eating* my babies!" She roared.

"You leave Bella out of this!" He bellowed. "She's done *nothing* to you and she's not *eating your flowers!"* He angrily gestured to the table. "And how do you even know it was *attached* when she got to it? It likely fell off before she chewed it," he argued.

Her brow furrowed. "I take *good care* of my herb-children! *Nothing* falls off of them! If it did, it means I'm not doing my job as a flower mom!"

"Flower mom?!" Earl mocked. "You need to stop talking like that. You're starting to sound like one of those dog psychos."

Maggie shot him a look of lividity. "Or one of those *cat psychos?*" She retaliated.

Earl took the leaf from her hand and held it in front of her. His hand trembled with malice. "Bella is a *living, breathing* mammal like you and me." His tone was soft but sore. "Your ..*weeds* are in the same genetic gene pool as the *mold* that forms on the inside of our toilets in mid July!" He spat.

She pushed his hand out of her face and smiled coldly through her teeth. "And yet they bring me *more joy* than you've *ever* given me," she hissed.

His face went white. Earl's brain inflamed with a fuming churn of indignancy and yet, he said nothing. Like most women, Maggie's emotions often swayed from one extreme to the next, laying behind a wake of words she hadn't actually meant in the heat of passion. Earl could usually dismiss these words through understanding. But not today. Not after what she had just said. He took his cup, took the cake from the plate and tossed the dish into the wet sink, smashing it to pieces and making her jump with dark surprise. Without further discussion, he left the kitchen and collapsed into a weathered recliner in front of a wall-mounted television in the living room. Maggie timidly went back to her flowers as her husband sharply snatched the remote and illuminated the TV.

Across the carpet and beside a tall lamp, Bella laid on her back, staring at him as he fumed. The lazy cat had an orange coat with white stripes. Her ivory paws seemed as though they had been dipped in white paint. Earl caught sight of her and smiled warmly. Unamused, Bella flipped, faced the other direction and ignored the gesture. In addition to his wife, Earl had almost forgotten that even his living, breathing housecat found no joy in his existence.

Maggie silently finished with the inside plants and hauled two more buckets of Forevergreen into the kitchen from the garage. She slid open the back door and began repotting the larger species of her nursery on her makeshift-patio-greenhouse. Not a word was spoken between them for the rest of the evening and into the night.

Earl woke just after midnight. His room was small, dark and sweltering. Years ago, he had moved into the guestroom due to Maggie's constant complaints about snoring. The complaints hadn't surfaced until his waistline began to increase. Now, the guest room was Earl's room. His clothes laid scattered across the floor, draped over the furniture and folded into neat stacks on the opposite side of the bed. No posters or pictures covered the walls and no decor was present to speak of. Earl liked it this way. He wouldn't call himself boring, just simple, unneeding and easy to please. Perhaps *that fact,* in itself, made him uninteresting.

He sat up, stood and yawned. Since the move into his new room, he would wake at this time every night, stewing over the past, analyzing his life's present state and yearning for times that once were. Months ago, he decided to replace the stewing with coffee, the analyzing with cake and the yearning with television. The habit was far less depressing and the nightly routine served him much needed happy time, without Maggie's cold shoulder or ridicule. Earl stepped into the hall, descended the stairs and entered the kitchen. He snapped the lights on. The scent of drain cleaner and the presence of broken ceramic in the sink was still present from hours before.

On the kitchen-garden-table, Bella gnawed vigorously on a small branch of Maggie's violet perennials. The tiny stems snapped and twisted between the feline's gnashing molars. Earl grinned. "Good girl," he whispered. As the cat chewed, he placed a filter in the coffee machine and filled it with grounds. With a click, he switched on the device as it popped and gurgled.

Earl leaned against the counter in his two-piece pajamas and glared with a narky scorn at the arrangement of blooming colors that had replaced him as a life partner. He scoffed at their impeccable beauty and thought on his wife's formidable and cruel words. Sadness battled with anger under his receding hairline and shiny head. The coffee continued to bubble.

Out of curiosity, Earl approached the table, lifted a bucket of growth booster and looked down his nose at the label. "Forevergreen," he read out loud. "Plantlife, long after you're gone." He turned the bucket and read from the fine print, "Water soluble, all-purpose plant supplement for extended life and overall health and wellness." Below the description, a paragraph in red caught his attention. "Do not mix with any other supplements, formulas or additives. Some ingredients may remain unidentified and/or unlisted until patent maturity, per Forevergreen Co. and the Environmental Protection Agency." His forehead wrinkled. "The hell does that mean?" He mumbled.

Bella meowed, interrupting him. Earl turned his attention to the cat, rested the bucket on the floor and attempted to place his hand on her furry head. *"Now* you want to talk to me you fuzzy, little rasc—?" Before he could finish his phrase, Bella pulled backward, hissed savagely and leapt from the table, vanishing into the dark of the living room. Earl glanced in the direction she had disappeared. "We used to be pals!" He called out.

The coffee maker finished its brewing cycle and steamed to a slow stop. As he readied his mug and poured a hot cup, the open bottle of drain cleaner beside the sink caught his eye. His sights moved over the lengthy warning label, brightly printed in yellow across green plastic. Earl paused as his thoughts stirred.

Maggie's painful words, her coveted weeds, the six-hundred dollars he had spent on growth formula and even the hateful cat piled in his head like weighted stones stacked one-by-one, atop a curse-spitting witch. Earl had taken far more than he could bear over the years and the emotions he had buried deep in the grave of his memory began to gestate, take root and sprout from mere thought—to physical action. He took the toxic cleaning product by the handle and sniffed the sharp, deadly scent of the open top. Bella entered the kitchen and meowed again, presumably looking for a midnight snack. Earl looked down at her. "Let's just see what Forevergreen does with a little competition," he said with a sinister smirk.

Earl sauntered over to his wife's table-top garden and simpered with amusement as he dosed every pot with a generous amount of sodium hydroxide, caustic oxidizer and hypochlorite. Bella curiously watched as he poisoned every petunia, begonia and marigold, adding an even heftier dose to Maggie's prized sunflower at the crown of the table. Smiling madly, he unlocked the sliding glass door and flipped on the patio lights. He did the same to the array in her makeshift greenhouse. Every beloved petal baby was sabotaged with malignant drain cleaner and left to absorb the lethal substance and left to die within hours of his vengeful exploit.

He tossed the empty bottle into the kitchen recycling bin and filled Maggie's daisy-printed watering can with the tap of the sink. One by one, he dissolved the poison with a light sprinkle of water, making sure that every indoor and outdoor pot was primed with H2O and laced with imminent death.

Earl returned the watering can to the floor and reveled at his deed. From his feet, Bella howled again. "I know," he concurred. "Mags is going to be mighty pissed when she wakes up in the morning," he chuckled. Earl didn't feel a modicum of remorse and actually looked forward to his wife's reaction to the massacre in seven, short hours. *More* than enough time for the additive to work its magic and show visually through wilting, discoloration and decay. "I'll tell you what..," he remarked to the cat. He pulled a can of Maggie's dolphin-safe, vegan tuna from the cupboard and removed the top with a steel opener. "You keep your furry little mouth shut.." He dumped a fresh helping of fish into her cat bowl. "..and I'll let you chow down on this bribe," he said. Bella eagerly consumed the tuna as Earl was finally permitted, after many years of resistance, to pet her.

His eyes opened. Beams of harsh sunlight emitted through the blinds and cast hot, midmorning stripes across his plain, white bed sheet. The house was silent and the position of the sun suggested late morning. Earl threw the warm sheet from his PJ's and touched his bare feet to the hickory floor.

Coming to life, Earl rubbed his eyes and mentally revisited the events from just after midnight. Maggie usually woke before eight. He should have woken up to screaming, crying ...some kind of outburst if the poison had taken effect. The quiet was odd. Sharply, Earl heard a metallic clank through his guestroom window followed by falling taps of wood. He stood, parted the blinds and squinted through the biting sun.

In the yard, just beyond the porch, Maggie was lining a row of newly-purchased oleander bushes wrapped in burlap, against the perimeter fence. A wheelbarrow filled with hand tools rested on the grass beside a rake, hoe and steel shovel. Earl's face twisted with perplexity. He departed from the room, jogged down the stairs and beheld the kitchen.

He quivered with frustration. Maggie's potted babies sat happily upon the table and exhibited no visible change. He stood over them, examining their obvious state of vigor and wellness. They almost appeared *healthier* than the day before. Blooming buds, crisp, hydrated edges and strong, hearty stems. He couldn't even find evidence of where Bella had chewed on the perennials. Irately, Earl leaned over the trash and retrieved the bottle of poison. The four paragraphs just above the number to poison control assured that the product could kill almost anything. He huffed through his nostrils and irritably dropped the container, returning it to the bin.

In addition to the new oleanders, Maggie had purchased several bags of top soil, a new pair of boots and hedge clippers. The items were neatly stacked by the glass door and a lengthy receipt exhibiting the Kipley's logo rested on the counter. He sickeningly refused to look upon the amount she had spent. The wholesome state of the plants he had attempted to assassinate was enough turmoil and grief.

Evidently, a new plant was added to her table-top collection as well. *Why the hell not,* he thought bitterly. The new orange flowers glowed brightly with white stripes and petal tips that looked as if they'd been dipped in bright, white paint. The coloring reminded him of Bella. On that thought, Earl dragged his body over to the pantry, pulled a bag of cat chow from a shelf and filled her dish.

The cockroach returned from the drain and watched the melancholy man go through the motions of his meaningless existence, exit the kitchen and return to his room to dress. On top of bringing joy to no one and becoming the most boring human being on earth, Earl K. Pike was also a failure.

The next thirty minutes went the way of every morning. Coffee, cake, his chair and the TV. Earl took a bite and a sip, viewing an infomercial for some kind of new facemask that retained hydration, absorbed caloric intake and gave your complexion a dewy and youthful appearance. He arbitrarily flipped through the channels. Every station wanted to sell him something and offered no entertainment on a Saturday morning filled with gloom and despair. He glanced to the floor beside the lamp. Bella was not in her usual place. The observation made him wary.

Pulling his phone from his drawstring pocket, he shot a text to Maggie. "Have you seen Bella this morning?" He'd get nothing in return. He wondered why he sent her messages at all. Perhaps *hope* still lingered in the recesses of his expectations. After four, long minutes with no return reply, that hope wilted and fell to decay. Out of vain curiosity, he composed another message. "You're spending too much money. I'm closing our account and taking your debit card." He tapped send. Six minutes passed. Earl laughed to himself, staring at his decade-long, one-sided string of texts to his wife. He tapped again, "You're a cruel woman and I poured extra strength DrainClear into all of your weeds last night." *Why the hell not,* he thought. It was now apparent that she had never even observed his massages to begin with.

The doorbell made him jolt in his seat. The alert was followed by a strong knock at the front door. Earl set his mug aside and rocked to his feet. The man at the door was dressed professionally in a blue and yellow uniform and held a long pesticide sprayer. "Pike?" He asked.

"Yes," he replied. His voice still scratched with morning grog.

"We're doing your weekly treatment? In-home and perimeter of the house?" He announced in the form of a question.

"Yeah, come on in," he welcomed.

The man pulled out a smart phone with a hefty case and read from it as he entered, "Says here, we spray for cockroaches in the bathrooms but not the kitchen or rear porch. Is that right?"

Earl was reminded of the strict specifics put in place by his wife and her paranoia about pest control spraying anything near her precious babies. He looked over his shoulder towards the kitchen. Silence loomed through the interior of his house. "Actually.." he started. "Let's do everything today."

"The entire home? Inside and out?" The man queried.

"Yeah," Earl said. "Everything. Spray everything."

The tech made adjustments to the previous instructions in his records with a few swift taps. "Ok. Sounds good," he chimed. He pushed the phone into his back pocket and proceeded up the stairs to begin with the hall bathroom. "Treatment should only take about ten minutes, then I'll be out of your hair."

Earl fell back into his chair. "No problem. Take your time," he replied courteously. He took a bite and a sip of coffee. "And let me know if you see an orange cat!" He added. In retrospect, Earl wondered why he mentioned his cat's color. If he saw a cat, it wouldn't matter what color it was. Bella was the only feline in the house. He dwelled on her unusual absence. Typically, Bella was only in two places, the kitchen and her place by the lamp. Even her litter box was kept beside the pantry, there was no reason she'd be anywhere else in the home. The longer he thought about it, the more he began to worry. *White stripes,* he thought to himself. Earl remembered Maggie's new plant. Curiously he stood and walked into the kitchen, standing over the new addition to the table.

The stunning orange flowers and ivory details of their curling petals were uncanny to Bella's fur pattern. He lifted the pot from the table and examined it closely. The scent of salted fish wafted past his nose and made him sick with bizarre confusion. His mind raced with unreasonable conclusions and anxiety.

Boots thundered down the oak staircase. Earl placed the pot back onto the table as the tech made his way past the kitchen and into the first floor toilet. Still riddled with questions, Earl floated into the living room and sat. He stared blankly at the televised ad for gluten-free nail polish remover as the pest-control tech entered the kitchen and resumed his light sprays of bug killer. He treated the floor beneath the cupboards, under the oven and along the glass exit to the rear deck. Earl heard the back door slide open, and then close. The same would be done with the greenhouse patio.

For five minutes, Earl waited to hear some kind of squabble take place. If Maggie caught the tech spraying anywhere near her pots, he would certainly hear her high-pitched squeals and shrieking objections. Immediately, it would be followed by another one of her angry rants directed at him. Only calm silence ensued as he drank from his mug. The kitchen glass slid open again, and shut. The tech returned, uninhibited.

"I'd like to come back tomorrow with a different solution to apply another treatment and lay out some traps, if you don't mind," he said sharply.

"*Another* treatment?" Earl asked curiously.

The man tapped notes into his phone. "You've got a roach infestation under your porch due to the aphids, spider mites and whiteflies in your above-ground garden."

Earl's expression went flat with ire. "The patio?" He growled.

"That's correct," he verified. "You have roaches getting into the home from below the patio and they're attracted to your indoor garden as well." Earl steamed with aggravation. "Not to worry," the man continued. "After a few more treatments with a new roach formula we've been using more frequently, you should see the matter clear up in a matter of weeks." He smiled and held his phone outward, presenting the screen to Earl. He cursed under his breath, fueled with animosity toward his wife as he signed on the digital line. The man pocketed the phone. "Same time tomorrow," he chirped. Earl opened the door for the tech. He watched as he made his way down the concrete path, past the garage and headed for the marked, white van across the street. Earl used every resistance he could muster to keep from slamming the door.

He always knew the roaches were an increasing problem but he had always assumed that their growing numbers were a result of changing climate, the time of year or even the constellation of the stars. Earl had *never once* thought that his pest control problem was a direct consequence of Maggie's overzealous green thumb and obsession with inanimate life. He knocked his head against the closed door, bathing in resentment.

He pulled out his phone. "I hate you. I want a divorce," he tapped in their ignored conversation. "Strike that, I want you dead." Earl sent the second message and felt a hint of remorse as it was sent at light speed, reflected off a nearby satellite and delivered directly to her phone. The remorse festered within him. Insults were one thing, suggesting divorce and moreso, her death, was borderline psychopathic.

The patio door slid open and slapped closed. Earl was jerked from his thoughts. Maggie's footsteps quaked into the living room. Her face was covered in dirt, sweat and what looked like outrage. She aggressively removed her gardening gloves. "So, what's *that* all about?!" She thundered.

Confused, Earl looked down at the message he had just sent. He became nauseous. Regret seized him by the throat and burned the pit of his stomach. *Had she actually seen the message, and all the others?* He kept his response neutral. "What's *what* all about?" He deflected.

Her voice became soft. She motioned her overworked hand toward the kitchen. "The orange pixie lilies," she squeaked. Wide prodigy and a childlike wonder showed in her bright eyes through the dingy smudges of topsoil. Her smile warmed him. "Where on earth did you find dwarf lilies with petunia stripes?" She asked in awe.

Earl just stood at a crossroads, speech impaired by a conflict of emotions. His fury towards her was still pumping through his veins. However, she hadn't looked at him like that in years. Many years. He spoke. "I just ..thought they looked nice," he mumbled.

Maggie jumped on her toes. Her braid swayed gleefully behind her moisture-drenched back. *"I love them!"* She shrieked happily. Maggie ran to her husband and wrapped her earth-encrusted arms around his neck. "Thank you," she clamored. Earl slowly and hesitantly returned the embrace. She smelled like the death of the rainforest, but the gratitude and affection she exhibited brought about feelings in him he had almost completely forgotten. His anger was still present, but for the moment, he gladly set it aside.

Maggie drew backward and joyously pulled out her phone. Earl became nervous. She opened an application and showed him a photo she had taken of the lilies above an endless string of likes and comments. "I posted them on BudSnap this morning." She flipped the phone around, scrolling down the post. "flowerchild312 says that they might be an orange pixie crossbreed with a swiss dancer and a red star!" She exclaimed. Her eyes landed on him again. "Where did you buy them? Everyone in my thread is *dying* to know!"

Earl's eyes shifted as he searched for a lie. He tried to remember the name of any nursery they had visited over the past several months, but no name came to memory. However, if he recalled every explosive argument that had taken place between them in public, a long list of crystal-clear garden centers came to mind. "Wilson's Growers And Landscape," he said quickly.

"You found them at Wilson's?!" Her face lit up with inspiration as she sent the word out to almost a hundred interested anthophiles. She pushed the device into her front, denim pocket and hugged him again.

Earl felt a loving fondness in her tight, adoring grasp. Her second embrace dislodged tender memories. Moments between them from before the fights, before the resentment and before the plants. They flooded into his head and made his heart hum with a slowly-cultivating bliss. Perhaps, he had not been replaced as he had thought. Maybe he had just fallen out of touch with what made her happy. It was possible that if he participated a little more in her interests and showed a little more support, things could go back to the way they were. And *that,* is what Earl K. Pike wanted more than anything else in the world.

Maggie released him and clapped her hands together. "Ok," she beamed brightly. "I have today's roster all planned out and I've already taken care of lots of items on the list! I'm *really* going to need your help today!" She announced. Earl's gut twisted at the thought of yard work. He assumed that's what she was referring to. "I went out this morning and got those oleander trees, but I *already* planted them so you won't have to get dirty today." He deflated with relief. Another opportunity for confrontation averted. She continued, "I called Wellsave and ordered a small pallet of Forevergreen, just in case they didn't have it all in stock. I figured, I already gave it to my babies, why neglect my trunk toddlers, ya' know?" Earl's neck trembled as he reluctantly raised his brow and nodded in false agreement. Furious goosebumps tingled across his arms and thinning scalp. "Oh, also," she snapped. "Our debit card stopped working so I checked ZonaBank to see if we were eligible for any credit cards, and guess what?" His eyes widened with feigned, positive anticipation. "Visa cleared us for a seven-thousand dollar limit!" She shrieked. "The card comes in about a week but I already put the Forevergreen on the digital card they sent me. We can pick up the pallet today!" She cheered happily. Maggie jumped again, hugged him a third time and raced into the kitchen. "I'm gonna' shower quick, then we can head out! You're the greatest, hun!"

Only a husk was left of Earl as he stood on the carpet. Every good feeling that had grazed him from moments before was dead, buried and memorialized on a stone epitaph covered in flowering vines and years of monetary debt. The regret about the spiteful messages he had sent her were reduced to mulch, right along with it.

Earl stoically followed his enthusiastic wife as she filled an oversized cart with a spree of garden-variety purchases. A new watering can, copper-infused gloves, more hand tools and an eighty-dollar gardening apron rested in their stash and threatened to max out their brand new Visa before it even had a chance to arrive. The twenty-four buckets of growth booster were loaded into his truck upon their arrival to Wellsave. Maggie had *insisted* on entering the store and browsing for anything she may have forgotten from her trip to Kipley's, generating even further spending. Who was he to argue? He was only responsible for the household's sole income and the only one who seemed to care about falling into bankruptcy.

Maggie rushed down an aisle and took a tray of pink zinnias from a tall rack and returned. She held them before Earl's nose. He sharply turned away. "Aren't they just the *sweetest things?!*" She cried. She held them close to her lips. "Hello little ones," she whispered lovingly. Turning to her husband, she exclaimed, "Well we *have* to buy them now! Did you see the way they *looked at us?!*" Maggie bent over the handle and gently added them to the cart.

Every time Maggie left the cart to retrieve another expensive item, her phone was left behind to Earl's devices. Each time she departed, he had the opportunity to open her texting app and delete his recent messages to her. Under the current circumstances and due to the state of his mood, he denied the venture, every time.

The couple passed the pet section where Earl noticed an abundant selection of bargain-sized cat food, treats and special-diet formulas. His attention changed tracks. "Have you seen Bella? He asked. "I didn't see her this morning."

Her eyes wandered sincerely. "I didn't. She wasn't in her spot by the TV?" She asked. "She didn't get out through the back door. I know that."

Earl decided to drop any further inquiry. He wondered if the tuna he had given her was somehow related to her disappearance. To his memory, she had never fallen sick in his care. He remembered reading somewhere that cats sometimes change their behavior if inflicted with any kind of ailment. He decided to check the house thoroughly as soon as they returned home.

They slowly approached the rear of the warehouse. To Earl's dreadful surprise, the Forevergreen demo table and its enthusiastic sales rep were still present from the day before. The banner now read, *Forevergreen Environmental Awareness Enhancer.* Maggie clapped her hands excitedly and raced to the display. Earl shat his metaphorical pants.

"Your chlorophyll-kiddos are far more attuned to their surroundings than you think, and this new consciousness-enhancing formula will open up their little receptors to the maximum amount of love and affection you give to them on a daily basis!" The woman bawled. Earl had forgotten her high-pitched shrill. The Forevergreen rep's blinding expression was the last face he needed to see today.

Maggie nudged him with her elbow. "See! I told you my petal-babies knew what I was saying to them!"

The woman's eyes fell on Earl. It was obvious she remembered his ignorant frown from yesterday. She resumed her pitch, "Just *four applications* of

Forevergreen's environmental awareness enhancer applied with this spray hose and solar-powered, electrical pump will have your root-rascals greeting you with the sunrise, gossiping over afternoon tea and bidding you a restful and sweet-dream goodnight!"

"Let me guess, it can't be used with any other stimulants or additives?" Earl mumbled.

"I'm sure that's implied," Maggie whispered. "We're definitely getting that."

He responded like a soleless robot. "Why the hell not," he surrendered.

"Before I open up the floor for sales, I'd like to give you a sneak peek at Forevergreen's upcoming, remote-interaction system that allows you to converse with your children from anywhere on mother earth!" The rep reached under the table and placed a large white box before her with the label facing a sea of astounded expressions. The product's image resembled a desktop monitor connected to a cylindrical canister of pressurized air. "Our soon-to-be-released FloraText station gives you the ability to send positive and encouraging words to your garden while simultaneously delivering a healthy spritz of carbon dioxide with every text message!" Earl was sent into a completely new dimension of perplexity and indignancy. Reality itself seemed to fall away, leaving him as the only logical mind among the irrational, overcredulous and absurd. He shuddered from the painful levels of stupidity. The rep continued, "Soon, you can take that trip to Maui, visit your Aunt in New York or visit Phoenix's breathtaking Desert Botanical Garden without the worry of denying your seedlings and cultivated cuties of your much-needed inspiration and life-giving breath."

Tears actually began to stream down the faces of every female onlooker, including Maggie. A slow clap began at the back of the crowd and erupted into thunderous applause as though a war had just ended and those oppressed by the conflict were freed from tyranny. "We're getting one of those," Maggie hummed in his ear.

"Are you insane?! He spat angrily. Earl shook with outrage as his argument went completely unheard due to the uproarious excitement. All he could do was glare bitterly at the sunny representative as the group continued to applaud. His financial state was doomed beyond time. For a moment he considered taking on a second job, joining the electrical worker's union to double his income or taking a detour past Echo Canyon forest preserve, strangling Maggie with a garden hose and leaving her in the desert for dead. The latter seemed the more reasonable of the three.

Maggie turned to him with a kind-eyed grin. "Don't worry," she said. "I'm not going to rack up our Visa with charges. I know how you get about major credit cards." Her tone was calm and earnest. She almost displayed a sense of responsibility. Earl eyed her. Her tone heightened, "I opened a Wellsave savers account. They only charge a twenty-eight percent interest rate and offer special financing options on purchases over two-thousand dollars per visit!"

Earl sat in his chair. He could hear the electrical whirr of the solar-powered pump as Maggie gave her second dose of awareness enhancer to the oleander trees and patio-greenhouse pots. Bella was still nowhere to be seen. As planned, he had checked every square foot of the house for her orange coat and white stripes when they had returned home. Alas, no Bella. He took a bite of cake and a sip of coffee. The flavor offered no relief to the hell Earl was inevitably spiraling into. All day, he had not raised a fuss to Maggie and all day, she had remained kind, affectionate and cooperative. *But at what expense?* Her mood would surely change when the credit dropped, the money ran dry and the house foreclosed. *That* was the cost of harmony.

The doorbell shook him in his seat. He set the dishes aside and answered the door. A different pest control tech stood happily on the step in the same uniform and equipped with the same sprayer as the man from before. "Mr. Pike," he chimed. Earl nodded. He didn't have the energy to display the same sunny attitude he retained yesterday. The man entered. "Cockroach treatment? Bathrooms and perimeter?" He asked cheerfully. Earl nodded again and gestured to his home's interior. The tech displayed a handsome tank strapped to his side and attached to the spraying apparatus. "This is PestEjector's new state-of-the-art formula that rids your home of roaches, rodents and rigors so you can rest easy, knowing tha—" The man halted his endorsement upon seeing Earl's face. His dead-pan expression exhibited absolute disinterest in the details.

"Just start spraying," Earl clapped.

The man checked his phone. "It says here to leave the kitchen and the patio untreated?" He asked.

"Everything," He barked.

"Apply treatment everywhere?" The tech inquired.

"Spray everything!" Earl confirmed. The pest control associate jogged up the stairs to begin his round as Earl collapsed into his chair. He resumed his spiral of depression, self-loathing and despondence as another obnoxious commercial danced across the television screen. Exasperated, he snatched the remote and switched off the TV completely. Silence fell over the room. Earl sat impassively still as the tech descended the steps, treated the bathroom and sprayed the perimeter of the kitchen. He slid open the patio doors and ventured out into the greenhouse. Another sip of coffee.

Within the span of five minutes, he heard Maggie's shrill voice boom against the double-paned glass. Earl raged, "Son of a—!" He leapt to his clogs and raced to the kitchen, mug in hand. In his rush, he tried coming up with an excuse for allowing the man on the porch. The easiest solution was to blame it on the tech. Claim that he never changed the instructions and just lie. He lacked the energy for any other option.

What Earl saw on the patio sent confusion, relief, fear and anxiety shattering through his body and caused his blood to run cold. He slowly slid the glass open as Maggie's delighted cries amplified. She clapped her hands and bounced before a tall, potted plant decorated in blue and yellow flowers and healthful, curling leaves. At her feet, the tank of PestEjector fluid and its long spray nozzle rested beside it. *"It's beautiful! I love it!"* Maggie screamed with elation. Earl stepped onto the deck and frantically began searching for the tech. He darted around the corner, vanishing from her sight. "Where are you going?" She called out. Earl zigged and zagged through the yard and to the opposite end of the house. He thundered past Maggie and ran back inside, checking every room, the garage and even the closets for the missing associate. At the top of the stairs, Earl snapped his fingers and remembered the van. He almost fell down the stairs, threw the front door open and stopped on the walkway. Parked across the street, the PestEjector cargo van sat silently and ominously.

Maggie watched her husband tremble with dread as he returned to the deck and stood beside her. His mug of coffee remained gripped in a white-knuckled fist. Earl's earlier suspicions about what had happened to the cat moved up a tier from unreasonable to probable as he beheld the six-foot, braided hibiscus before him. His wife continued to gush over its beauty and rarity as he lifted the tank and sprayer from the deck and set them against the house. In her excitement, she hadn't seemed to notice it. "Where did you find it?!" She rejoiced.

"Uh, Wilson's," he lied again. He figured she'd believe anything after that ridiculous display at Wellsave. Anyway, she only wanted a name she could share with her online plant freaks. Maggie pulled out her phone and began taking various pictures of the new addition, attaching a swiftly-tapped comment to each one. Earl closed his eyes tightly, processing all he had witnessed over the past twenty-four hours and what the evidence suggested. His knees rattled and his spine twitched.

If the Forevergreen supplements did what they claimed and their warnings were justified, it was possible that the drain cleaner had some kind of effect on whatever ungodly thing they used in the formula. He remembered what he had read on the bucket's label and how discretely it avoided listing several ingredients, shrouded by the excuse of patent complications. Earl couldn't believe he was accepting the ideas that shifted through his head. He rubbed his eyes. His grip on reason was becoming irrational, overcredulous and absurd.

Maggie threw her arms around his neck and kissed him on the cheek, squeezing him tightly. "Thank you so much! *I love it!*" She beamed with affection. Earl just stood in place, unresponsive and dispassionate. His expression vacant and his sanity slipping into madness.

That night, Earl sat on the bed of his guest room and watched the clock slowly tick to midnight in the light of the bedside lamp. Maggie had long been asleep and his coffee mug was still clenched tightly in his fist. He stood. Wary not to make a sound, he crept to the door and cracked it open. Darkness dampened the hall. Earl tiptoed past his wife's room and carefully descended the stairs. The kitchen was dark as he stood in the entryway. Swiftly he switched on the lights. There was the table-top garden, just as it always was. The crown sunflower at the center stared back at him. Gulping in the back of his throat, he approached the group of suspects. No motion, no sound, just a normal, everyday anthophile's kitchen. Lifting a nervous finger, he reached over and tapped on the sunflower's center. No response. His wariness subsided. He snapped on the patio bulb and glared through the glass. The greenhouse remained in the same, customary state. And so did the hibiscus.

Sliding open the door, Earl carefully approached the new plant. He needed something. Some kind of proof. Proof he was sane, or proof he had lost his mind. He didn't care which. He examined the petals, leaves and stems. He felt them in his fingers and even smelled them. Nothing seemed out of place. Earl lowered to his knees and rested his mug on the deck. Taking a preparatory breath, he pushed his hand into the potted soil, feeling around for anything other than roots. The fresh dirt was silky, wet and warm. *Was soil supposed to be warm?* He thought. He dismissed the observation and continued to feel around, deeper and deeper into the pot. Suddenly, something rigid brushed against his middle finger. Gripping it softly in his fingers, it felt metallic and made up of several parts like a stack of coins. He wrapped his fist around the object and pulled it out of the pot.

Crushing horror drained the color from Earl's face as he fell backward, knocking his mug to its side. Cold coffee spilled onto the treated cedar as he crawled backward in terror, moaning with unhinged panic at the sight and the state of his hand. From his wrist to his fingers, Earl's trembling fist dripped with coagulated blood. In his fingers and coated in crimson gore, he held a set of vehicle keys. The PestEjector logo was printed boldly on a hanging key fob.

He looked with terror upon every plant on the patio. He saw every blooming bud as a face of vile evil, staring gruesomely back at him. He shot to his feet as thick drops of blood spotted the porch like rose petals. He stumbled into the house, threw on the sink faucet and rinsed the human bodily fluid off of his flesh and into the drain. Earl tossed the set of keys into the sink and applied gobs of dish cleaner all over his hand and up his arms, frantically washing like a panicked surgeon. He made sure that every bit of gruesome evidence left by the affliction was scrubbed away, bleached and sanitized, leaving nothing behind but spotless flesh, polished steel and the overpowering scent of detergent. Earl turned off the water and eased his breathing. Nausea and trepidation raced through his trembling body and quivering lips. He looked to the plants resting on the table. Probability for his suspicions had now become absolute certainty. Something had to be done. They had already taken the cat and the pest control man, and it was only a matter of time before they got their murderous vines on himself and on Maggie as well. With no other options to think of, Earl snapped into action.

The indoor garden watched wickedly as he threw open the cabinets below the sink and retrieved every single bottle that displayed a warning label. Soaps, sanitizers, powders and sprays were gathered between the sink and the coffee machine. He rushed to the pantry and pulled bleaches, surface finishers and a Wellsave-sized box of weed killer from the floor and added them to his arsenal below the glow of the kitchen light. For a second, he thought of dousing both gardens in gasoline and setting them on fire, but the scent of smoke would surely wake Maggie. There was also the chance of burning down the house. For a moment, Earl considered *that* as an option as well. Then, quickly dismissed it. Drowning the potted demons in every lethal chemical he owned was his only option. Upon finding them dead, Maggie would surely never use a Forevergreen product again.

Earl slid open the patio door and worked quickly. He added a life-killing dose of household poison to every pot, and with sickening hesitation, to the hibiscus and the orange pixie as well. He smiled madly as sweat dripped down his forehead. "Take that you little monsters! You won't get your thorns into me! *Never!*" He whispered insanely. Earl could almost hear their delicious little screams as he flooded their pots with imminent death. He lifted the last, tall bottle of bleach in his armory and shifted on his bare feet to the table-top garden, unscrewing the child-proof top.

"Earl?" A groggy voice moaned from behind him. He jerked his head away from the prize-winning sunflower and melted with dread. His body froze, holding the white bottle of bleach over his wife's most coveted of potted babies. "What are you doing?" She asked. Maggie stood in the entryway to the kitchen in daisy-print underwear and a thin, forest-green top whimsically displaying the words, *Sometimes I Wet My Plants.* Her messy, red bangs framed her timid and horrified expression. Her breaths quickened with panic. This had been the *first time* in Earl's hundreds of midnight visits to the kitchen that Maggie had woken up and descended upon him.

His mouth fumbled for words. He was left with nothing but the truth to explain his actions. "Forevergreen is turning everyone in the house into plants!" He blurted out. "That's where the lilies and the hibiscus came from! Bella and the pest control guy were turned into flowers! They need to be stopped!" His voice cracked. He heard the faint chatter of laughter resonate from the flowers behind him. *"Shut up!"* He roared at them.

Maggie was smitten with malignancy and disbelief. "You said you bought those from Wilson's!" She moaned with dejection. Earl grew aggravated. After everything he had just told her, the fact that he had lied about buying her flowers was the first piece of information she had reacted to.

"Why the *hell* would I buy you more weeds!" He barked. "And did you *not just hear* what I told you?!"

Maggie eyed the bleach. She brought her shaking hand to her mouth and began to sob. "Are you ...killing my babies?" She asked tearfully.

Earl straightened his back and slammed the bleach bottle on the counter beside him. He spoke coldly. "Not if *they* can help it! The drain cleaner I poisoned them with yesterday didn't stop them, why would anything else?" He growled. "What I *should* do is burn them alive!"

She sharply drew a finger in his direction. "Get away from them!" She screeched. Tears cascaded down her face. "If I see *one sign* that you've harmed them in any way—" Maggie's sentence was cut short. One by one, every plant on the table shriveled, wilted and turned from a healthful green to an anorexic gray. Small, dehydrated leaves fell from their stems and floated to the wood of the table.

Earl was on to their ruse. He boiled with contempt for their phony display. "You melodramatic little bastards!" He muttered through his teeth.

"*I want you out!*" Maggie screamed. "Get your things and *get out!* I don't want to see you here in the morning! Not then and not *ever again!*" She slapped her ankle-socked foot against the tile.

"And *then what,* Mags?!" Earl belted. "You'll sell everything we own to finance a new row of azalea bushes for the front yard and continue to sing to your flowers and *not work* like you've done for the past ten years?! I've paid for *everything* in this house and your new obsession with Forevergreen is going to leave you forever in the red and out on the street! Not to mention those new credit cards you opened *without* my permission! *Who's going to pay those off?!*" His breaths shook.

Maggie wiped the moisture from her reddening cheeks and crossed her arms. She lifted her brow in preparation to deliver a logical and rational response to his well-grounded objection. She spoke, "Azaleas *don't grow* in this climate, Earl! Arizona is too dry and too hot for their ideal growth and seasonal bloom!" Earl closed his eyes and sighed with resignation. "You'd know that if you *ever once* paid attention to me and what *I'm* interested in!" She cried.

The couple stood in silence. The hum of the kitchen light buzzed over the thick and wavering tension. Earl shook his head. Maggie would never open her eyes to the real-world problems that affected adult life. He had kept her too long and too far detached from financial planning, budgeting and anything else that sustained her carefree lifestyle. Every time he complained about money, she saw only gripes and bitterness towards what she was spending their money *on*. She wouldn't survive without him, his income or his administrative responsibility. And sadly, she didn't have a clue.

Earl's voice softened with mercy. "Look, Mags. If you'd just please listen to me for a second," he begged.

"*No!*" She barked. "I want you *out*." She turned her back. Her braid swayed as she ascended the stairs. "I don't want to see you in this house again," she said. Maggie stepped to the landing and continued to cry. Earl heard the hollow slap of her bedroom door close with adamant conclusion.

Alone in the kitchen, Earl exhaled through his nose. He did his husband-best to think of everything through his wife's perspective. Alas, every thought that came to him was met with stern protest. He began to question himself. *Had he actually gone crazy? Were the plants completely innocent? Did the cat finally take enough of his monotonousness and run away, along with the missing pest control tech? What about the blood on the deck and in the hibiscus? That* was the only sure proof he possessed. The only proof he hadn't gone completely insane.

He walked to the open, glass door and flipped on the lights. The thick drops of blood were nowhere to be seen. Only small piles of topsoil were spotted across the deck. He approached the tall hibiscus. Evidence that he had dug through the pot was present, along with spilled dirt left in clumsy mounds surrounding it. Earl fell to his knees and began to dig. He uprooted the entire plant and found nothing but potting soil and smelled nothing but earthy must and Forevergreen additive. No gore and no blood. To his confusion, the spray nozzle and PestEjector tank were gone as well.

Leaving the hibiscus askew, he ran into the kitchen. The keys were no longer in the sink and any trace of bodily fluid was washed away by his earlier tenacity. *The van,* he thought. Earl rushed to the front door and threw it open. Across the street, he clearly viewed the neighbor's house. No van and no evidence that pest control had ever been there. *Had it been towed?* He thought. *Or had his company come by to pick it up? If they had, why had nobody showed up to question him about the missing employee?*

Earl slowly closed the door and gave up. *He was insane,* he concluded. It finally happened. Maggie had finally driven him to the end of his rope and plunged him headlong into mental instability, just as he'd always feared. He locked the front door, did the same with the back patio and took one last look at the kitchen garden. Earl flipped off the lights, sighed with defeat and began the long, depressing hike to his personal guestroom.

Every stair creaked and every grip on the banister's handrail moaned as he ascended to the lightless hall. His bare foot made contact with the landing just as a sharp, familiar sound echoed from the kitchen below. Earl froze. After a series of ominous seconds, the meow came again. Then again. Bella's hungry cries could clearly be heard from her spot beside the filled bowl of cat chow on the kitchen floor. He whirled around. "Bella?" His voice cut through the darkness. She meowed again.

With everything having gone seemingly back to normal and his perception clear of illusions, he realized Bella's return wasn't completely unreasonable. *Had he not noticed her during his brush with dementia? Had he been ignoring her this whole time?* Those were the only logical answers. Excitedly, Earl jogged down the steps, jumped into the kitchen and illuminated the lights.

His terror returned in full force as he beheld the dining-room table. Every potted flower in Maggie's indoor display was gone, with the exception of *one*. The striped, orange pixie lilies sat in their pot at the center of the table, healthful, vibrant and sinister. The weight of the sight was suffocating. Earl gulped in his throat. The meow came again. Not from the floor, but from the lilies.

Against his better judgement, Earl approached. "Bella?" He called again. His tone vibrated with fear. Standing over the blooming petals and curling leaves, he shivered. The tile was cold against his feet. His heart pounded like a funeral drum. Suddenly, the largest of the flowers retched forward and began to cough. Earl stumbled backward. The lily spat and choked as if regurgitating a hairball as the pot shifted across the table's surface. With one last heave, the orange and white flower coughed up a red collar attached to a dangling, copper tag. The name *Bella* reflected across the tag's surface, in the glint of the kitchen bulb.

Earl reacted. His plunge into madness resumed as he whirled around and flailed out of the kitchen. His shoulder collided with the edge of the drywall, sending his body's weight onto the rug of the living room. Gripping his arm and clenching with pain, he attempted to push himself up.

Inches from his nose and resting on the carpet, was Maggie's new tray of pink zinnias. The sight sent him stumbling back again. Earl got to his feet, and flipped on the lights. Every plant in Maggie's collection was positioned in various locations throughout the living room, blocking his path to the front door and every window. The end tables, the couch, his recliner and the coffee table were decorated with roses, orchids, geraniums and violets. Every petal stared lifelessly and demonically back at him as he hyperventilated with panic.

He heard a sound behind him. Earl turned to see every patio plant in the same array obstructing his escape through the opened patio door. His only clear path from certain death was up the stairs and to the hall. Without a second to think, Earl took it. He gripped the handrail with white knuckles and tumbled up the steps. Abruptly, he felt something leafy seize his ankle, causing him to fall. His throbbing shoulder hit the stairs and his chin crashed against one of the rungs of the banister. Blood dripped from his mouth upon biting into his tongue. He yelped in pain, but did not dare give up.

Crawling as hastily as he could, Earl climbed up the steps and reached the landing. Chirping giggles and maniacal cackling erupted from the living room as he attempted to flee the diabolical garden of possessed plantlife. He dragged himself to the foot of Maggie's door and opened his eyes. There, just between his face and the door to Maggie's master bedroom, her prized, spotted sunflower stood imminently waiting for his approach. Eyes glazed by tears and his throat dry with anxiety, Earl looked upon its featureless face.

In one atrocious instant, two, green, horrendous eyes opened at the center of its flowering, canary mane. The threatening glare of its abominable, serpentine pupils sent Earl into a formidable fit of transcendental horror.

At the heart of Earl's Arizona subdivision, his fearful and panicked screams boomed across the empty streets, through the sleeping trees and into the humid, Arizona air.

Weeks later, Earl rested in a comfortable flower pot on Maggie's table-top garden. He was positioned beside Bella's white stripes and ivory-tipped petals. A cockroach happily perched on one of his leaves and ate aphids from his healthy stems. Before him on the table, was Forevergreen's newly-released FloraText station. With a friendly chime, a message from Maggie appeared across the screen as a healthy spritz of carbon dioxide emitted from the life-giving device. Her message read, *I miss you, babies! Mommy will be right back with more growth booster for you all! I love you, my botanical beauties!*

Earl K. Pike was a happy plant. Likely, this was due to the fact that his receding hairline was no longer a problem, he had a new pet that found him interesting and money was no longer a problem he possessed. Even more likely, his happiness was due to the fact that after a decade of loveless marriage — his wife had *finally* sent him a text message.

GRIMMBERRIES FOR SAMHAIN
The Feast Of Halloween

The old chant goes,

Come and sup for every turn,
Let the old ones join our earn.
Another grind against the churn,
Watch the flames of Samhain burn.

These words are long since forgotten. Their message has died with the passing of time and the failure of the generations. However, the rules that accompany them — are still very, very much alive.

Beginning as long ago as five-thousand years, the festival of Samhain was celebrated by the ancient Celts between October 31st and the first day of November. This short, two-day window represented the end of the harvest season and the time in which the boundary between the living and the dead decayed to its weakest point, before the beginning of the new year. Large bonfires were lit, offerings of food were presented to deceased ancestors and the living adorned themselves in animal skins to ward off corrupted evils.

Over centuries, the pagan rituals of Samhain fell to tradition and devolved from divine purpose, to inconsequential frivolity. Samhain became the eve of All Saints Day and eventually, Halloween, as the world found new religion by the end of the tenth century. Pagan *traditions* remained the same, although their meanings became rebranded and repurposed to fit the changing years. After World War II in the United States, Halloween fully commercialized after the war-time ban on sugar was lifted and suburban growth cultivated. Offerings for the dead became trick-or-treating and animal skins transitioned to store-bought costumes for children. Today, the holiday has reached all new lows of ludicrosity and in many countries, holds as robust a commercial income stream as Christmas. Throughout the entire month of October and growing, many participants rhapsodize death, darkness and gore as millions justify the worship of deviltry, embracing their own diabolical natures without the fear of persecution. The days of Samhain remain lost, misconstrued and abandoned by arrogance.

Only wickedness can thrive in a modern world where villainy is celebrated, the dead fall to starvation and disencumbered evils treading on the living earth — need no place to hide.

The high-pitched beep of a rolling forklift echoed against the towering walls of the massive hardware store. A wrapped pallet was positioned into place and lowered to the floor. A young, lethargic employee ran his blade through the stretched film, freeing the new shipment of Halloween lawn inflatables. He took each box from the pine pallet and dropped them to his feet, kicking them across the shiny concrete and against a wide, green display rack. The forklift pulled its tongs free and continued to scream as it departed for the rear stockroom and left the sales floor.

A tap came at the boy's shoulder as he folded his blade and whirled around. "Happy Halloween!" An overenthusiastic man in an appalling gray and orange sweater greeted him beside an equally-avid wife, in an equally-hideous top. The words *This Is My Ugly Halloween Sweater,* were woven into both, with thick, crimson yarn.

The wife repeated, "Happy Halloween!" Beams of unwanted cheerfulness emitted from her wide stare and blinding teeth. Behind the couple, a flat, rolling cart held at least two dozen seasonal lawn inflatables, yard props and over two-thousand feet of orange and purple lights.

The boy felt a suspecting chill run up his spine. He had heard stories about customers like this — Halloween freaks seeking exclusive favors in exchange for harassment and boisterous persistence. Interaction with them always took a turn for the worst. The date was currently September 7th but in order to retain his minimum-wage job, the customer had to be right. He mumbled without dispute, "Happy Halloween."

"I'm Dave, and this is my beautiful wife Betty..," the man introduced. He gestured to his wife.

She waved her hand eagerly. "Hi!" She squeaked.

The kid halfheartedly returned the wave. "Hi."

"And you are..!" Dave slapped his hand against the boy's plastic nametag. "Jason!" He shouted. "Jason, my wife and I are the most devout Halloween-ers you'll ever meet! You've heard of us?"

"Halloween-ers?" Jason asked. He had never heard the term before, but was sure he was mere seconds away from learning all about it. Immediately, he regretted his inquiry.

Dave blushed with a smile as his wife jumped excitedly. "It's a term we're trying to get going online," he said proudly. "Soon It'll be a household name, we hope! Currently, our social media has over ten-thousand, dedicated Halloween-ers. We take the holiday *very seriously*. It's a lot more than a *holiday* for us, more of a *way of life* that lasts all year." Betty nodded dramatically. "We think Christmas is overstuffed and offers no real substance or morality when applied to life. God is overrated," he whispered covertly. "And, come on, has anyone ever really met Him?" He turned to his wife. "Have you ever met the big guy?"

Betty's brow rose as she shrugged and shook her head. "Nope!" She answered.

"There it is!" Dave confirmed. The couple kissed. "It's time for the Halloween-ers! Halloween-ers all the way!"

Dave's face narrowed with a sense of seriousness as he captiously examined the stockboy. "Jason, are *you* a

Halloween-er?" He asked. They stared him down like a pair of Quakers during a witch hunt.

"Um, well..," he stuttered. He searched for any way to relate, even just to get through the interrogation. "..I did take my little brother trick-or-treating last year. My mom made me do it because she found pot under my bed," he blurted out. Fear set in as he wondered if drug possession was a detail better left omitted when speaking with a customer.

Dave grinned as he raised his hand and a request for a high-five into the air. "Atta boy!" He cheered. Jason returned the gesture with a soft slap. He chuckled nervously. No negative judgement seemed to follow the confession. "Jason, my wife and I are wondering if you could help us out," Dave petitioned as he gestured to the pallet.

The kid returned his arms to his sides and stood awkwardly. "How can I help you today?" He asked. *Here it came,* Jason thought. *The favors.*

"We are on the hunt for..." Dave began. He leaned backward as his wife lifted her phone into view. Betty pointed to a list of items on her screen. "We are looking for.. *ghost in pumpkin with witch hat, Frankenstein teddy bear* and *skeleton playing banjo on gravestone,*" he listed.

Jason turned to the pallet and began searching through the large, black boxes. "Um.. ok.. here's banjo.." He handed them a large box.

"Fantastic!" Dave erupted.

He handed over a second box. "..Ghost witch.."

"Outstanding!" Dave chimed.

Jason searched for the final request. He peeled back the plastic wrap, exposing the shipment of yard decor. Slowly he dismantled the stack. After sifting through the inventory, he spotted the bear and presented it to them. "Frankenstein teddy bear," he said. The package depicted the image of a green, statuesque monster holding a small, zombified bear.

Dave's expression narrowed with disappointment. "No, we have that one already. That's Frankenstein *with* teddy bear. We're looking for Frankenstein teddy bear. A teddy bear that *is* Frankenstein."

"Oh," Jason groaned. He placed the box on the floor and continued to search. "If it's not on the pallet, we have a lot more in the back," he muttered.

"Ooh!" Betty gasped. "Oh my gods, David look!" Raw elation shined from her blue eyes as she pointed to a box on the pallet. Dave's euphoria was equal to his wife's, but expressed with more reservation. He bent down and retrieved an item from the pallet.

"Jason, you've been holding out on us!" He accused with felicity. The kid stood and eyed the item with mild perplexity. "This.. is *Rooster with pumpkin scarecrow!*"

"Yeah, looks like it," Jason agreed.

"*This* lawn decoration isn't supposed to be out this year," Dave stated. Betty was overwhelmed with emotion. She pocketed her phone and quickly began fanning her eyes as they moistened with joy. "*Rooster with pumpkin scarecrow* is part of the farm friends collection that was supposed to, but did not release, in 2021 because of manpower complications during Covid," Dave said. He stared at Jason with astonishment.

"I think I'm going to cry," Betty choked. "I never thought I'd ever see it in person!"

Jason scratched his head. "Oh yeah," he remembered. "Management told us something about getting backstock this year," he said. "There's more in back, I think."

Dave looked at his wife. Betty folded her fingers in front of her nose as tears streamed down her cheeks. He looked back at the boy. "Jason, are you telling me that *pig with candy corn, horse grim reaper* and *cow flying over moon on broomstick* could be in *this building?*" Dave and Betty stared at Jason with a level of desperation commonly witnessed just before a murder verdict.

"Um.." He squeaked. "Yeah, I think I saw those." Dave became weak in the knees as Betty threw her hands in the air in unbridled praise. She jumped on her toes again as the couple hugged, whispering words of endearment and celebration to one another. Jason interrupted, "There's others too, like one with a hatching chicken, a haunted barn and a raccoon dressed like a Dracula." The stunned surprise returned to their faces. "But there's a lot more in the collection," he said. He eyed their full cart of boxes. "I don't know what kind of car you guys have but you'd need a truck to move them all."

"How many farm friends do you have back there?" Dave asked intensely.

Jason thought for a second. "Fourteen, I think."

"Do you rent trailers?" Dave inquired.

"Yeah," he replied.

Dave took a close step to the young employee and spoke candidly. "Jason, if you hook up that trailer and get every lawn spook you have in stock loaded up, there's two tips in it for ya'."

"Ok!" Jason gasped.

"The first is this.." Dave reached into his pocket and handed the stockboy a folded up fifty-dollar bill. The kid took it into his hand with wild disbelief. "And the second tip is this..," Dave growled. He brought his lips close to Jason's ear and whispered, "Next time, hide the pot in your mom's bedroom closet. She'll never find it in ten years and if your dad finds it, the argument that follows won't involve you." The man slapped the boy on the shoulder, winked surreptitiously and departed with his wife. Jason chuckled nervously as he stared at the cash in his hand. "Black SUV is already parked out front!" Dave called out. "License plate is WEENERS!"

The boy's lips twisted into a dumbfounded simper. His interaction with the Halloween freaks had taken an unexpected, yet profitable and opportunistic, turn for the best.

Dave and Betty drove through an unfamiliar town located about sixty miles from their new home in Bradbury Ash. The eight-foot trailer and rear cabin was stocked high with enough Halloween supplies to open a store of their own. The bumper and rear window of their jet-black Suburban was covered in a clutter of occult-themed stickers, horror film decals and a looping, orange ribbon that read, *Support Halloween*. Sunday traffic crowded the streets as gray daylight showed through a thick layer of dimming clouds.

Betty fussed with her long, blonde hair and showed obvious signs of distress. Her husband fought through the neverending stream of oncoming vehicles, attempting to make a wide, left turn. "What are you so nervous about, hun?" He asked.

She folded her fingers and slapped her hands into her lap. "What if they don't have it?!" She squawked. "I'll just die if they don't have it!"

"They'll have it," he assured her. "I called ahead last week and again yesterday. Patrick is holding it for us, and I even Venmo'd him a hundred bucks to put a guarantee on it. It'll be there."

She tapped on her teeth with manicured fingernails. "Well, couldn't they have shipped it to a location closer to home?" She asked. "We must have passed six stores on the way here."

Dave huffed through his nose. "Sweetie, the book has been in Germany for the last thousand years. It's only been in the U.S. for a handful of months and that was Cincinnati. I don't think that it's *completely unreasonable* that we drive an hour out of our way to pick it up." She nodded, subserviently agreeing with him. "Anyway, moving it again would just put more hands and more interest on it. Especially during this time of year."

"Oh!" Betty puffed, distracted by another thought. She slapped her hands together. "I'm gonna look at their baking recipe books! I might find something new, or even better, something old!"

"That's the spirit," he encouraged. "Also, start thinking about what theme we're doing this year for trick-or-treat. We've only got 54 days to prep before the big event."

His wife died with unease. "I know!" She moaned. "You must think I'm a terrible wife! Last year I had everything planned out by July!" She rested her forehead on her fingers. "But with the stress of the move and setting up the new place, I've barely had time to decide how we're decorating the inside of the house, what we're doing for costumes and what wine to pour when we're watching our show after Halloween midnight! Everything forms into a big, illegible ball of tasks in my brain, and *you know* stress makes me forgetful!"

"Nonsense," He eased. "We've got plenty of time. The move put us both off our game. If it makes you feel any better, I didn't update my Facebook status to *Feeling Halloweeney* until just last month."

Betty dropped her jaw and stared at him in horror. "I don't even *know* you anymore!" She gasped.

"I know, I know," he concurred with shame. "The move's been hell on us both."

They pulled into a small, stripmall parking lot. The black Suburban pulled into two, empty spaces leaving room for the trailer. David geared the truck into park and rested his elbow on the wheel. "Don't go nuts in here now. I don't know what this little venture is going to cost us, so

I don't need you spending our entire Halloween budget on books," he warned.

"You're the one tossing cash around with your generous tips!" She argued.

"It's not about generosity," he said. "It's about giving credit where credit is due. The world is inherently ignorant. It's an inconvenience I gladly pay to avoid."

Buy And Sell Books was wedged between an office supply store and a Mexican supermarket. The couple exited the SUV and approached the bookstore. The closer they drew to the shop, the more panicked Betty became. Dave noticed her discomfort and threw a sympathizing arm around her. "Long, calming breaths, sweetie. Remember the exercises we practiced? Three seconds in, three seconds out, and think about how amazing Halloween is going to be. That'll get you through it. They'll have the book, I promise."

Inside, the atmosphere smelled of aged parchment and old-world must. The air was thick with earthy elements. If the day had been sunny, swirling clouds of dust would have been visible against the tall windows. Betty stood before a seasonal display of books presenting titles by Anne Rice, Edgar Allan Poe and R.L. Stine. Paper skeletons reminiscent of a kindergarten classroom decorated the display with dangling, rubber bats. She took a long, devouring breath and grinned with serenity. "Ok, ok. I'm calm now," she whispered. "I'm in my happy place."

Passing the front registers, Dave traveled to the far back of the shop. He stood before a long, wooden counter below the words, *Buy And Sell In Store Or Online.* Not a soul could be seen behind the counter. However, a service bell was provided for just such a circumstance. He tapped the bell and waited for service as Betty joined his side. After a long moment, an elderly woman approached, holding a classical music guide and a Hostess Twinkie. Her pale complexion matched the tedium of her motif-print top and corduroy skirt. She set the book on the counter, opened it to an arbitrary section and took a bite of her treat. She chewed as she openly ignored the couple before her.

"Hi," Dave began. "Uh, Patrick is holding a book for us. We arranged a pickup today. My name is David Wallace. He said he'd be here until noon," he said. The woman made no eye contact. She continued to eat as she lifted a finger, prompting the couple to wait until she either finished reading, or finished chewing. A gold cross dangled from her wrist. With a glint of aggravation, Dave waited patiently, drumming his fingers against the counter. After two more bites and a drawn-out minute, the clerk slapped the crumbs from her fingers and closed the book. She lifted her eyes. "Breaktime finally over?" Dave asked sarcastically.

She swallowed her remaining cake and folded her hands slowly on the wooden surface. "How can I help you?" She asked flatly.

Dave repeated, "Patrick is holding a book for us. We're picking it up today."

"What is the title of the book?" She asked.

Dave knocked at the counter with his knuckle and struggled to recall the exact title. "Umm, ..Compenditures of Abraxi something, something.. It's an old Celtic spellbook, creepy-ass, old-looking witch book." Betty spoke over him, attempting to correct him as he answered. Her words were inaudible under the volume of his voice. Dave leaned back. "Sorry, what was that, hun?"

His wife spoke again, "Compendium Of The Abramati And Mage, Volume Six. The title printed inside is in old Gaelic but it translates to the Compendium Of The Abramati and Mage, Volume Six."

Dave tilted his head toward his wife. "What she said. Compendium Mage book. Big one." He held his hands out in front of him, spacing them about a foot apart. "It's about yay big, looks old and haunted, probably *actually* haunted come to think of it. It looks like something your grandmother's grandmother's grandmother would own if she had been burned at the stake for turning children into small rodents for sustenance," he explained. The woman just stared at them. Her expression had twisted into a whole new level of adversity during the course of the book's description. Disinterest became raw repugnance. Seconds passed. "Do you know that book?" David asked.

The clerk removed her thin glasses and thumbed at her nose. She petulantly observed the foolish whimsicality of the couple's matching sweaters. She looked directly into David's eyes and addressed him coldly. "Yes I know that book," she hissed. Tensions rose. "And the likes of you nor anyone else should ever lay a hand on it." Dave's face flattened with incredulity. "And if I had my way, It would be burned in the same furnace that awaits the both of you, and anyone else celebrating that wretched holiday!"

Betty gasped with offense. "You unbelievable bitch!"

Dave raised his palm and calmed his wife as her breathing went into spasms. "Ok, ok. No need for insults, we're all adults here. Do your breathing like we talked about and think about Halloween." He turned back to the woman. "Look, ...Miss?" He prompted her.

"I'm *not* giving my name to *you.*" She growled.

He relinquished the request. "Look, Miss. We're just here to pick up our book, pay our tab and be on our way," he said calmly.

"Please leave," She scratched. "That book is the devil's work."

Dave became pettish. "Which devil? Because there's about *six* of them in the Old Testament, not to mention unclean spirits, lying spirits, the Legion and Abaddon. I just want to make sure we're talking about the same guy, here," he snarked. "I'd hate for this altercation to continue based on misunderstanding alone." Formidable rage flushed in the clerk's thin, bony cheeks. He leaned in closer to her. His condescension sharpened. "If the nature of my book scares you because of what they taught you in Sunday school in the late 1940's, that's not on us. Personally, I'm afraid of any books about rabid, wild animals. Cujo — absolutely terrifying, couldn't finish it! But, I can see by your fire-and-brimstone visage that our conversation has reached an impasse. So, if you could just get my boy Patrick, I'm sure he could be of better service to us."

"You have no idea of the powers you are tinkering with!" She barked. Her neck began to twitch and her hands trembled.

Dave closed his eyes and nodded. "I'm pretty sure we do. In fact, I'm *so unafraid* of that book, I'll read it in the can with my pants down and tinker with its powers to conjure me more toilet paper. And I'll think of you when I do it."

"Blasphemy!" The woman cried.

"Blasphemy is the act or offense of speaking sacrilegiously about God or sacred things, but *nice try*. I only addressed the book you've *failed* to retrieve," Dave countered.

From a back room, a tall, wide man holding a large, flat box against his belly emerged. He stood beside the flustered, old woman as she writhed with outrage. "Agatha," he said. "Why don't you see to the out-of-print's in Home And Garden. I'll take care of these folks," he requested casually.

"Agatha," Dave repeated with a grin.

"Agatha," Betty murmured through her teeth.

"Now we have your name, Agatha. What now?" Dave teased.

"You will both answer for your sins, you can bet on that!" She grunted. "The Lord brings judgement to us all." She turned on her heel and stepped away from the counter.

Dave called to her as she stormed away. "Uh, to our credit, you *are* working on a Sunday, are you not?! That's a big no no in your book, you gonna get judged for that?! Hopefully patriotism makes up for disobedience!"

"Bye bye!" Betty shouted with a taunt. No words were returned. Agatha turned a corner and disappeared.

"Sorry about that," The man said kindly. "Agatha's been on edge a bit lately since your book arrived. She says it's the devil's book or some religious hoo-ha. The Twinkies seem to take her edge off." He rested the box on the counter.

"Ha!" Betty cried with a laugh.

"Well, hopefully it *is* the devil's book. That's what we're paying for," Dave beamed. "My *wife's* been on edge ever since we found out it entered the market. We've been looking for it for some time. You're Patrick, I presume?"

Patrick extended his large hand and shook Dave's. "I am. Lemme get you all sorted out." After shaking Betty's tiny paw, he positioned the box directly under Dave's nose and retrieved a blade.

Dave looked upon the box. "Is that it?" He asked.

"Yup," the man croaked. "Straight from Ohio and Munich, Germany." Betty leaped with excitement and tapped her teeth. "Before that it was in Geneva, Switzerland. It's been kicked around the states for a year or so. Big collector's item, but it never seems to stay in the same place for long."

"That's promising," Dave remarked.

"In so many words," he half-agreed. "How it ended up at a Buy And Sell Books is beyond me. Idiot clerk in Vermont paid the seller twenty dollars for it."

"Does that mean I'm paying forty?" Dave joked.

Patrick laughed, "Nope. Misappraisal and acquisition cost does not affect resale price. Store policy."

Dave moaned, "I figured as much." The man opened the box and swung the top open. He unfolded several layers of acid-free tissue paper and exposed the book's magnificent cover. Countless centuries of wear and the punishment of history's wars, plagues and atrocities aged the codex to a gnarled perfection. The birch covering was wrapped delicately in ruby-dyed leather and reinforced with worn, bronze hinges. No inscriptions were present on the front cover, nor the book's ribbed and weather-beaten spine. Dave took a short second to observe it. He raised his nose to the clerk. "Looks good to me," he said. "But honestly, I'd say the same thing to an unmarked, leatherbound print of Sorcery For Dummies." He turned to his wife. "Sweetheart, this is your department. You're the bookworm. Is this your book?" He asked as he stepped aside.

Betty approached and stood before the codex. She pulled out an eccentric pair of jack-o-lantern-print reading glasses and placed them on her face. After fastening back her hair with a purple scrunchie, she carelessly threw open the book's cover and sifted through its pages. With apparent disinterest in the text's preservation or condition, Betty flipped through the book in chunks, searching diligently. Towards the back of the codex, Betty stopped.

She eyed a small, yellow stain smeared across hand-written, Gaelic print. She rubbed at the stain with her thumb. She smiled, bounced on her toes and slapped her hands together. "This is it!" She chirped.

Her husband looked up at Patrick and shrugged. "The lady says it's legit! What do I owe you?" He asked.

The clerk carefully closed the book, replaced the tissue and sealed the box. "For the Compendium Of The Abramati And Mage, Volume Six.. you're looking at about four big ones, four thousand," he said. Dave winced and whistled through his teeth at the figure. "But.." Patrick lowered his voice. "Since you dealt with me so graciously with your manners, your patience and your ..wallet, the best I can do as a *Buy And Sell* employee, is give you our associate discount. That's ten percent." He slid over a plastic calculator and tapped the buttons. "..bringing you down to thirty-six hundred dollars."

"Well..," Dave stammered. "I very much appreciate your graciousness in return, but even thirty-six hundred threatens to break the bank." He stewed for a moment, then glanced at Betty. She folded her fingers in front of her face and begged with her eyes. Dave sighed and looked back at Patrick. "I'd be neglecting my self-indulgent need to haggle if I didn't ask if there were any other ways we could lower the price," he haggled.

"Fair enough," the clerk said. "I'll knock off twenty bucks if you buy a book today."

Dave's expression warmed with satisfaction. He turned to his wife. "Sweetheart, you said you were in the market for some baking books?" He asked. Betty squealed with glee as she jogged away and headed for the culinary section of the bookstore. Her slapping steps faded into silence. Dave released a long breath as he pulled out his wallet. "Happy wife, happy life, right?" He said to the clerk.

Patrick shook his head and giggled. "Ain't that the truth," he laughed. He peeled a large, round sticker from a roll and slapped it onto the box encasing the codex. The shiny, Halloweeny font read, *Scare You Again Soon!*

The day's errand-run came to a close as the Suburban cruised home, trailer in tow. Dave gripped the wheel as Betty cheerfully studied the Compendium. She used her phone's translation app to convert each inscription from old Gaelic to modern English. The box and tissue paper laid discarded on the rear seat as she reviewed every page, snapped a picture and read with a childlike wonder. A second book entitled *The Vintage Baker,* rested on the high dashboard.

"Good read?" Dave asked.

"This is remarkable, David," she gushed. "This volume actually lists real spells, conjuring practices and summons. It's full of them! And the recipes aren't that complex. Most of these ingredients can be bought at Whole Foods or the farmers market downtown."

Dave eyed her suspiciously. "I don't have to worry about you turning into one of those teen, Hot Topic witches, do I?" He asked in jest.

Betty dropped her phone to the book. She flashed her husband a look of ire. Her Halloween reading glasses were still perched on her nose. "You know I'm not that naive," she groaned.

"Ok," he replied cautiously. "But If I see a new nose piercing or Harry Potter tattoo, I'm gonna start to judge."

His wife ignored him, her eyes back on the codex. "This recipe for example..," she said. She tilted the book in his direction. "Meadowsweet, yarrow, hazelnut and wild garlic with grimmberry mash and hare."

Dave made a one-second attempt to understand a single word she had just said before shaking off the confusion. "All I got from that was garlic, because garlic is in pizza," he said.

Betty smiled widely and presented the screen of her phone as he drove. "And look at that!" She squeaked. "Google searches for each ingredient and tells you where you can buy them locally!" She went through the shopping list. "With the exception of a few," she groaned.

"Exception?" He asked.

"Grimmberries," she replied. She looked over the book and searched for the ingredient online, yielding no results. "What the *hell* is a Grimmberry?" She irked.

"Search under Franken Berry and Boo Berry. Sounds like a new addition to the General Mills lineup," he jested.

Betty became flustered. "Baby, ..would you just ..please cut the dad-joke sarcasm?! You know this is my thing. Books are my thing, films are your thing. I don't roast you on your horror movie trivia shit and which mask Freddy wore in what movie in what decade!" She barked.

"Ok, ok," he backed off. "Do your thing and I'll do mine. And it was Jason, not Freddy by the way. Jason wore the mask, and Michael."

"Exactly," she concluded.

"Just be careful," he feigned caution. "You may have *no idea of the powers you are tinkering with.*" He mocked the woman at the bookstore.

"Ugh! Good gods, that bitch! Could you even believe her gall?! Where does she get off talking to us like that?" Betty bawled.

"The benightedness of the mislead," Dave cited. "Poor Agatha."

"Burn everything you disagree with!" She satirized. "I can't believe with all the advancements in human society, we still have psychological witch trials. Although, I *was* impressed with your Old Testament knowledge."

"You'd be surprised how much of the horror film industry relies heavily on Catholic influence," he said. "Useful information, though. Helps me deal with freaks like Agatha. They hate it when heathens know more about their book than they do. Drives 'em crazy. There's no finer wine than watching the ignorant cry by the feast of their own famine," he quoted.

"Bitch," Betty murmured.

Her husband reached over and patted her on the knee. "Don't sink to her level, hun. Her negativity only affects you as much as you let it," he said. "She's going through some tough trials herself if she's spitting curses like that to complete strangers."

"I damn hope so," she spat bitterly. Slapping the codex closed, Betty took the vintage baking book from the dashboard and placed both books in a neat stack on her lap. Her grin became as wide as the promises of a Cheshire cat. She beamed with mirth as she sat in her seat, holding the books tightly together.

Her husband noticed the change in her demeanor. "What?" He asked. She showed her teeth and shrugged innocently. "What's that look all about?" Dave giggled.

Betty walked her fingers across the cover of the baking book, teasing his intrigue. "I may.. know what we're going to do for trick-or-treat this year," she sang.

"Oh?!" He inquired. "Well, do tell! What are you concocting?" She lifted both books from her lap and presented them together with extended, eager arms. Dave figured it out immediately. "Oh!" He howled. "I like it! I like it a lot." A moment passed as Dave's face softened with skepticism. "You sure it'll work?" He asked.

"Of course it'll work. I'll make it work," she said confidently. "And you know I don't go for an idea without testing it first. As always, everything that comes out of my kitchen will taste amazing." Betty held the books against her chest. Her anxiety from earlier in the day eased as the couple sat side by side, shining with enthusiasm, ambition and bliss.

"I'll tell you what," Dave chimed. "This idea of yours may be a little belated, but I'd be lying if I said it wasn't the best theme you've come up with in years."

Betty cooed, "Thank you, baby." They leaned in and kissed. They both reached for their Starbucks

Pumpkin Cream Coldbrews in the center console, lifted them high and tapped their edges together in a toast.

"To the Halloween-ers," David cheered.

"To the Halloween-ers," His wife returned.

September chilled to an ebbing brisk as autumn winds brought October tides. The warming colors of nature's course were welcomed with hot beverages, harvest themes and pungent scents. Every creature adorned patterned wool and frosted breath as the end of year neared and spirits came to life.

The Wallace household was the first to embrace the fall — and with furthermost enthusiasm. Dave worked vigorously through the month of September, transforming the home to a robust display of Halloween charm. Thirty-seven inflatables decorated the lawn as an oversized skeleton towered over the walkway. The purple and orange lights covering the house reached Griswold levels of overembellishment as cotton ghosts, polystyrene jack-o-lanters, and pun-laden headstones haunted every square foot of the property. Only the driveway and garage door were left untouched by the ghoulish invasion — reserved, and ready for the day itself.

Night fell as Betty busied herself in the large kitchen. The interior of the home matched the lawn. Autumn wreaths and veiling cobwebs covered ivory walls and a library of countless in-set bookshelves. She stood before a veritable cornucopia of ingredients, sprawled across the kitchen's island in a disorienting mess. Pie plates, cake pans and cookie trays were stacked along with mixing bowls, whisks and wooden spoons. A pair of Kitchenaid mixers stood adjacent to one another, one violet and one orange. Not a single tool or supply was left to compromise. At the center of it all, the Compendium Of The Abramati And Mage, Volume Six laid open to a selected section and soiled with dry splashes of baking flour. A long-stem dandelion was placed neatly beside it.

Dave descended the curving staircase wearing ghostface-print pajamas. He entered the kitchen, eyes on his phone. "During all of your journeys in the literature world..," he began. He looked up from his device to see Betty covered in white splotches and a black-and-orange, polka dot apron. "..did Bram Stoker ever explain what the pendant around Dracula's neck was supposed to signify?" He asked.

"Taste this!" She spat. She brought a spoonful of marigold custard to his lips as he took the sample into his mouth.

"Mmm," he hummed. "That's *really good.* Nutmeg and ginger?" He guessed.

"Hawthorn and all spice," she announced.

"Really?" He humored. "I might be more impressed or less impressed if I knew what Hawthorn was."

Betty tossed the tasting spoon into the sink and wiped her hands with her apron. "Umm, Dracula's medallion wasn't in the novel. It was added to the 1931 film as an aristocratic rank to give him the look of a nobleman," she answered. His brow furrowed, surprised by her answer. Her face lit up and her mouth dropped open. "Ooh!" She hooted. "Did I just bruise your movie-trivia ego?"

"You did! You *absolutely* did. How did you know that if it wasn't in the book?" He asked.

His wife took a taste of pumpkin mousse and licked her lips. "A different book," she chirped.

Dave rolled his eyes. "Naturally." He showed her his screen. "I've narrowed it down to these two Dracula costumes. One has the pendant and one doesn't. But, I really like the renaissance-era style of the one without. I need a dealbreaker. Help me out."

Betty tossed the spoon. "That depends, do you want to be inaccurate Dracula from the film, or renaissance-faire Dracula? Which is also inaccurate. Vlad the impaler missed the renaissance by about a hundred years," she said.

He looked defeated. "Well, when you put it like that, I think I might keep browsing. What are *you* going as?" He asked.

"Ughhh!" She roared. "Don't stress me out! I'm *really* getting into the trick-or-treat spread. Don't remind me about the things I'm neglecting!"

"I understand you're on a roll and you're doing a bang-up job of it, but Halloween is in two weeks," he cautioned. "Your costume is your uniform. Soldiers prep, clean and maintain their uniforms as representatives of their country. We need to do the same if we're showing respect for the holiday."

"I have two-hundred and forty-seven costumes in my closet upstairs. Would It be *completely unreasonable* to wear one of them again? We live in a new neighborhood, nobody will notice!" She shouted.

Her husband dropped his jaw and stared at her in feigned horror. "It's like I don't even *know* you anymore," he gasped. Betty raised her white, powdery hands and shook off the anxiety, returning to her work. Dave stood behind her and lovingly placed his hand on her shoulder as she whisked sugar into raw egg and milk. "So, how's it going in the bakery?" He asked. "You're not putting anything weird or dangerous other than curses and toad transformation into these pies, are you?"

"Of course not! I'm not in the business of poisoning our entire neighborhood," she snapped. She placed the bowl on the island and rested her palms. "Honestly, it's going really, really good."

"That's good," he praised.

"But..," she stipulated.

"Uh oh, what's the but?" He hummed.

She took a long breath. "The ingredients in the spells are jiving *very well* with the ingredients in the pastries and cakes — *but,* most of the book requires grimmberries, and it would be really, really awesome if we could identify what they were and get ahold of some. A *lot* of some. Like, sacks of them," she emphasized. "Veronica next door said she had about five-hundred trick-or-treators last year, there'll be a lot of mouths to feed. And I want to go *all in* with what the compendium has to offer in keeping with our theme for handouts this year."

"Veronica next door?" He queried.

"Yeah, sweet old lady in the gray one-story. Smells like kitty litter and pee. I brought her a pie earlier," Betty said. "Our first test victim."

"Look at you, mingling with the neighbors!" He taunted kindly. She rolled her eyes dramatically. "I'll tell you what, start practicing as if you have the berries — use blueberries or something instead — and I'll hunt down your grayberries and see what I can get. Maybe that'll take some stress off and you can start thinking about your costume."

She turned and faced him with a thankful smile. "Grimmberries," she corrected him.

"Grimmberries," he repeated. "I doubt it's something completely unavailable, or extinct." Betty jumped, slapped her hands together and kissed him on the chin. A thick cloud of flour engulfed them both. "And I'll take care of picking out the wine," he said. "There's no better feeling than sitting down and watching our show after the chaos is over, and knowing we did our part for the season." He stepped toward the hall. "You coming to bed?"

Betty untied her apron and tossed it onto a hook beside the fridge. "Yeah, I'll clean everything up in the morning." The lights were doused as the couple floated down the hall and ascended the stairs to the bedroom. A door was closed and the entirety of the first floor became drenched in ominous blackness. An unease began to linger. A sickening, sense of vile corruption bloomed from the center of the kitchen. Its villainous stain of enormity tainted the walls and claimed the home.

On the cluttered island and shrouded in night, the open codex hummed with an enigmatic lifeforce. As if manipulated by a ghost, the pages of the compendium turned. Page after page flipped at a rapid pace and suddenly stopped on a section of the book defiled by baking flour and canola oil. Amber light cast a haunting glow onto the kitchen ceiling as an old rune was etched into one lambskin page. The marking burned like searing coals, only to quickly vanish into darkened ash. The light obscured, the hum seized and the codex slapped closed. All that remained was a puff of white and the scent of powdered sugar, in the darkness of polyester cobwebs, plastic spiders and synthetic Halloween charm.

Later that night, in the small, gray one-story house next door, a single light kindled from the dim living room. Veronica sat in a large recliner beside a tall, four-point cane standing upright beside her elderly hand. The woman was large and draped warmly in a fall-themed muu-muu. About a dozen cats crowded her as she watched the television and ate from a family-sized pan of microwaved lasagna. Crying felines pawed at her feet, laid in her lap and perched on every free space upon the cushiony chair. Behind Veronica's seat and mounted on the wall, a large, wooden crucifix hung portentously above her screaming pets and bleach-blonde hairdo. Cat-themed scriptures and photos of deceased furry friends decorated the rest of the home's interior.

Her program ended as a series of reverse mortgage and medicare commercials began their parade. The woman sighed, rested her lasagna on a wooden side table and began shooing the cats off her lap. Two leaped away but one remained, stubbornly refusing to budge.

"Casey, babygirl, down." She whispered softly, snapping her fingers. The solid-black Bombay cat ignored her. "Casey, baby! Off mommy's lap!" She shouted. Nothing. "Casey," she said. "Mommy's gotta feed you, It's time to eat. Who wants to eat?" She sang. The finicky beast turned on its back and raised its paws into the air, begging for affection. Veronica lost her patience, grabbed the cat with both hands and tossed it violently onto the floor. "Get the hell off me!" She screamed.

Shifting her weight slowly to her feet, the woman stood, leaned on the cane and lethargically made her way to the kitchen pantry. All the way, her fuzzy companions pawed, cried and followed. She flipped on the kitchen lights and illuminated the disaster of filthy litter pans, open cans and flies. She noticed the pantry door ajar and shook with fever. "Shit, I left it open again!" She gnashed. About six steps and a minute later, she swung the door open and yanked on the chain switch. A buzzing bulb cast a mechanical light onto a toppled bag of feed. The paper sack had been torn to shreds and only remnants of dry cat food and brown dust was left behind. Veronica turned and faced the living room. Her forehead went red with rage. "God dammit, Casey, you little bitch!" She hollered. Casey watched her fit from the seat of the recliner. She licked her jaws below wide, moonlike eyes. The woman left the mess, closed the door and hobbled to the refrigerator. A bright blue light blinded her as she swung open the door and searched. Depleted cans of cat-chow, expired condiments and tupperware containers filled with vet-requested urine samples took up most of the fridge's real estate. The only fresh item available was a large, round pie provided by her new neighbor. Veronica took the pie by the edge, pulled it from the grate and closed the door.

The pie was perfectly crafted. Crimped edges, a buttered, crusty weave and the face of an orange jack-o-lantern applied with dollops of cheesecake icing. A feast for the tongue as well as the eyes. The woman bent at the waist and tossed the pie onto the floor beside a moist litter box. Crumbs flew and custard spilled onto the stained tile. The cats sniffed at the treat, showed no interest in their substitute dinner and continued to harp. "I'll go shopping in the morning, babies," Veronica said softly. She straightened her back and glared at the cat in her chair. "Casey, you can wait until morning! This isn't for you, fat ass!" She barked. The fellowship of beggars followed Veronica as she returned to her seat, slapped Casey off the cushion and fell into position. She released the cane and shifted into comfortability. The next program was introduced and commenced its broadcast.

Casey watched her brothers and sisters crowd around her angry mother. She licked her paws, and then her coat. Catching a whiff of what was offered in the kitchen, she curiously traveled across the carpet and tapped her paws against the tile floor. The pie was bright, attractive and sweet. Its brown and citrus colors matched the bag she had destroyed in the pantry. Without hesitation, she sniffed at the cheesecake and began to eat. Frosting dotted her whiskers and lips.

Veronica's eyes began to close behind her large-framed lenses. The television screen reflected in her glasses as she fell asleep and began to snore. Abruptly, Casey ran into the room and stood before the recliner, pie smeared across her face and crumbs stuck in her fur. Her eyes were larger than usual. Her pupils had retracted to razor-thin slits. She shook, then convulsed. The impact knocked her to her side and made her yelp. Suddenly, she stood upright and began to urinate. The thick stream of pee struck the carpet and continued to flow so loudly, Veronica woke. She opened her eyes, adjusted her glasses and noticed the cat. "God dammit, Casey! Use your box!" She spat. Casey looked her directly in the eye as the pee stream became thicker and more powerful. Spray spattered against the floor and pooled into a large puddle beneath the feline's feet. "Casey?" Veronica squeaked. The situation reached alarming levels of extremity when Casey began spasming violently as her limbs flayed and urine fountained in all directions. The cat began to scream as the sound of snapping limbs and tearing tendons overpowered the volume of the TV. "Casey!" Veronica cried. Long, black, bone-like protrusions spidered out from the beast's body, snatching each cat one-by-one, from the recliner and pulling their bodies into Casey's, creating a howling, twisting ball of fur and claws. Veronica trembled as she attempted to stand. She gripped her cane and struggled to peel herself from the chair in the midst of the panic.

The ball of cats mutated into one, deformed monstrosity, constructed of torn fur, black bones, white teeth and green eyeballs. The creature was the size of a panther and laid sprawled across the carpet. It looked unconscious, even dead. Veronica gave up on trying to move. The sight sent her heart into convulsions as she stared in stunned dismay. Shockingly, the panther stood. It fixated its hellish gaze on Veronica and leapt forward. The old woman screamed as her cane knocked to the floor, the lasagna slapped the carpet and the recliner fell backward. The woman screamed in pain and anguish. A hot dose of blood splashed a hand-knit sign mounted on a nearby wall, reading, *Bless This Home And All Who Meow In It.*

Daylight poured through the Wallace's front doorway. Hay bails and pumpkins decorated the hall and a wooden scarecrow smiled beneath the in-set window. With a jar, the boundary was thrown open. Dave entered wearing a long, brown coat and a festive scarf. He carried a tall stack of pine trays that rose from his fingers and touched his chin. He swung his leg around and kicked the door closed behind him.

In the kitchen, both mixers emitted a low-pitched whirr as flour, granulated sugar and yeast was kneaded into dough. The island was a buffet of meticulously-prepped pies, cakes, cupcakes and foldovers. Their glowing crusts, artistic toppings and violet colors exhibited a standard of visual presentation worthy of a royal banquet. Betty stood over the sink, washing her hands. Her husband trotted into the kitchen and placed the trays carefully beside a plate of green-apple hand pies. The shipment rose three feet from the granite island. Dave shouted to Betty over the working mixers and running water. She turned and noticed him. Quickly, she shut off the fawcett and switched off the motors. "What?" She asked. She stared at the trays.

Dave threw out his hands and proudly presented the stack. "Grimmberries!" He announced.

His wife gawked with a wide, awestruck gape. "No way!" She halloed. "Where did you find them?!" She took a tray from the top, placed it before her and began tearing off the mesh.

"Remember that farmer's market you mentioned?" He asked.

"Yeah." Betty peeled back foam exposing hundreds of marble-sized fruits colored enigmatically in vibrant hues of gray, purple and blue. She took one into her fingers and sniffed it curiously.

"Well, there's an old-timer there by the name of Percy Caldwell, who runs a pickled-venison-jerky table — very delicious by the way, I bought some. You gotta' try it," Dave said. He leaned in and kissed his wife.

"He sold you the berries?" She asked. She popped the berry into her mouth and chewed. Her eyes lit up with delight.

"No," He clarified. "But he knew a guy, who knew a guy, who knew a woman who runs a market down in Evans Park that grows them in an old barn converted into a greenhouse on her father's property. *She* sold me the berries, and at a very reasonable rate. I, of course, tipped her for her time since she took a couple hours out of her schedule to meet me out there. Typically, she only visits the barn twice a week and today wasn't one of her days."

Betty ignored his inclination to hand away money. Her smile upon tasting the berry lit up the kitchen. "They taste like ..butter and taffy." She ate two more. "Gods, they're amazing! Grimmberries. Who knew?" She gushed.

"Phytologically, they're called..," Dave pulled out his phone and read out loud. "..Genus Vaccinium Calvaria. A large group of flowering plants in the heath family. Native to Europe and Aisia, this species of antioxidant-rich fruit only grows in temperatures under forty-five degrees Fahrenheit and when dehydrated, retains a shape similar to that of a *human skull,* earning them the colloquialisms Moritsberry, Necroberry and Death Fruit." He flashed her a jovial gaze and stowed his phone. "..Which is striaght-up *killer* for the Halloween season, wouldn't you say?"

Betty bounced and cheerfully ate another handful of death berries. She swallowed and excitedly threw her hands out over her buffet of sweets. "Ok, I'm going to start baking on Thursday at five a.m. That should give me plenty of time before Friday evening. I'm making twenty-five pies, twenty 8-inch cakes, and about two-hundred cookies, mini pies and cupcakes. That'll yield about six-hundred servings and I can always toss in a few more trays of single-serves while you man the tables," she explained. "Flavors are going to vary based on stock." She placed a hand on the stack of grimmberry trays. "Please tell me we can get more of *these* this week?" She asked.

"I've got six more stacks in the car," Dave said.

"Holy shit. Ok, I think we're good then," she hummed.

"Did you think about all the variables that might hinder us, keeping an entire smorgasbord of baked goods out on the driveway Halloween night?" He asked.

Betty's smile frowned. She shook her head with irritable confusion. "Like what?"

His eyes widened. "Like if it rains, it gets windy or the birds get wise?"

She ground her teeth and stomped her foot. "You always have to do this, don't you?! I'm in a harmonistic, tension-free flow and you have to drop another stress bomb! When has it ever rained us out on Halloween?!" She bellowed.

"2019, 2013 and 1991. Ninety-one was that Halloween blizzard, remember? We had to wear antarctic survival gear over our costumes," he replied.

Betty huffed, "Then, we go door to door and hand-deliver like we did during Covid. People loved that. ..And if birds show up, our theme can be Alfred Hitchcock."

Dave grinned lovingly. He leaned in and kissed her on the lips. "You really *did* think of everything," he cooed. "I'm gonna unload the rest of the flats, where do you want 'em?" He headed down the hall for the door.

"Kitchen table's fine!" She shouted. She switched the mixers back on. They continued to moan and churn. "And no more stress bombs!" She demanded.

"What are you going to be for Halloween?" He half-joked.

"Shut up!" She cried.

Thursday morning and the day before the big evening arrived. Betty woke to her alarm, leapt out of bed and tied on her apron. The baking commenced as she floured the island, kneaded dough, and boiled grimmberries down to a thick, sugared syrup. Hawthorne, wild garlic, dock leaves and sea spaghetti was added to egg, salt, butter and baking powder as ingredients from the codex and *The Vintage Baker* were merged precariously together. Through the rest of the day and throughout the night, Betty slaved and labored. She produced thirty pies, twenty-four cakes and over two-hundred and fifty single-serve baked goods. After six crates of Granny Smith apples, twelve flats of black raspberries and every last grimmberry from the kitchen table, the banquet was tediously prepared. Every available surface was covered in sugary sweets and tantalizing desires. Betty scrubbed the pans, and wiped down the sink. She removed her bleached apron, tossed it into the washing machine and dragged her body upstairs and into bed. Eleven hours until showtime, and the work was complete.

Halloween night. Dave thundered down the oak staircase and sauntered into the living room. His expression conveyed flat outrage as he stood in a bright-orange t-shirt that read, *This Is My Halloween Costume,* in a playful, ghoulish font. His wife sat on the sofa wearing a violet, flowing witch costume. She ate from a bowl of sugared blackberries and cackled gaily upon seeing his sour frown and unappreciated attire. He spoke sternly, "This shirt is blasphemy. And I mean that to the *very degree* of the word's definition."

"It looks good on you," she smirked.

"It's contemptuous," he spat.

She popped a raspberry into her mouth. "Well, think of it this way," she said. "It's new, you've never worn it before and it's prepped, cleaned and ironed. All of your standards met, as a representative of Halloween."

Dave exhaled sharply through his nose. "Can we just get the festivities underway?" He said impatiently. "I still have to set up the table, get the projector going and pull out the lawn chairs to start scouting out early bird trick-or-treaters. We don't want to miss anyone." Betty rested the berries on the coffee table and stood. She pulled an oversized witch hat from the cushion beside her and placed it on her blonde head. "If I keep myself busy, I can start forgetting about this stupid shirt," he griped. They began heading for the front door.

"*Now* who's stressed?!" She taunted him.

"I'm not stressed, I'm unnerved," he snipped.

"Did you pick out the wine for tonight?" She asked, still poking at his nerves.

"Shut up!" He snapped.

Long plastic tables were dragged out of the garage, unfolded and positioned into place. Mummy-print, vinyl tablecloths were stretched over them and pinned at each corner. Two, large adirondack-style chairs were placed at the foot of the driveway, painted festively in orange and black jack-o-lanterns. A box projector was plugged in and planted on one of the tables, facing the garage. The wide door was closed as *The Beast From 20,000 Fathoms* was dimly projected onto the garage door like a drive-in theater, in black-and-white monochrome. The first round of baked goods were brought out, sliced and divided into servings on ebony paper plates. The weather displayed no signs of obstruction. The air was still and not a single bird was in sight. Six p.m. struck as the couple planted their bodies in their chairs and waited for the rush.

Dave took a bite of pickled venison jerky as he peered through a pair of safari-grade binoculars. Their home was situated at the very center of a cul-de-sac and faced directly down their street. Any costumed treat-seekers would be traveling to the house head-on. "Do you see anyone?" Betty asked.

He chewed as he spoke. "Nope, not yet — *hang on!*" He leaned forward, examining both corners of the distant, crossing Avenue. "Nevermind. It's just the mailman. Or, someone in a mailman *costume.* Hand me a plate just in case," he requested. Betty reached behind her and took a thin serving of grimmberry pie with buttercream icing from the table.

Relaxing, he lowered the binoculars and rested his back against the chair. He took a long, pleasing breath. His eyes wandered delightfully. Betty placed an affectionate hand on his. "Smell that?" He asked. She nodded happily. "The decomposition of the leaves.. the smell of cooking meat, pumpkin spice, ginger tea, moisture soaking into maplewood..," he drifted. *"That's* Halloween." He nodded jovially. "A lot of things come and go over the years. A lot of things change. The outfits, the food, the attitude, the taboos ..but the *smell* — that has *always* stayed the same." He took another delicious breath. Now, all we need is a bonfire." They sat together smiling from ear to ear, their hearts beating as one and their spirits as free as death. In the midst of their most treasured time of year, Dave and Betty were home at last.

Movement faintly came into view from down the street. Dave lifted his heavy lenses and scoped the situation. A small family with two children approached from around the corner. "Ok, look alive," he said. "We've got unicorn princess, robot zombie and vampire Mom and Dad coming in at twelve-o-clock." Dave winced as he studied them. "Ah, damn!"

"What's the matter?" Betty asked.

"Dad went for the renaissance look *and* he's wearing the Dracula pendant. And it looks really becoming." He complained.

"Oh," she replied.

"Dammit, why didn't I think of that?" He griped.

Betty stood and grabbed a pie server. "Four plates?" She asked.

"Four plates," he confirmed. Dave stood and took a second plate into his hand. The enthusiastic pair stood on the sidewalk awaiting the family's arrival with four servings at the ready. They smiled widely and waited patiently as the group stopped at every-single house on the way to their cul-de-sac. Ten, long minutes passed before the family finally arrived at their driveway. "Happy Halloween!" Dave greeted brightly.

Betty repeated him, "Happy Halloween!"

Piercing the moment of welcoming pleasantry, a rottweiler began howling and snapping upon spotting the Wallace's. It was restrained by the father with a silver chain and choker collar. The dog viciously barked and lunged as Dave stumbled backward in terror, almost dropping his plates. Betty's eyes went wide with fear.

"Oh, don't worry! He's a big softie, he's just saying hi!" The mother said. She was about eight months pregnant and kept a single hand on her wide, distended belly. She snapped her fingers at the animal. "Igor! No! Stop!" She shouted. The dog silenced but its contempt remained. It sat and growled behind nipping teeth, refusing to take its eyes off Dave.

"Of course," Dave chimed. He failed to come up with an off-handed compliment regarding the dog's name. At any other given moment, he had all the confidence in the world. However, in the presence of clapping jaws and matted fur, he was reduced to formidable apprehension.

The two children hurriedly approached the offering of baked crust and sugar. A small girl in a pink, unicorn hoodie wore a ballroom-style dress and held a glittering scepter. Her big-boned older brother wore a box sprayed in silver paint and undead makeup smeared on his face. The boy was the first to speak. "Pie! Fuggin-A! I'm first!" He howled.

"Joseph! Language!" His mother spat.

Dave handed a plate to each child. A plastic fork stood embedded and upright from each slice. "There you are, the feast is served! One for each of you," he said pleasantly.

"Thank you," the girl chirped politely.

Joseph dropped his candy bag and tossed the fork on the pavement. He began eating the slice with a bare hand. "I want two!" He barked.

"Two? We've got two, no problem!" Dave replied. He snatched another plate from the table and handed it over. "We've also got three, four, five and six if the mood strikes you right!"

His mother interjected. "No, no, Joseph. Two is enough, you just ate that whole tray of rice crispy treats. You'll throw up again," she warned. Betty handed servings to the adults as they thanked her graciously.

Dave bent over and addressed the girl. "How 'bout you? You want two slices of pie as well?" He asked.

The little angel spoke sweetly in an even, courteous tone. "No, thank you," she squeaked. "I'm gonna save mine for later when I watch Maisy Sprinkle."

"That's her TV show, she saves everything for watching Maisy before bed," her mother said. Her husband melted with desire as he ate the pie.

"Maisy Sprinkle, huh?" Dave repeated. "Well, I'll tell you what.." He grabbed a pumpkin foldover from the buffet and placed it on her plate beside the slice. "Just in case you want some dessert to go with your dessert when you're watching Maisy, you'll have that. Sound good?" The girl showed her oversized teeth and nodded favorably.

"Say thank you, Claire," her mom requested.

"I did!" The angel cried.

Mom gestured to their overzealous lawn. "I love what you did with the house! We could see it all the way from down the street. We almost didn't come down this way," she praised.

Dave grinned. He glanced back at his decorations. "That was the plan! If you're gonna go at all, you may as well go big! You should see the backyard!" He joked.

The woman laughed. She took her first bite of pie and shivered with delectation. Her eyes went wide with revelation. "Oh my *God!* What is *in* this?! It's amazing!" She moaned.

Betty's expression emitted rainbows as her husband answered. "Oh, that's *all* my wife! I can take credit for the lawn, but I'm completely useless in the kitchen! She makes everything from scratch!"

She took another large bite and addressed Betty. "Remind me to come back and get your recipe, this is fabulous!"

"Absoluetly," Betty graced.

The woman shook her head as she chewed. "I'm so sorry, where are my manners?" She extended her hand. "Henny Kensings, this is my husband Robert. We live down on Sycamore Ranch."

Dave and Betty shook Henny's hand, keeping a good distance from Robert and his chained beast.

"Henny, Robert. Pleased to meet you, we're David and Betty Wallace. New blood in the neighborhood. Moved in last June," Dave greeted. He pointed to the woman's pregnant tummy. "And should we expect to see a *fifth* Kensings trick-or-treator next year?" He grinned.

"Oh! I hope so! With the way *this* pregnancy is going, it almost feels like it'll never end!" She laughed.

"Do you know what you're having?" Betty asked. Her voice was quiet and shy.

"Not this time," She replied. "We wanted to know ahead of time for the first two, but we want this one to be a surprise."

"They always are!" Dave remarked.

Henny shook her head and motioned pettishly to her son, "Ain't that the truth."

From down the street, a decent flow of trick-or-treaters made their path from house to house, approaching the cul-de-sac. Dave noticed. "Here we go! Here come the crowds! Halloween's officially begun!" He said happily.

Henny turned and waved genially at the people approaching. She whirled back around. "Say, are you guys going to the Dark Hollow Faire downtown? Bradbury does it every year, there's games and food and prizes.." Dave and Betty looked at one another and shrugged, unaware that the event even existed. "It starts at eight, an hour after trick-or-treating starts," Henny said. "Everyone in town goes after collecting candy. It's a hoot!" She pointed a thumb at her husband. "I'm gonna try and get Robert to enter one of the contests with me, he never participates in anything," she whispered. "Do you think you'll be there?"

The Wallace's hesitated awkwardly, attempting to hide their complete disinterest in the faire. "Sounds spooktacular, Henny! But if we did go..," Dave started. He gestured to his tables. "There'd be nobody to man the inventory, and we want to make sure we get everybody!" He chuckled. "Also, the misses and I have a ritual we do every Halloween when the night is out. It's kind of our Midnight Mass to All Hollow's Eve."

"Awww!" Henny moaned. "Well, think about it for next year, It's a riot!"

"Sure thing!" Dave chirped.

The crowds neared the Wallace driveway. Henny and her family began to move along. "Anyway, it's been great to meet you both!" Henny said. "Welcome to the neighborhood!"

"Likewise!" Dave bid. The Kensings continued their route around the cul-de-sac loop and approached the next house on their path.

The sun set as hundreds of costumed participants traveled the subdivision and solicited candy from every home, taking part in the tradition of sugar distribution. Children, teens and adults crowded the streets, knocked on doors and rang doorbells. The entire town was alive with Halloween spirit and ghoulish excitement. Dave and Betty handed out plate after plate of pie, cake and singles as each family happily and with delightful surprise, accepted their corrupted confections. Some partakers found the offerings so profound, they circled back again and even twice to take another helping. Dark consumed the evening as the festivities went on and became even more lively. Lawn decorations blazed, flashlights flashed and glowing accessories accompanied costume attire in the midst of the celebratory night.

Dark Hollow Faire was a buzz of excitement and haunted Halloween fun. The entire celebration took place in Town Square, a large, open space situated in the downtown district of Bradbury Ash. Each family found their way to the event after collecting as much candy as they could carry, joining the already-overcrowded grounds. Illuminated rides, carnival games, a beauty contest, two haunted houses and endless food trucks added to the excitement of the yearly reception. High-energy Pop songs from the last two decades echoed against the surrounding, downtown structures as the smell of popcorn and funnel cakes delectably wafted in the gentle breeze.

The Kensings family happily traveled through the thick crowds and booming music. Claire continued to carefully preserve her pie plate as her father kept Igor on a tight tether. "I want to go home and eat my candy!" Joseph shrieked.

"You've already eaten enough candy, Joseph. You'll get sick," his mother replied. "Give me your bag." She supported her belly with one hand and snatched the treat-filled sack from her son's hand.

"What's the *Goddamned deal!*" He screamed. "Give it back!"

"You can have it back tomorrow," she scowled.

Claire pointed across the grounds to a small petting zoo. "Mom, can I go see the ponies?!" She asked.

Her mother spotted a large booth with a long table. A row of ten seats were placed before ten, oversized, tin buckets. The banner above read, *Battle Of The Bobbers.* A large screen displayed a digital timer counting down from three minutes until the next battle. Henny seized her husband by his wrist. "Bobbing for apples, Robert! Look!" She cried. Robert eyed the booth with objection. His lips frowned into a sour grimace. Henny became agitated. She slapped him on the meat of his upper arm. "I told you we were doing a contest this year and *this* is the one I'm picking!" She turned to her children. "Joseph, take your sister to see the ponies! Your father and I are doing the apple contest," she commanded.

"Ponies are assholes!" He screamed. "I want fudge!"

"Fine," she compromised. "We'll get fudge after the ponies and apples."

The boy crossed his arms stubbornly. "Not good enough," he complained.

Henny sighed and handed over the candy bag. Her son eagerly took it. "Take your sister and Igor, we'll be done in a few minutes." Joseph took the dog by his chain and ran with his sister through the costumed hoards, headed for the petting zoo. "And watch your language!" She cried out.

Henny and Robert approached the booth, signed up and took their seats. Over the next several minutes, the remaining eight chairs filled with participants and the timer dropped to zero. Henny clapped her hands and heartily nudged her husband. His sour expression had not changed. He glowered at the empty bucket before him.

A tall, overenthused host in a ringmaster-style coat and hat grabbed a microphone and leapt onto the grass. A glow-in-the-dark skull was painted over his face and brightened under the cast of blacklight bulbs. A small group of onlookers gathered around the booth. "Welcome to the *fifty-third* Bradbury Ash Dark Hollow Faire and the *second* Battle Of The Bobbers tournament of the evening!" He announced. Windswept concert speakers emitted his voice across the entirety of Town Square and over the music. "Our boo-hungry bobbers will have *no more* than *two minutes* to empty their troughs with hands behind their backs, using nothing but werewolf fangs and howling determination!" A handful of volunteers sporting Dark Hollow t-shirts emptied gallons of distilled water into the buckets. A second round of locals added one box of Honeycrisp apples to every trough, counting them to be sure the prospects were even. "Show me two minutes on the clock!" The host shouted. The screen obliged, displaying the time. He pointed a finger at the avid row of contestants. "Are we ready?!" Henny, Robert and their contenders nodded eagerly. The announcer held up his fingers as he counted down, "Three, Two, One, and begin!" He screamed. The crowd cheered as the bobbers crossed the starting line.

Hands behind her back, Henny stood and furiously slapped her face into the cold water, submerging her entire head and soaking her shoulders. She took an apple almost instantly into her teeth and let it fall onto the table. It bounced, rolled and fell onto the stage. Uninhibited by her swollen gut and unborn child, she did the same with two more, letting them drop and scatter. All that mattered was emptying the bucket.

Robert found it difficult to snatch even one apple from his tin. He made several attempts as frustration reddened his forehead. His wife noticed his struggle and leaned in close. Her hair splashed water onto his angry face. "You have to hold the apple against the bottom and bite into it!" She shouted over the chaos. He followed her instructions and began plucking apples of his own, releasing them from his teeth and letting them bounce.

A minute passed as every contestant splashed, bit and spat in the heat of the countdown. After Henny's eighth apple, she began to feel a short wave of nausea. Dizziness struck her as she took a break and sat in her chair. Robert went wild with enthusiasm as he emptied his bucket and caught up to the others. He pulled his tenth Honeycrisp from the water and tossed it aside. Oddly, dark circles began to form above his cheeks and his eyes were beginning to cloud. A deathly gray replaced chestnut brown as the entire surface of his eyeballs rotted into an unusual form of pallor mortis. He dunked his head into the bucket, seized another apple and spat it onto the table. His eyes were now bright white. Black scales were beginning to form, spreading from his eye sockets and webbing across his face.

"Rob, I don't feel so good," Henny moaned. The night began to spin as she supported herself against the table, trying not to fall.

Robert soaked his face again. An apple slipped from his jaws and floated to the top. Before he could lift his head to make another attempt, something fleshy grazed his nose. He sank his teeth in and pulled. Robert's dripping face erupted from the bucket. His eyes now emitted a bright yellow sheen and the scales had spread all the way to his chin. In his mutating teeth, he held a dangling, human ear. Blood oozed from the appendage and dripped onto his remaining, bobbing apples.

Down the table and five seats from Robert, a competitor pulled his head from his tin and began shrieking wildly and painfully. Blood spewed from the back of his jaw and the top of his neck. His ear had been bitten and torn cleanly from his head.

Robert spat the ear onto the table and continued to bob. His face continued to transform as he pulled a nose, a fleshy cheek and a human eye from the thick, red water of his bucket and added them to his collection of body parts. Three more contestants began to wail, covering their faces and spraying blood onto the stage. The volunteers panicked, the host began to tremble and the crowd screamed in terror at the gore-drenched display.

Unaware of the grotesque turn of events, Henny collapsed and fell onto the stage. A growing pain blossomed from her belly and made her quake with sickness and churning discomfort. She lifted the edge of her costume and beheld her stomach. Her protruding gut had turned a dark, bruising purple and shivered with movement. "Rob!" She cried. "I think the baby's coming!" Her husband was distracted. He had gathered all the fleshy appendages he collected from his bucket and began eating them with a primal vigor. Bloody participants ran from the booth, screams and disorder echoed from the crowd and the host had already abandoned the contest. Henny screamed in pain as her belly split. Ruby-red fluid exploded from her gut as twisting tree branches spiraled from her body and reached towards the sky. The branches thickened and became the rough, blood-soaked trunk of an appletree as the woman went limp and pale with death.

The tree slowed its growth and curled into shape. On one, protruding branch, an apple began to form. The oversized fruit ripened and matured in seconds, hanging heavily from the limb. The scratching cries of an infant cut through the havoc as the face of a baby howled from the surface of the apple. The apple screeched and shook as tears fell from its tightly-closed eyes. Rob finished his meal of human flesh and ears. He jumped from his seat, approached the screaming fruit and plucked it from the branch. Crazed starvation showed violently in his lizard-like eyes as he sank his teeth in — and devoured the apple. The baby's cries intensified to yowling fits of agony.

Claire and her brother stood on the wooden fence surrounding the petting zoo. They hugged the top rung of the barrier against their chests as they watched the livestock graze. Igor licked his chops as a rooster passed the interlacing, wire mesh, taunting his instincts. "Ponies are stupid!" Joseph spat. He crammed a popcorn ball against his lips and took a messy bite, his bag gripped tightly in his fist.

"They're not stupid, they're magical," his sister argued sweetly. Holding her pie plate close, she turned her head and noticed intense shouts coming from the center of the fairgrounds. "People are screaming," she said with unease.

"Of course they're screaming, dummy. *It's Halloween,*" he cracked.

Claire noticed other children paying for cups of dried corn to feed to the animals. Goats, sheep and llamas gladly licked it from their unsanitary hands. "Can we feed them too?" The girl asked.

"Mom didn't give me any money and I'm *not* giving them any of my candy. They can starve!" He yelled.

She gave her brother a look of adolescent criticism. "They're not gonna starve. Everybody's feeding them," she peeped.

"Then *you* don't need to!" Joseph snapped. A vile grin crept across his face as he eyed his sister's plate. "I have an idea."

"What?" She asked curiously.

"Let's see if they like pie!" He grabbed Claire's plate and tossed it into the pen. The paper dish landed upside down onto grime and scattered hay.

His sister spewed with outrage, "I was saving that for Maisy, you jerk!"

"Maisy's an asshole!" He objected. He turned his eyes to the pen. "Let's see if they eat it."

Claire frowned as a llama neared the plate and sniffed. Disinterested, the animal trotted away and approached a group of corn-offering kids. A few chickens passed the plate and a pony galloped by, stepping onto the paper and flattening the desserts into mush. "I don't think they want it," Claire pouted. "You ruined my Halloween for nothing."

From the rear corner of the miniature zoo, a black goat slowly made its way to the defiled desserts. It lowered its head and took the paper into its teeth. The goat began to chew as the slice of pie smeared down the plate and fell onto the ground beside the pumpkin foldover. Consuming the frosting-covered trash, the goat swallowed and bleated loudly. It stared at Joseph and Claire with an impartial, lifeless gaze.

"Eat the pie!" The boy shrieked. The goat bleated again, then again. "Stupid idiot," Joseph moaned.

Suddenly, the animal went still. As still as a statue. Its eyes fixated on the brother and sister as a strange breeze blew through the petting zoo. Its coat hardened and its hue faded from a healthy, black sheen to a tablet gray. The creature's entire body turned to limestone as cracks began to form and a green moss began to grow like the northern-facing edge of a rock formation. After momentary seconds of shock and surprise, the goat exploded into chunks sending rocky debris in every direction. The other animals in the pen panicked, going into discombobulated fits and darting from left to right, trapped by their enclosure.

Where the creature stood just seconds ago and in a cloud of airborne dust, a black specter in the image of a goat hovered above the ground. The menacing ghost snarled below roasting, crimson eyes. Its clawing horns rose high above gnashing teeth and dangling hooves.

Joseph was the first to react. *"Oh, fuck! Demon goat!"* He wailed. Igor yanked his chain out of the boy's hand and darted across the faire. Joseph and his sister dropped from the fence and sprinted into the crowds. Others joined them. Frightened faire-goers and terrified families fled from the event and dispersed into the adjoining streets. Other anomalies had taken place throughout the celebration simultaneously, mutilating victims and claiming lives. The tiny-tots haunted house was eating every child that approached, the winner of the Dark Hollow beauty contest had become an enormous, flesh-hungry squid and the food trucks exploded into flames sending wave-after-wave of devouring fire over the devastated and affrighted grounds.

Claire ran beside her brother as a fever struck him. He fell to his knees and dropped his bag onto the sidewalk, moaning grievously. Crowds of people ran by them, crying and squealing, shouting and weeping. The fires spread quickly as the heat engulfed Town Square. "Get up!" Claire squeaked. "We have to go!"

Her brother's face had turned a pale green as he pawed at his tummy. "I can't. I have to ..I have to..," Before he could finish, he lurched forward and vomited onto the pavement. Wrapped candy and freshly packaged treats struck the street and scattered. He heaved again. Lollipops, single-sized packs of Halloween gummies and soft circus peanuts spewed from his jaws and piled onto the ground.

Claire stepped backward in terror, watching Joseph spray pound after pound of trick-or-treat-ready candy into an enormous heap between his quivering hands. With every wave of vomit, Joseph thinned. His belly disappeared, his baby fat dissolved and his bones began to show under tightening flesh. With one final choke, Joseph coughed up an entire tray of rice crispy treats. The metal pan clanked against the sidewalk as Joseph collapsed onto the pile and expired, a gangly mass of flesh and bone. Claire dropped her candy bag and screamed in fear. Her piercing cry was muted by the deafening disorder and fleeing swarms. Dark Hollow Faire became a blaze of fire and brimstone, as if hell itself had swallowed it whole. Charred, deformed bodies, frosting-covered forks and burning paper plates were left scattered across the desolated fairgrounds.

Dave and Betty laughed maniacally at the top of their lungs. They stood before a man dressed as a clown accompanied by at least eight children and eager mouths. He had just finished showing the Wallace's the fake, naked butt hanging from the rear of his costume. "At least you won't have to worry about how to use the bathroom when you're out and about, that's for sure!" Dave chuckled.

"Very funny," Betty remarked. They handed out the final plates of the evening and fell into their patio chairs. The clown and his kids continued their trick-or-treat venture, around the cul-de-sac and down the street. The driveway tables held nothing but dirty plates, soiled pans and discarded, elastic film.

"Wow!" Dave exclaimed. "Six hundred and forty-five treats to five-hundred and ninety treators. That is *definitely* a new record for us."

Betty released a long, exhausted sigh. She glanced at her bare arm. "I think I'm developing a tan from overusing the oven," she said. She rested her head against the wood and took her husband's hand. "Did we do good?" She asked.

Dave smiled and squeezed her small palm. "I think we did," he said confidently. "We did *really* good." They relaxed as the stress of Halloween night oozed from their aching bodies and fatigue set in.

"Can't we just skip the rest of tonight and go straight to bed?" She whined.

"You know we can't," he replied. "The night's just getting started." He sniffed the air, a grin stretched his lips. "You smell that?" He asked. Betty took a pleasant breath and closed her eyes with euphoria. "Bonfire," he said happily. "Now it's official. It's Halloween!"

Down the street and from around a corner, a family jogged past their cul-de-sac, screaming and shouting. Dave lifted his binoculars and peered at them as they passed. "Tell me that's not more trick-or-treators. I'm spent," Betty groaned.

"No. Wherever they're going, they're not coming down here. Although, they're hard to make out." He held the lenses in front of his face and examined them. "Remind me to get night-vision binoculars for next year. These things are useless when the sun goes down," he said.

He squeezed her hand again. "Ready to pack up?" He asked.

"No," she griped. "But here I go." They stood, stretched their backs and opened the garage. In the same manner everything was brought out, the tables, chairs, projector and supplies were dragged inside. In minutes, Dave and Betty stacked the pans, folded the tables and cleared the driveway. The garage door was closed and the decorative lights were left on. The first phase of Halloween night had come to a satisfying and triumphant close.

The kitchen was a clutter of baking debris and dishes as they collapsed onto the sofa. Dave in his contemptuous t-shirt and Betty in her slightly-used witch outfit. She held the codex against her chest and a long dandelion in her fingers as Dave took the remote and illuminated the TV. He checked the large, Victorian clock on the wall and then the time on his phone. "Six minutes until showtime," he said. Betty ate from a bowl of sugared grimmberries as her husband flipped through the channels. He halted at a station broadcasting a solid-black screen. A small, digital bat flapped its wings above a message stating, *Stream Will Begin Shortly!*

Dave threw his tired feet onto the coffee table and tossed the remote aside. "So," he began. He gazed merrily into distant nothingness. "How many people do you think we killed tonight?" He asked. He grinned as Betty ran generalized figures through her head.

"At least eight hundred," she replied. "I know we only served about six hundred, but I put some nasty, nasty recipes into those pies. We definitely topped last year's numbers."

"Fantastic!" He clamoured. "Those grimmberries really did the trick!" His voice hardened. "Remember when we handed out those hexed idols one year? That was a disaster. Kids want candy for Halloween, not toys. Win some, lose some, I guess."

Betty opened the compendium and thumbed through the pages. "Some of the spells were *astoundingly* gruesome. Even to me," she commented.

"Well, you *are* the one who wrote them," he said. "I'm surprised you couldn't remember a *single one* all these years."

She writhed with aggravation. "The last time I put hands on this book was Samhain of ten seventy-three! Since then, we've had four hundred plagues and over three thousand wars. Not to mention the one that was taking place when it was taken from me. And you know stress makes me forget! I'd say a thousand years brings a lot of stressful events and plenty of forgetfulness!" She barked. "And my Gaelic needs some serious practice."

"Fair enough, fair enough," he eased. "At least the book is back where it belongs with the others."

Betty simpered and sniffed the dandelion. "It is, isn't it?" She cooed. She ran her hand across a page in the codex, stuck the flower into the book as a marker and closed the cover, flattening the dandelion between the pages. She stood and placed it on a bookshelf between volumes five and seven. The entire bible of the Compendium Of The Abramati And Mage was reunited at last, after centuries of curses, famines, museums and auction houses. The deadly books warmed with an amber glow as the last volume was shelved and slid into place. Each codex was bookmarked with the long stem of a flower. Betty sauntered over to the sofa and sat.

"You think there's enough spells in that book to use again next year?" Dave asked.

"Oh yeah!" She said. "I barely cracked the cover."

His grin straightened. "We'll have to be careful," he cautioned. "If we keep doing numbers like this, we'll have to move again before the neighbors get wise. I want to limit us to one move every four years. Anything more frequent than that is exhausting, and stressful for *you.*"

"You don't want to do the same thing next year as we did tonight? After how *this* Halloween turned out, I don't mind the moves," she asked.

Dave's smile brought a rosy glow to his cheeks. "All right," he admitted. "Tonight *was* pretty spectacular. We can do it again."

"Is there anything you'd change?" she asked.

"There is," he said. "The decorations were perfect, the spread was perfect.. Only *one thing* has been bugging me all night that we'll never do again, and I'm sure you can guess what it is."

"What's that?" She inquired curiously.

He pointed his finger directly at Betty's witch gown and hat. *"Neither one of us* wore costumes this year," he stated grudgingly.

His wife laughed as they leaned in and kissed. Dave reached to the floor beside the couch and retrieved a tall bottle. He held it with both hands, displaying it to the witch. She covered her mouth with her hands in surprise. "Oh my gods! I completely forgot!" She laughed.

"Well I did not," he hummed. "Feast your eyes on Pumpkin Ginger Granny Smith Merlot, made right here locally in our great state!"

Betty took the bottle. A happy ghost holding a pumpkin shined from the label. "Where did you get this?" She gasped.

"Percy Caldwell, at the farmer's market. The guy who sold me the venison jerky. He makes wine too, I thought I'd surprise you," he said sweetly. She slipped off the couch and retrieved two wine glasses and a bottle opener from the kitchen. Dave popped the top and poured the bouquet of pumpkin-ginger and fermented grapes. They tapped their glasses together and sipped.

Abruptly, the black screen of the TV faded as midnight struck. The broadcast displayed the dark blue caverns of the Abramati and the tenth level of the nether; a desolate, inhospitable realm where only the most neglected of the deceased go to feed. Cruelly, the Abramati was also where souls ended up when afflicted by death caused by supernatural evils. Evils, that when left unchecked, roam between worlds and claim lives as they please.

A large stone rolled away from a black entrance to the cavern. The camera views switched between four different perspectives and showed the cave from agreeable angles. "Here we go, here we go!" Dave spat excitedly.

"Tell me if you recognize anyone. I always try to pick them out."

"Shouldn't be too hard with the resolution we have now," Betty said. This screen is an 8K, remember when we had to actually *be there* to watch this?"

"Don't remind me," Dave growled.

Thousands of naked bodies were herded through the gateway and onto the darkened rocky plain. They cried, wept and screamed as the stone rolled closed, sealing them inside. Dave leaned forward and examined the frightened souls, beaming giddily as the stream changed angles. From the shadows surrounding the crowd, enormous starving bodies crawled into view and approached the mass. Thousands of ravenous giants crept from the darkness and began devouring the confused flock of newcomers, one after the other. Flesh tore and blood spilled as the feast took hold and the crowd was consumed. Dave was unable to recognize anyone he had handed a plate to over the course of the night. "Poor bastards," he noted. "But, that's what happens when you don't leave a dinner plate for great, great Grandma."

"None of them do anymore," Betty commented. "Not after the dark ages. The world is ruled by ignorance."

Dave sat back and took a sip from his glass. He smacked his lips and exhaled with satisfaction. "And there's no finer wine, than watching the ignorant cry by the feast of their own famine," he cited. "Oh! I almost forgot to check our rank!" He grabbed his phone, opened his social media and pulled up his page. His handle read, *Halloween-ers United* beside a glowing full-moon avatar.

He reviewed posts pouring in, submitted by other entities. "Looks like Cleveland did four hundred, Washington did five hundred and Salem did *three hundred and twenty?*" He clicked his tongue with a scold. "Shame on you Salem, you've got a reputation to uphold."

"Anything close to what *we did?*" Betty asked.

He continued to scroll. "Not that I'm seeing. So far we hold the torch. Polls aren't completely closed just yet," he said. Suddenly, his phone chimed with the sound of a haunted mansion doorbell. "Ok, nevermind, polls are closed!" He squawked. A post popped up ranking every participating group by amount of spirits harvested. Dave rose to his feet and victoriously raised his fist into the air. "Number three, Jenny and Patty O'Mally, seven sixty four! Number two, Steve and Olivia Gutenberg, seven hundred and seventy six!" He stuffed his phone into his pocket and opened his arms. His wife rose and excitedly took him by the hands. He kissed her on her left cheek. "Number one.." He kissed her on her right cheek. "David and Betty Wallace, eight hundred and twenty lives collected — and served up to their ancestors!" He kissed Betty on the lips as she jumped on her toes with glee. They hugged and celebrated with waltz and wine.

After a quick slow-dance and a few sips, they returned to the couch, beaming with pride. Betty smiled at Dave as if harboring a dark secret. She chuckled with anticipation. Her husband noticed her delighted hesitation. "What?" He asked. "What's that grin all about? He laughed.

Betty slowly raised a finger. "Eight twenty-*one*," she whispered.

"Eight twenty-one, what?" He asked with perplexity. His wife gleamed with a devilish smirk and tapped her nails against her teeth. Dave caught on almost immediately. "Oh.." He shook his head with a satisfied sneer and blushed with Halloween bliss. *"You little witch,"* he cursed.

Sunlight poured into *Buy And Sell Books* as swirls of dust danced before the tall windows. A bell chimed as Agatha entered. She locked the door behind her and approached the rear counter. She noticed a plate resting beside a stack of Home And Garden issues with no one in sight and silence looming through the aisles. She stepped closer to the counter and rested her purse. The plate presented a large slice of berry pie and a note written on an index card. The words, *Have a blessed day,* were written in Old English, calligraphic handwriting. She checked her surroundings, claimed the pie and took a bite. She melted with delectation as a gold cross dangled from her wrist. She turned to the open backroom door with a full mouth and shouted, "Patrick, you really shouldn't have!"

ABOUT THE AUTHOR

Mark Steven Nordlund grew up in the suburbs of Chicago, Illinois and loved writing and illustrating, beginning at a very young age. In 2010 he created the comic strip *Dead End County Monster* that ran successfully until 2017. The strip was ranked in the top 50 webcomics in 2015 by Comic Chameleon and one of his strips was awarded Daily Deviant on DeviantArt in ten out of thousands of submissions. Mark ended the venture after seven years in pursuit of larger ambitions.

In November of 2023 Mark published his first novel, *Mining For Teeth, Wilstrom Territories*. From that point on, his love of short story and novel writing has never ceased. In 2024 he founded Boohouse Books. Thereafter, every publication he released was produced under that name and today, boohousebooks.com offers free short, horror stories, a podcast featuring free works and a store selling book-related merchandise.

Mark continues to write free stories and purchasable collections and novels. His free works can be found on his website, Boohouse Books Podcast and Patreon.com. His collections and novels are available everywhere books are sold online.

MARK STEVEN NORDLUND

WHERE TOY BOATS SINK

A COLLECTION OF DARK STORIES

BOOHOUSE **BHB** BOOKS

boohousebooks.com

www.ingramcontent.com/pod-product-compliance
Lightning Source LLC
Chambersburg PA
CBHW020243010826

48973CB00006B/1641